FRANCI
THE NIN1

GW00496560

Francis Vivian was born Arthur Ernest Ashley in 1906 at East Retford, Nottinghamshire. He was the younger brother of noted photographer Hallam Ashley. Vivian laboured for a decade as a painter and decorator before becoming an author of popular fiction in 1932. In 1940 he married schoolteacher Dorothy Wallwork, and the couple had a daughter.

After the Second World War he became assistant editor at the Nottinghamshire Free Press and circuit lecturer on many subjects, ranging from crime to bee-keeping (the latter forming a major theme in the Inspector Knollis mystery *The Singing Masons*). A founding member of the Nottingham Writers' Club, Vivian once awarded first prize in a writing competition to a young Alan Sillitoe, the future bestselling author.

The ten Inspector Knollis mysteries were published between 1941 and 1956. In the novels, ingenious plotting and fair play are paramount. A colleague recalled that 'the reader could always arrive at a correct solution from the given data. Inspector Knollis never picked up an undisclosed clue which, it was later revealed, held the solution to the mystery all along.'

Francis Vivian died on April 2, 1979 at the age of 73.

THE INSPECTOR KNOLLIS MYSTERIES
Available from Dean Street Press

FRANCIS VIVIAN

THE NINTH ENEMY

With an introduction by Curtis Evans

DEAN STREET PRESS

INTRODUCTION

SHORTLY BEFORE his death in 1951, American agriculturalist and scholar Everett Franklin Phillips, then Professor Emeritus of Apiculture (beekeeping) at Cornell University, wrote British newspaperman Arthur Ernest Ashley (1906-1979), author of detective novels under the pseudonym Francis Vivian, requesting a copy of his beekeeping mystery *The Singing Masons*, the sixth Inspector Gordon Knollis investigation, which had been published the previous year in the United Kingdom. The eminent professor wanted the book for Cornell's Everett F. Phillips Beekeeping Collection, "one of the largest and most complete apiculture libraries in the world" (currently in the process of digitization at Cornell's The Hive and the Honeybee website). Sixteen years later Ernest Ashely, or Francis Vivian as I shall henceforward name him, to an American fan requesting an autograph ("Why anyone in the United States, where I am not known," he self-deprecatingly observed, "should want my autograph I cannot imagine, but I am flattered by your request and return your card, duly signed.") declared that fulfilling Professor Phillip's donation request was his "greatest satisfaction as a writer." With ghoulish relish he added, "I believe there was some objection by the Librarian, but the good doctor insisted, and so in it went! It was probably destroyed after Dr. Phillips died. Stung to death."

After investigation I have found no indication that the August 1951 death of Professor Phillips, who was 73 years old at the time, was due to anything other than natural causes. One assumes that what would have been the painfully ironic demise of the American nation's most distinguished apiculturist from bee stings would have merited some mention in his death notices. Yet Francis Vivian's fabulistic claim otherwise provides us with a glimpse of that mordant sense of humor and storytelling relish which glint throughout the eighteen mystery novels Vivian published between 1937 and 1959.

Ten of these mysteries were tales of the ingenious sleuthing exploits of series detective Inspector Gordon Knollis, head of the Burnham C.I.D. in the first novel in the series and a Scotland Yard detective in the rest. (Knollis returns to Burnham in later novels.) The debut Inspector Knollis mystery, *The Death of Mr. Lomas*, which was published in 1941, is actually the seventh Francis Vivian detective novel. However, after the Second World War, when the author belatedly returned to his vocation of mystery writing, all of the remaining detective novels he published, with two exceptions, chronicle the criminal cases of the keen and clever Knollis. These other Inspector Knollis tales are: *Sable Messenger* (1947), *The Threefold Cord* (1947), *The Ninth Enemy* (1948), *The Laughing Dog* (1949), *The Singing Masons* (1950), *The Elusive Bowman* (1951), *The Sleeping Island* (1951), *The Ladies of Locksley* (1953) and *Darkling Death* (1956). (Inspector Knollis also is passingly mentioned in Francis Vivian's final mystery, published in 1959, *Dead Opposite the Church*.) By the late Forties and early Fifties, when Hodder & Stoughton, one of England's most important purveyors of crime and mystery fiction, was publishing the Francis Vivian novels, the Inspector Knollis mysteries had achieved wide popularity in the UK, where "according to the booksellers and librarians," the author's newspaper colleague John Hall later recalled in the *Guardian* (possibly with some exaggeration), "Francis Vivian was neck and neck with Ngaio Marsh in second place after Agatha Christie." (Hardcover sales and penny library rentals must be meant here, as with one exception--a paperback original--Francis Vivian, in great contrast with Crime Queens Marsh and Christie, both mainstays of Penguin Books in the UK, was never published in softcover.)

John Hall asserted that in Francis Vivian's native coal and iron county of Nottinghamshire, where Vivian from the 1940s through the 1960s was an assistant editor and "colour man" (writer of local color stories) on the Nottingham, or Notts, *Free Press*, the detective novelist "through a large stretch of the coalfield is reckoned the best local author after Byron and D. H. Lawrence." Hall added that "People who wouldn't know Alan

Sillitoe from George Eliot will stop Ernest in the street and tell him they solved his last detective story." Somewhat ironically, given this assertion, Vivian in his capacity as a founding member of the Nottingham Writers Club awarded first prize in a 1950 Nottingham writing competition to no other than 22-year-old local aspirant Alan Sillitoe, future "angry young man" author of *Saturday Night and Sunday Morning* (1958) and *The Loneliness of the Long Distance Runner* (1959). In his 1995 autobiography Sillitoe recollected that Vivian, "a crime novelist who earned his living by writing . . . gave [my story] first prize, telling me it was so well written and original that nothing further need be done, and that I should try to get it published." This was "The General's Dilemma," which Sillitoe later expanded into his second novel, *The General* (1960).

While never himself an angry young man (he was, rather, a "ragged-trousered" philosopher), Francis Vivian came from fairly humble origins in life and well knew how to wield both the hammer and the pen. Born on March 23, 1906, Vivian was one of two children of Arthur Ernest Ashley, Sr., a photographer and picture framer in East Retford, Nottinghamshire, and Elizabeth Hallam. His elder brother, Hallam Ashley (1900-1987), moved to Norwich and became a freelance photographer. Today he is known for his photographs, taken from the 1940s through the 1960s, chronicling rural labor in East Anglia (many of which were collected in the 2010 book *Traditional Crafts and Industries in East Anglia: The Photographs of Hallam Ashley*). For his part, Francis Vivian started working at age 15 as a gas meter emptier, then labored for 11 years as a housepainter and decorator before successfully establishing himself in 1932 as a writer of short fiction for newspapers and general magazines. In 1937, he published his first detective novel, *Death at the Salutation.* Three years later, he wed schoolteacher Dorothy Wallwork, with whom he had one daughter.

After the Second World War Francis Vivian's work with the Notts *Free Press* consumed much of his time, yet he was still able for the next half-dozen years to publish annually a detective novel (or two), as well as to give popular lectures on a plethora of intriguing subjects, including, naturally enough, crime, but also fiction writing (he published two guidebooks on that subject), psychic forces (he believed himself to be psychic), black magic, Greek civilization, drama, psychology and beekeeping. The latter occupation he himself took up as a hobby, following in the path of Sherlock Holmes. Vivian's fascination with such esoterica invariably found its way into his detective novels, much to the delight of his loyal readership.

As a detective novelist, John Hall recalled, Francis Vivian "took great pride in the fact that the reader could always arrive at a correct solution from the given data. His Inspector never picked up an undisclosed clue which, it was later revealed, held the solution to the mystery all along." Vivian died on April 2, 1979, at the respectable if not quite venerable age of 73, just like Professor Everett Franklin Phillips. To my knowledge the late mystery writer had not been stung to death by bees.

Curtis Evans

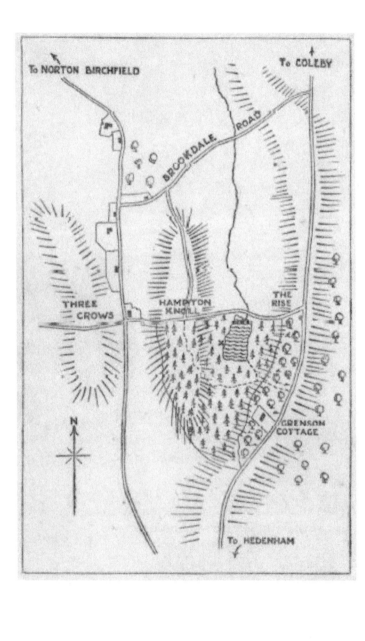

Chapter I
THE EVIDENCE OF DEATH

JOHN BAMFORD, inspector in charge of the Borough of Coleby's Criminal Investigation Department, replaced the telephone receiver and slowly walked back to the lounge, where his weekend guest was idling in the depths of the settee.

"So you are looking forward to a nice quiet week-end, Gordon."

"That is my earnest hope," sighed Gordon Knollis. He glanced up with a suspicious air. "Nothing cropped up, surely?"

Bamford perched himself on the arm of the settee. "One of the town's leading burgesses has managed to get himself shot to death on the edge of a dam just outside the town. Bad show, too, for he was a good fellow!" Knollis relaxed, and pulled on his pipe. "Accidental deaths can be troublesome, especially if the coroner happens to be one of the officious breed. Ah, well!" Bamford shook his head. "No accident, I'm afraid."

Knollis grimaced. "Suicides are still worse. I used to hate them when I was in Burnham."

"It isn't suicide, and it isn't accidental death," Bamford said slowly. "One of our mobile patrols is on the spot, and the sergeant says that the circumstances look horribly suspicious. He's a cautious type is Drayton, and I'm fearing the worst. Anyway, I'm afraid it will break up our pow-wow. Shall I find you an armful of detective novels?"

Knollis got to his feet and knocked out his pipe in the grate. "Don't be an idiot, Bam. I'm coming out with you. A busman's holiday won't do me any harm for once in a way."

"Decent of you," Bamford said with a relieved air.

As he backed his car from the drive to the main road and slid the gears into top, he briefly sketched the setting of the tragedy for Knollis's benefit.

"Three-Acre Dam is on this side of the town, about two miles on and lying between two hills. We shall turn right and descend Coleby Rise, a gradient of one-in-nine. The hill then facing us is Hampton Knoll, a one-in-seven slope. The dam lies between them, to the left of the road. The by-road over the hills leads into the urban district of Norton Birchfield. The stretch of water is at the northern end of a Forestry Commission plantation, amply shrouded by conifers, most of them about ten to twelve feet high."

And then, as Knollis's eyes were closed, Bamford asked if he was bored.

"Carry on, Bam," said Knollis. "I'm vastly interested. You possess the worthy gift of being able to describe in the vivid manner."

"Well," continued Bamford, "the trees come down to about twenty yards of the water's edge, and that twenty yards is thick with hawthorn and gorse bushes—an ideal spot for a murder. The water passes through a small sluice-gate and is culverted under the road. The resulting stream meanders for a mile to join the river that flows through the town—you'll remember that we passed over it in Bridge Street on our way from the railway station."

Knollis nodded. "The dead man. Who and what is he?"

"Richard Huntingdon," said Bamford. "It would be quicker to tell you what he isn't than what he is. His name is to be found in the local paper practically every week. He makes speeches—lots of 'em. Made a pile in engineering and then retired, although he still has a seat on the board and draws a retainer as consultant. He spends his time doing good works, playing golf, and imploring the youth of the town to grow into good and righteous men. His favourite speech is *Chivalry in this Modern Age*. It is alleged that the compositors on the *Herald* staff keep the speech made up in type and merely alter the name of the hall in which the thing is made, and the group he happens to be addressing. That is by the way. He is people's warden at his church, president of about five youth clubs, an athletic club, the town cricket club, the church football club, a Rotarian, amateur operatic singer—quite a decent baritone—member of the Borough Council, alderman, and has been mayor."

"Pooh Bah?" commented Knollis.

"Something like that, yes, except that he is possessed of great dignity and glories in his own good works."

"When social service becomes self-conscious it loses its virtue," Knollis remarked quietly. "Anyway, he's dead and beyond all that now. Murdered, eh?"

"Drayton seems to think so."

"Sounds like being an interesting case," Knollis said in a too-casual voice. "The more connections a man has, the more angles there are to explore. What is your county superintendent like?"

Bamford chuckled. "He won't want to handle the case, if that is what you are getting at. He has never handled a murder case—apart from the usual infanticide cases—and he has more sense than to want to take the case for the sake of his pride. He's one of those level-headed fellows who appreciates the difference between the general practitioner and the specialist. I'll wager a fiver that the Yard will be asked to assist. Still, it may not be murder. We don't know yet."

Knollis settled deeper into his seat as the car sped along the road. "They'll assign me to it as I happen to be in the district."

"Don't be a darned hypocrite," returned Bamford. "The light of battle was in your eyes almost before I had mouthed the word murder. You are itching to get at it!"

Knollis gave a sheepish smile. "Well, I must admit that I am interested," he admitted reluctantly.

"Personally, I hope you do get it," said Bamford. "I'd like to see you at work. You've gained something of a reputation for your work on your last three cases, and I'm keen on seeing how you do it."

"Heaven forbid that you should watch me," Knollis exclaimed in a tone of alarm. "I'm horribly self-conscious."

"Nuts!" said Bamford. He put out an arm and swung the car to the right to begin the descent of Coleby Rise.

"How far is it from here to Norton Birchfield?" Knollis asked idly.

"Two miles and a half. A mile and a half to the so-called level crossing in a slow right-hand curve, and then a straight mile into the sleepiest and worst-planned little industrial town in the whole of England. I hate the place! It is a stretched-out ribbon of shops and houses; an urban district formed from what were once three hamlets."

"And the main road we have just left leads on to the county town?"

"Fourteen miles straight on to Hedenham."

"I see," said Knollis, which he could not have done because his eyes were closed again. "This plantation? Any footpaths or bridle-paths through it?"

"Not officially. It is forbidden land, well-fenced and liberally bespattered with notices warning off the general public, although I dare say that they can still claim way-leave on the paths which are established by long custom."

"Any angling in the dam?"

"Only by children, for tiddlers."

"The water? How does it get here?"

"The draining of the surrounding hills. You do ask a lot of questions, don't you!"

They reached the bottom of the hill, and pulled in to the grass verge, a few yards from the first of the four cars that faced them. There was a small group of people on the bank of the dam.

"Sergeant Drayton and P.C. Harrison," explained Bamford. "The woman leaning on the shoulder of the other woman must be Mrs. Huntingdon, although I'm blessed if I know how she's got here so soon."

"The little fellow in chauffeur's uniform; who is he?" murmured Knollis.

"Haven't a notion. The car looks like the Bishop of Northcote's, but I'm not sure."

"And there lies the body," said Knollis. He indicated a blue melton cape which lay outspread, and from beneath which stretched a pair of tweed-trousered legs.

As they walked from the car Knollis caught at Bamford's arm. "Look!"

A green-and-white model yacht was riding on the dam, drifting slowly towards them, towards the sluice-gate and the culvert.

"Was the man a model yacht enthusiast by any chance?"

"I've never heard of it," said Bamford. "Queer. Still, we shall learn about it eventually."

Drayton came forward, vaulting the fence, a three-barred affair of a rickety nature. He saluted Bamford, and grimaced. "A nasty job, sir. Shot through the back, between the shoulder-blades. The bullet has lodged inside him, or seems to have done, because I can't find any second wound."

"Not shot at close quarters then," commented Knollis.

"That Mrs. Huntingdon?" asked Bamford, nodding towards the woman he had pointed out to Knollis.

"Mrs. Huntingdon and Mrs. Frampton, sir," said Drayton. "The story goes like this as far as I can make out. The Huntingdons have a little girl of eleven years of age. She is at a party in town—at Mrs. Castle's, just above your own house. She went alone, and there doesn't appear to be anything out of the way in that as she takes herself to school every day. Anyway, she had a birthday a fortnight ago, and among her presents was a model yacht. She took this to the party with her, as kids will, and left home about half-past three—"

Knollis glanced at his watch and remarked that it was now twenty-one minutes past four.

"Yes, sir," said Drayton. "Her mother was playing golf on the town course, and she left home about half-past one, straight after an early lunch. Mr. Huntingdon stayed home to prepare a speech for a meeting of the Young Templars to-night—him and the mayor and the Bishop of Northcote were all speaking at the same meeting. According to Mrs. Huntingdon, a message was brought to her from the club-house about ten to four. It was from her husband, and it was to say that the kiddie had met with a serious accident down here, and would she meet him. She had a fair distance to walk back to the car-park, and then she and Mrs. Frampton set out.

"Harrison and myself were patrolling the top road when she passed us doing about fifty-five, and of course we went after her. She took the corner on two wheels, and we fully expected her to turn over, but she made it, and just pelted down the Rise. We were forty-five seconds behind her when she drew in. She jumped out, scrambled over the fence, and was dashing about among the bushes. We hurried after her. Mrs. Frampton was standing by the car and said something about an accident. Then Mrs. Huntingdon came to a sudden halt, screamed, and went down in a heap. And then we found *him*; she had fallen over his body. It didn't take many seconds to decide that he was dead, and so we haven't disturbed his position."

Knollis touched Drayton lightly on the sleeve to engage his attention. "The yacht, Sergeant; how did she react to that?"

Drayton nodded significantly. "That was what came next, sir. She was muttering her husband's name when she came out of the faint, and then she saw the little boat and started chasing round and calling the child's name—Dorrie it is. She went hysterical, and Mrs. Frampton smacked her face until she was quiet enough to question. It seems that the kiddie's name was painted on both sides of her own yacht, and even from here I could see that there was no name on the one on the water, so she calmed down a bit at that. Once I found out where the child was supposed to be, I sent Harrison down to the Three Crows at the cross-roads to 'phone Mrs. Castle. She reported that the child was safe at the party, and that the boat was with her."

"Who is the fellow in livery?" asked Knollis.

"Chauffeur to the Bishop of Northcote, sir. He was driving down the hill, and pulled in when he saw that something was going off."

"Suppose you dismiss the two ladies, Bamford," Knollis murmured quietly. "We can't examine the body while they are on the scene."

Bamford climbed the fence and had a word with them, as a result of which Mrs. Frampton led her friend back to the car and drove away.

Knollis joined Bamford beside the body. "So that's the widow, eh? Age about forty, and attempts to disguise the fact. The dark hair shows signs of dye which is growing out, and her complexion is too sallow for a younger woman in good health. Loud check tweeds and brogues naturally indicate the woman-about-town."

"Secretary or chairman of every club not monopolized by her husband," Bamford supplemented. "She's noted for spending more time out of the house than in it. Huntingdon is a second husband, and the child is by the first marriage. Isn't there some tragedy connected with that first marriage, Drayton? I seem to recall something of the kind."

"First husband committed suicide on the south coast, sir," said Drayton. "The child was born after his death, and Mr. Huntingdon married her about a year later."

"That's interesting," said Knollis. "Let's have a look at the body before the photographers and the surgeon get working on him."

Drayton removed the cape, revealing the corpse. It was lying face down. There was a broad splurge of blood between the shoulder-blades, from which stretched seven narrow streams, so that it looked as if an evil blood-red spider was sitting on the dead man and endeavouring to embrace his body.

Huntingdon was about five feet eleven in height, and exceptionally broad. His head was large, well-shaped, and covered with dark brown hair. The ears were large and somewhat coarse in texture, and set low over a short and very thick neck.

"How old was he?" asked Knollis.

"About fifty-one, I believe."

"Considerably older than the wife, eh?"

Bamford nodded. "He was, but I don't see that the fact is in any way significant."

"Neither do I," Knollis admitted. "I'm merely collecting data. I take it that he was well on the way to success when she met and married him?"

"Drayton has been in the town longer than myself."

Drayton pushed back his cap and scratched his head.

"I seem to remember that they were married some ten and a half years ago, sir. He retired five years ago, so I think you are correct."

"Been through his pockets?" asked Knollis.

Drayton had not, so they went to work, examining the pockets after they had turned him over, and replacing each article when it had been listed. Knollis did the work. He was already right inside the skin of the case, and identifying himself with the investigation.

"Pipe and matches in left jacket pocket. Handkerchief tucked up right sleeve. Money in left trousers. Small bunch of keys in right trousers. Wallet in right inside breast pocket. Five one-pound notes and cheque-book. Light gold half-hunter. The man travelled light. Over with him. Now replace the cape, Drayton."

He got to his feet, his features tense, and his eyes mere slits. "He was left-handed, and he wasn't killed for his money."

He turned to the chauffeur, who up to now had been a mere interested onlooker. "Who are you?"

"Burton, the Bishop of Northcote's chauffeur, sir. I dropped him down the road some time ago. He wanted to walk among the trees while he meditated on his speech for to-night's meeting. I forgot about him when I dropped across this business, so I expect he'll be waiting for me on the main road."

"I've very much afraid that he'll have to wait a little longer," said Knollis. "Does he usually walk in plantations when he wants to meditate?"

Burton, a little man with querulous eyebrows, shook his head. "As a matter of fact, he doesn't, sir. It's the first time I've known him to do it. The Old Dear generally prefers the comfort of his study."

"I can understand that," said Knollis.

At that moment the 'Old Dear' emerged from the plantation, an expression of wide-eyed astonishment on his bland features. He walked round the southern end of the dam in a dignified and stately manner, treading as daintily as a cat on the springy turf, an incongruous figure in his frock coat, gaiters, and top hat.

Burton bobbed obsequiously as he joined the group. "My lord, I was—"

"Seemingly delayed, Burton," said the Bishop solemnly. He glanced round the assembled figures and indicated the covered body with a cautious finger. "An—er—accident?"

Knollis removed the cape as deftly as a matador performing a veronica. "Do you happen to recognize him, my lord?"

The Bishop blinked at the blood, and his jaw tightened. He removed his hat, and bent over the body, his wispy grey hair frisking frivolously in the light breeze that was running through the valley.

"Mr. Richard Huntingdon. Dear, dear!"

"You know him, of course?" asked Knollis.

The Bishop did not heed Knollis's question. Instead he stared fixedly at the corpse. "God has a way of sending His angel Azrael when the time is—"

He broke off in some embarrassment and glanced uncomfortably at Knollis. He coughed apologetically behind his hand. "'Life,' said the Immortal Bard, 'is but a poor player upon the stage—a brief candle.'"

"Which has been abruptly snuffed," said Knollis.

The Bishop turned his eyes to the heavens, where great creamy cumulous clouds sailed majestically against a filmy blue backcloth. "It would seem that Richard Huntingdon has had his hour upon the stage. *Requiescat in pace!*"

He shook his head sorrowfully, replaced his hat, and walked sedately to the car, Burton following respectfully. Once the Bishop had negotiated the fence, Burton hurried forward, opened the door of the car, tucked a rug round his gaitered legs, and drove away.

Knollis watched the whole performance through near-shut eyes. As the car rolled smoothly up the hill towards the main Hedenham-Coleby road, he sniffed cautiously. "Candle-snuffers *have* been made in fine porcelain."

CHAPTER II
THE EVIDENCE OF THE CHILD

BY MIDNIGHT Knollis was in charge of the case, and his sergeant, Ellis, entrained for Coleby. In the meantime, Bamford had interviewed Mrs. Huntingdon, Mrs. Frampton, and the secretary of the golf club who had taken the telephone message. The latter was not prepared to swear that it was Richard Huntingdon who had telephoned, but, as he said, he had no reason at the time to suspect that the speaker was any other than Huntingdon. Mrs. Frampton's statement was mere corroboration of Mrs. Huntingdon's recital of the facts, and Knollis was left with very little to tell Sergeant Ellis about the case when he reported at Divisional Headquarters at nine o'clock on the following morning.

"Looks like being a sticky job," commented the black-haired Ellis as he brushed his heavy walrus moustache away from his mouth. "Where are we going to start?"

"I don't know," replied Knollis thoughtfully. "I wish it was any day but Sunday. The Old Dear will be preaching and we shan't be able to get at him very easily."

"The Old Dear?" queried Ellis, cocking an eyebrow.

"The Bishop of Northcote, as described by his chauffeur. Being near the scene of the crime he might have seen something important to which he paid little attention."

Ellis stroked the moustache. "Bishop of Northcote. He's the one who's constantly airing his views on the depravity of modern youth in my Sunday paper—the *Argus*."

Knollis looked up. "Oh? Explain."

"He pans modern youth pretty badly," Ellis further explained. "He's doing a series of articles in the *Argus*, and facing a constant barrage of indignant letters—most of them under pseudonyms."

"Might be interesting," Knollis murmured softly. "He was due to speak at a meeting of the Young Templars last night, and that is an association for reviving chivalry in everyday life. Huntingdon was due at the same meeting. I wonder if there is anything there? It's ridiculous on the face of it, but you never know!"

"You say he was wandering in the plantation?" asked Ellis. "And during the commission of the murder?" Knollis nodded. "Yes, and there was a point which intrigued me, Ellis. He blinked a wee bit on seeing the exposed body, but he didn't seem as perturbed as I should have expected. The mess of blood startled him temporarily, but it *was* a mere temporary reaction. He recovered on the instant and then examined Huntingdon's body with all the professional detachment of a doctor."

"And the inference?" said Ellis.

"Well," Knollis replied slowly, "I take it that a bishop, by virtue of his position, is expected to appear dignified and composed at all times, so I'm wondering if he heard the shot, saw the arrival of the mobile patrol and Mrs. Huntingdon, and stayed under cover until he had obtained control of himself. He was so smooth and placid that he might well have been putting on an act—and a doubt about him remains in my mind as a consequence."

Bamford entered the office, waved a good morning, and with admirable brevity asked: "What's happening?"

"Let me introduce my invaluable lieutenant, Sergeant Ellis," said Knollis. "Ellis, this is my good friend, Inspector Bamford."

Bamford grinned. "I've heard a lot about you, Sergeant."

"I count him as one of my friends these days," said Knollis. "We only keep up the officialese when there are any big chiefs about. Anyway, Bam, we're thinking of making a trip to the Huntingdon house. Care to join us?"

Bamford shook his head. "Sorry, no. I'll be busy all day with reports, coroner, Hackett's autopsy, and the rest of it. I'll be your inside man from now on. There's a car waiting downstairs, complete with driver, so I'll give you both my blessing and wish you all the luck in the world—and you'll need it!"

"Luck has nothing to do with it," Knollis said severely. "It is a mixture of thought, tears, and perspiration that solves murder cases. Ask Ellis: he's been in at more than myself."

"'Sright," said Ellis flatly.

"I still wish you luck," smiled Bamford.

The Huntingdon home, Red Gables, stood in spacious grounds in the eastern suburbs of Coleby, a tall red-roofed villa with cream-and-green painted woodwork and pebble-dashed walls. Wide and carefully-kept lawns fronted the house, and were surrounded by deep herbaceous borders on which two gardeners were working in the yellow April sunlight.

"They won't grow," said Ellis. "Flowers planted on a Sunday never do. My old granny was all against it. They should be planted on a weekday, and on a waxing moon."

Knollis leaned over and asked the driver to pull up by the two gardeners. "Now," he said to Ellis, "ask them why they are working on a Sunday."

Ellis, although displaying his surprise, wound down the window, and did so.

"Mr. Huntingdon skidded into the border yesterday afternoon, sir," said the elder of the gardeners. "We don't usually work Sundays."

"Now," asked Ellis as he withdrew his head and closed the window; "why did you want me to do that?"

"I was curious. There is a reason for all things, and I'm particularly fond of discovering reasons. Simple though it looks, that work might have held a more important reason."

Ellis grunted. The car drew up before the house, and Knollis stepped out. "I wonder what is the rate of flow?" he murmured as they stood facing the front door. "You see, Ellis—but we can go into that later; that and the movements of the Old Dear. We'll see what Mrs. Huntingdon has to tell us. Bamford was too impetuous. He should have given her time to become coherent. However, that's his method and I shouldn't criticize him. He's no fool."

Ellis rang the bell, and they were shown into a mahogany-furnished morning-room in which the yellow sunlight competed unsuccessfully with three bowls of deep gold King Alfred daffodils.

"Solid and reassuring," commented Knollis as he looked around. "The home of a man whose finances are sound. Some day I'm going to summon up the courage to write an essay or a monograph or something on the psychology of furnishings. People reveal themselves by the settings in which they place themselves. Colour, too, is equally revealing. See this room! Mahogany furniture, old gold walls, deep-yellow flowers; warmth, solidity, and security."

"He was a bit old-fashioned in his ideas, too," said Ellis from the bay window.

"How do you reach that conclusion?"

"The monkey-puzzle tree in the garden. That, according to your theories, fits in with his Edwardian ideas on chivalry. I mean, can you imagine a believer in sex equality having a monkey-puzzle tree in his garden?"

The door opened before Knollis could comment on Ellis's observation, and Mrs. Huntingdon joined them. About five feet four in height, she was sallow-complexioned, brown-haired and blue-eyed. There was a trace of brusque arrogance in the lift of her firm chin, and Knollis recalled Bamford's statement that she was a leader, with a stake in nearly every woman's club and society in the town. He could easily visualize her taking a meeting, holding the members to the business in hand, and allowing no side tracking nor wandering from the printed agenda.

"Your husband's death will have been a terrible shock to you, Mrs. Huntingdon," he murmured softly as his eyes ran over her with professional thoroughness.

"Death has to come some day, Inspector," she replied crisply. "Even in my own case it is not death *per se* that I fear, but the manner of its coming. The suddenness, the unexpectedness, and the very nature of Richard's terrible end has been a shock which has rendered me almost incapable of thought. For what is probably the first time in my life I find myself in a situation with which I am unable to cope. I am bewildered!"

"The normal effect of shock," said Knollis gently. "I hate disturbing you at such a time, but I am sure you will appreciate the necessity of answering a few questions about your husband, and will assist us to the best of your ability."

She clenched her small fists and nodded. "Anything I can do, I will do, Inspector. Richard and my child were all my life."

Knollis took her arm and led her to a chair. "Can you suggest any reason why your husband should have been done to death in this way? Or any person who would, in your opinion, be capable of killing him?"

"Inspector," she said flatly, "I am at a complete loss. I have lain awake through the night trying to find the answers to those two questions. My husband was well-liked and respected. He was a prominent man in the town, and a hard worker for the less fortunate. He was in very great demand as a speaker, and I have a cuttings-album filled with press reports of his many public appearances."

"There were people who disliked him, Mrs. Huntingdon?"

"Well, yes," she said reluctantly. "Richard was outspoken, and was certainly not all things to all men. There were people he disliked, and people who disliked him, but I cannot honestly say that I know of any who disliked him to the extent that they could be ranked as enemies."

"Perhaps you could name a few of these people?"

She hesitated, toying with the square neck of her brown dress. "It is ridiculous to name such a person, of course, but perhaps his most bitter antagonist was the Bishop."

"The Bishop of Northcote?" Knollis asked sharply.

She nodded. "His antagonism had been a disturbing factor in Richard's life for several years. They were at variance on a number of subjects. The Bishop is a firm believer in the equality of the sexes, and believes that women should stand beside men as equals and not ask nor expect any consideration as an alleged weaker sex. Richard was of a chivalrous nature, and believed that women actually were the weaker sex, and should be treated as such. Again, Richard believed in the inherent good in human nature, while the Bishop is a member of the old hell-and-brimstone school, believing in original sin and the literal truth of the Adam and Eve legend. He lectures on the necessity of wrestling with the evil side of man's nature, whereas poor dear Richard believed we should concentrate on the development of one's better self—which he said was the better psychology."

She smiled wistfully. "I don't profess to know a great deal about such matters myself, but Richard was accustomed to practising his speeches and addresses on me, and so I know what he spoke about even if I do not understand it. Richard was a good man, Inspector!"

"I am sure he was," murmured Knollis. "Your married life was obviously a very happy one?"

She hesitated, and Knollis looked at her keenly as a shadow quickly crossed her eyes and vanished again. "A very happy one, Inspector."

"Your second marriage, I believe, Mrs. Huntingdon?"

"Ye-es," she answered slowly. "My first marriage ended tragically. My husband fell to his death over the Seven Sisters cliffs, outside Eastbourne. We had only been married a very short time."

"Tell me, Mrs. Huntingdon," said Knollis; "when you received the message via the secretary of the golf club, and Mrs. Frampton went down with you to the dam, what was the first thing that attracted your attention?"

"My husband's car, standing on the roadside."

"And the next?"

"The yacht on the water. My little daughter had received a similar one as a present a fortnight ago, and I straightway thought that the Angel Child had—had—well, been drowned, and that my husband was trying to revive her somewhere amongst the bushes."

"Quite a logical line of reasoning," said Knollis. "You called your husband's name in an effort to locate him?"

"Yes, I thought he must be somewhere amongst the bushes, and as he would be bending over my daughter applying artificial respiration it was natural that I could not see him. And then, of course I tripped over him."

"The message that took him to the dam; it was received in this house, Mrs. Huntingdon?"

She rose, and touched a bell-push on the wall. "Marie, my housemaid, can tell you all there is to be known about that, Inspector. I think you should ask her yourself."

A slight-built girl of about seventeen years entered the room, and stood awkwardly looking from one to the other.

"Marie, dear," said Mrs. Huntingdon, "the Inspector wishes you to tell him what happened when your master received the telephone message about Dorrie."

"Well, sir," said the girl, "I was dusting in the hall and arranging the flowers on the table, and Mr. Huntingdon was in the study. I heard the telephone bell ring, and then it sounded as if he was shouting into the telephone. He rushed out and said that Miss Dorrie had met with an accident, and we were to get her bed ready and put hot-water bottles in it. He rushed from the house without his hat, and a minute or so afterwards I heard the car racing down the drive. I looked out of the front door, and saw him drive into the flower-beds. He went straight on, got back on the drive, and turned right when he got through the gateway. Then I hurried to the kitchen and put the kettles on."

"He didn't say where Miss Dorrie was, or where the message had come from?"

"Not a word, sir."

"I see," Knollis said slowly. "That will be all, thank you."

Knollis turned back to Mrs. Huntingdon. She was sitting with her hands clasped tightly between her knees, staring vacantly at the Indian carpet.

"Your daughter did go to the party, Mrs. Huntingdon?"

She raised her head. "Oh, yes! Mrs. Castle says that she arrived about ten minutes to four."

"How long would it take her to get from home to the house where the party was held?"

"Twenty minutes, Inspector. She would catch a bus at the end of this road which would deliver her within a few yards of Mrs. Castle's house."

"And she left here at half-past three?"

"So Marie tells me; yes."

"Whereabouts in the town is the Castle home situated?"

"On the Hedenham Road."

"Near Inspector Bamford's house, by any chance?"

"About twenty yards beyond. The bus halts higher up."

Knollis fingered his ear and grunted. He stared slowly at Mrs. Huntingdon. "The message was brought to you about ten minutes to four!"

"Why yes," she said in a surprised voice. "Between ten minutes to four and four o'clock, anyway. I couldn't swear to a few minutes either way."

"And the secretary of the golf club says he was satisfied that it was your husband's voice. Would you mind recalling your maid, please?"

She stretched a hand to the bell-push, and Marie re-entered the room a moment or so later.

"Marie," said Knollis, "can you say whether Mr. Huntingdon made any outgoing calls before leaving the house?"

"He did not, sir. The bell rang, and I heard him shouting down it, and then he thumped the receiver back into place and rushed into the hall. He did not go into the study again."

"Thank you," said Knollis, and dismissed her.

"What are you wondering about, Inspector?" asked Mrs. Huntingdon. "The times coincide, surely!"

"That is the whole point," returned Knollis. "They *coincide*, and I don't think they should. There doesn't appear to be any time lapse between them. Another point, Mrs. Huntingdon; why didn't your husband call you from the house? He must have called from a kiosk, and that entails the delays caused by the insertion of coins and the pushing of the button. And surely the idea of 'phoning you to tell you about your own daughter could not have been a mere afterthought! There's something wrong somewhere."

Mrs. Huntingdon appeared to be intensely interested in the suggestion. She wrinkled her brows as if in deep thought, and then said, very deliberately: "Richard did not use a kiosk, Inspector. He would not use one. He was a fine man, but like the rest of the human family he had his little oddities and idiosyncrasies. For instance, he would not ride in a public vehicle—a bus or train, and similarly he would not use a telephone box. He regarded both as being provided for the people who had neither a car nor a private 'phone, and said that we must never infringe the privileges of the less fortunate. And to tell you the truth, I don't think he would know how to operate a public telephone!"

"Is there a kiosk near the Castle home?"

"I believe there is one about two minutes' walk up the road."

"And the next one in the direction of Hedenham?" She paused in thought, a finger to her lip. "That will surely be the R.A.C. box a few yards beyond the turning down Coleby Rise."

Knollis nodded. "As I surmised. One other point troubles me, Mrs. Huntingdon. From what I know of the district—which I admit is little enough—your husband would have to pass the Castle home on his way to Three-Acre Dam?"

"Oh, yes!"

"And he was aware that Dorrie was supposed to be at the Castle party?"

"Why yes, of course!"

"That is the point," said Knollis. "Why didn't he call there to make sure?"

"Surely he would be so concerned about Dorrie."

Knollis nodded. His tongue ran over his upper lip. "Yes, I suppose that is the true explanation—but I wonder what *name*, if any, was given by the person who telephoned him? The matter is intriguing."

He returned to his brisk official manner. "Now, Mrs. Huntingdon, I would like to look through your husband's private papers. I trust you have no objections?"

For answer, she rose and conducted them across the hall, pushed open a door, and silently invited them to enter a room furnished in much the same style as the morning-room they had just left. "This was Richard's study, library, and den-in-general. Do you wish me to assist you, or do you prefer to be left alone?"

"It is immaterial," said Knollis. "We can manage, and the business is likely to distress you, so I suggest—"

She inclined her head. "In which case I will leave you, Inspector. The bell is behind the door should you require anything."

"Well?" asked Ellis a minute later.

"On the face of it," said Knollis, "it would seem that the killer waited for young Dorrie entering the Castle house, and then rang

Huntingdon. I assume that a car was used by him, because he would be pushed for time. The schedule would run something like this: make sure that Dorrie arrived at the Castles'—ring Richard—hurry to the dam to await his arrival—kill him—hurry to a 'phone and inform Mrs. Huntingdon—make a getaway. There is an alternative, naturally. He could have 'phoned Mrs. Huntingdon before he informed Richard. A further alternative is that he made both calls from the same box at the same time."

He stroked his hair back over his head. "Ellis, I'm glad I was not that man! Those ten minutes must have been horribly crowded and full of risks and hazards. In fact, at the moment I don't see at all clearly how the deuce he pulled it all in during the time. There is an explanation, of course, but it doesn't leap to meet the mental eye. However, let's see if there is anything to interest us here."

He pulled down the desk-flap and silently regarded the tidy nests of envelopes.

"Business-like, anyway," said Ellis with a grunt.

"Very business-like, Ellis. Everything filed in foolscap and quarto envelopes. Rates receipts, electricity receipts, provision dealer, butcher—all household accounts in the foolscap ones, so let's try the quarto department. Council minutes, Town Planning Committee minutes, correspondence between R.H. and Mayor. Marriage licence—this should be interesting. Two of 'em? Oh, yes, of course! Jean Montague and Walter Froggatt, August sixth, Nineteen-thirty-four. Second one: Jean Montague Froggatt to Richard Huntingdon, August sixth, 'Thirty-five. Exactly a year later, eh? Sentimental reasons? I wonder."

"There's an envelope of birth certificates here," said Ellis, fishing in the other end of the desk.

"Give," Knollis said briefly. "Ah, Richard Huntingdon, born May seventeenth, Eighteen-ninety-eight. That makes him forty-eight all but a month. Jean Montague, born September eighth, Nineteen-hundred-and-four—forty-two this year. That was a good guess of mine. Young Dorrie's here, too. March twenty-first, Nineteen-thirty-five. See, that makes her a seven-month baby unless the marriage had to be rushed. That fact may be useful; you can never tell. Both marriages solemnized in London registry offices; Streatham for the first marriage, and Marylebone for the second."

"She isn't a persistent husband-killer, is she?" queried Ellis in a low voice.

"She couldn't have killed Huntingdon, at all events," Knollis replied, "and there is nothing whatsoever to suggest that she killed the first one. Nevertheless, we'll contact the Eastbourne police and ask for details of Froggatt's death. If he fell over the cliff he was just plain careless. If he jumped over he must have had some bad trouble in the offing. And if he was pushed over—well, we must seek the reason. That someone at the door?"

Ellis opened it. A small girl cautiously entered the room, looking behind the door before she ventured further progress. Knollis smiled at her, and then looked down his long nose and considered her more carefully. She looked less like a child than a doll. Large blue eyes shone from an oval face whose complexion was perfect. Her hair was golden, cropped close to her head, and arranged in tight curls that could not be mistaken for anything else but the handiwork of a professional hairdresser. Her legs were bare to the ankles, brown sturdy legs without blemish. Her frock was tight at the waist, and emphatically flared, but so short that Knollis silently thanked heaven on Mrs. Grundy's behalf that she was wearing knickers. She stood watching him silently, one hand lightly holding the hem of her frock, and the other poised in a graceful gesture that was the product of her dancing school.

"Which is Mr. Knollis, please?" she asked after a minute or so.

Knollis repressed a smile at her adult manner, and made a slight bow. "I am, my dear. You will be Miss Doreen Huntingdon?"

She curtseyed. "Yes, sir, although everyone calls me Dorrie. My mummy's name is Jean, but she is always called Dinney because when I was quite small I couldn't say her name properly."

"I'm very pleased to make your acquaintance," Knollis said solemnly. "Is there anything I can do for you?"

She glanced nervously over her shoulder. "Is Dinney coming back, sir?"

"Your mother? I don't think so, Dorrie," said Knollis.

"You see, sir, she doesn't know I've come to see you. I heard your name from Marie, our maid, and I wondered if you could . . ."

She stared down at her toes and plucked nervously at her frock.

"Yes?" coaxed Knollis with an amused glance at Ellis. "If there is anything I can do for you, I will. In fact we are both at your service. This is Sergeant Ellis."

"You really are a 'tective, sir?" she asked anxiously.

Knollis gravely admitted the fact.

The earnestness of her expression relaxed, and a more human smile came over her pretty face. "You are a nice man, sir."

"That is nice of you," said Knollis.

"Mr. Knollis?"

"Well, my dear?"

"Dinney will be awf'lly annoyed if she knows I've asked you."

"We won't tell her then," said Knollis.

"Please," she said, stepping a foot nearer to him; "please could you find out who sent the ship for my birthday?"

Knollis shot a quick glance at Ellis.

"You mean that you don't know who sent it, Dorrie?"

"Oh, no, sir! It came wrapped up ever so nicely, but there wasn't a card with it. Dinney and Daddy said I must have lost it with the paper from my other presents, but I know I didn't! Cross my heart, I didn't. There really wasn't one—and how can I thank somebody for a lovely present when I don't know who it is?"

Footsteps sounded in the hall, and Mrs. Huntingdon hurried into the room. "So here you are! Now come along, my darling, and don't bother the gentlemen! They are very busy indeed!"

"But, Dinney darling," exclaimed the child, "Mr. Knollis is going to find out about my ship! He really is, aren't you, sir?"

Mrs. Huntingdon made a gesture of impatience. "My darling, both your—your Daddy and myself have told you that the card must have got lost with the wrappings. You shouldn't come bothering the gentlemen!"

She glanced apologetically at Knollis. "I'm sorry about the interruption, Inspector, but perhaps you have children of your own, in which case you will understand."

Knollis gave her a direct stare. "I have two boys," he said, "and that is exactly why I am interested in Dorrie's yacht. Both yourself and your husband may have been able to take the easier way by convincing yourselves that the card was lost, but you cannot fool a child! They are far more observant than a so-called grown-up person. With your permission I would like Dorrie to tell her story in her own way. Is your permission granted?"

Dinney Huntingdon stared unbelievingly, and then something like a sob escaped her. "You cannot seriously suggest that any foul person would use a *child*! Heavens above, I feel sick at the very thought!"

Knollis shrugged his shoulders. "The possibility is there, Mrs. Huntingdon, and further I dare not go. I grant you that the thought is a sickening one, and surely we should try to prove or disprove it?"

Her mouth tightened, and a dangerous gleam came into her eyes. She turned and slammed the door, then laid her hands on her child's shoulders. "Darling, your Dinney is as blind as a bat. The Inspector shall help you to find who sent the boat. Tell him all about it, darling!"

"Can I fetch it first, Dinney darling?" Dorrie asked eagerly.

"Yes, dear, and hurry!"

As the child hurried away, Dinney Huntingdon beat her right fist into the palm of her left hand. "But Inspector, it's—it's dastardly!"

"Mrs. Huntingdon," said Knollis, "your choice of words is admirable!"

Chapter III
THE EVIDENCE OF THE MAID

THE YACHT WAS fourteen inches long, white-painted, and had a narrow green band running round the gunwale and the name *Doreen* on either side of the bow. Knollis pointed to the name and raised an enquiring eyebrow. "The name has been written since Dorrie received the present?"

"You see the yacht exactly as it arrived, Inspector."

"You unwrapped this yourself, Dorrie?" asked Knollis.

"Oh, yes, sir! I unwrapped all my presents, didn't I, Dinney darling?"

Dinney darling agreed. "She was downstairs half an hour before Richard and myself. When I came down the Angel Child was sitting on the hearth in the dining-room with her parcels around her—and you had so *many* presents, hadn't you, darling!"

"Mm!" purred Dorrie contentedly. "Fourteen!"

"And there was a card with each of them?" asked Knollis.

Dorrie shook her golden curls. "Only thirteen cards, sir, but fourteen presents."

"The wrappings? I suppose they went to salvage?" Dinney Huntingdon shrugged her shoulders. "I suppose so, Inspector. Marie cleared the room after breakfast."

Dorrie interrupted: "I saved the paper from my ship, if that is what you want, sir."

Knollis heaved a great sigh. "That is exactly what I do want. Can you get it for me?"

"And the string, sir?"

"And the string, please."

She scampered round the table towards the door until her mother said "Dorrie darling!" in a reproachful voice, when she quickly came to attention and walked sedately from the room with a straight back and chin held high.

"I try so hard to teach her to be a Young Lady," said Dinney Huntingdon with an apologetic smile. "You see, we cannot afford to let her behave in the *gamin* manner, for it is people like ourselves who must set examples. She is really quite good, but tends to forget herself when excited."

Ellis brushed his moustache with the back of his hand and sniffed.

Dorrie returned with a neatly-folded square of brown paper, several squares of white tissue paper, a white cardboard box, and a length of string, all of which she laid in Knollis's lap. "That is all of it, sir."

Knollis thanked her, and unfolded the brown paper.

"The sail was rolled round the mast, and packed in the bottom of the box, sir," Dorrie explained. "Daddy put it together for me."

Knollis examined the name and address. "The usual block letters. *To Miss Dorrie Huntingdon, Red Gables, Chestnut Road, Coleby.* Postmark indecipherable, which is generally the case on parcels. I've never yet discovered whether the post-town is included in the franking-stamp!"

He took up the box and turned it over. On the bottom were two sets of private marks as made by tradesmen: NA/W in one corner, and underneath it OT/NN. "Very useful," he commented. "Mrs. Huntingdon, have you seen similar yachts on display in Coleby shop windows?"

"I'm afraid I have not, Inspector."

Dorrie had. Oh, yes, she knew three shops which sold exactly the same type of yacht. "There is Franklin's shop in Carter Gate, Mrs. Spencer's shop in Harrow Road, and I've seen one in a little green shop with no name in Hedenham Road, just past the railway bridge."

Ellis made notes, and gave vent to a grunt of deep satisfaction. "Children make excellent detectives!"

"They are twenty-four and elevenpence," Dorrie added gratuitously, "and none of my other presents cost all that except those from Daddy and Dinney."

"Have you sailed it yet?" Knollis asked absently.

The golden curls danced again as she shook her head. "Oh, no! But Daddy promised to take me to some water. I wanted to go alone, and I asked Marie which was the best place, but she said I must wait until someone went with me—in case I fell in, you know."

A strange gleam came into Knollis's eyes.

"Mrs. Huntingdon, what stretches of water are there in and around Coleby?"

"Stretches of water?" she asked with a surprised air. "Why, there are three. There is the reservoir on the road between Coleby and Norton Birchfield, and the small pond in the Bentinck Pleasure Gardens, and—of course—the dam!"

Knollis thoughtfully fingered the lobe of his right ear, looked at the floor, and then raised his eyes to Dinney Huntingdon.

"I have a queer idea running in my mind, Mrs. Huntingdon. First, may I take it for granted that the pond in the Gardens is well patronized? What I mean is that there is nearly always someone there—children playing, people walking round, and nursemaids with prams?"

"Yes," she replied; "yes, that is correct."

"And the reservoir? That is in no way secluded?"

"Oh, no! The main road runs within a few yards of the bank, and it is frequented by anglers during the season, and skiffs and rowing-boats are available for hire from Easter Monday onwards. The naval cadets train there, too, and the Rover Scouts."

"As I suspected," said Knollis. "Now, the road that runs from the Coleby-Hedenham road to Norton Birchfield, and by Three-Acre Dam, is that used a great deal?"

"Very seldom, I should say," she replied. "You see, Inspector, there is the cross-roads farther on, and the right and left turns lead respectively to Norton Birchfield and the same Hedenham main road. It is an easier gradient than Hampton Knoll—and actually the more direct route from Hedenham."

"I see," Knollis said slowly. "Inspector Bamford tells me that there is no angling in the dam. That raises a very interesting possibility."

He turned to the child. "Dorrie, I want you to answer a question. Am I correct in saying that you do not want to sail your ship because of dirtying it?"

"Oh, but I do want to sail it, sir!" she protested. "All the other girls and boys sail theirs!"

"You can leave us now, my dear," said Knollis. "Please ask Marie to come, will you?"

Dorrie caught her mother's warning eye, and proceeded to leave the room in a sedate manner, the treasured yacht held tight in her arms.

Knollis was silent until Marie rejoined them, when he glanced up and gave a ghost of a smile. "Sorry to keep bothering you like this," he apologized, "but you seem to be a key witness, and a very valuable one. Tell me; do you remember Miss Dorrie's birthday?"

"It was Spring Day, sir, the twenty-first of March."

"Who met the postman with the child's presents?"

"I did, sir, at the side door."

"Any idea how many parcels there were?"

"Fourteen, sir, and five birthday cards."

"Richard and I posted our presents to her," Dinney Huntingdon interrupted. "We thought it would be more fun for her to have them that way. You know how children love undoing parcels!"

Knollis nodded, and turned back to Marie. "What happened after you had taken in the post?"

"I took them through to the dining-room, sir, and Miss Dorrie ran downstairs a few minutes afterwards and started opening them."

"The breakfast-room was being redecorated," Dinney Huntingdon again interrupted.

"I see," nodded Knollis. "Now, Marie, you were present when she opened them?"

"Yes, sir. Her father and mother were not down, and she asked me to look at them as she opened them."

"So that you saw her open the parcel containing the model yacht? Is that correct?"

"Why, yes, sir!"

"She insists that there was no card indicating the giver of the present. Can you say whether that is correct?"

Marie hesitated. "Well, I must say that I never saw one. Miss Dorrie said that there was no card with it, and when I cleared away the paper after breakfast I went through it carefully, but I didn't find one."

Knollis held out the sheet of brown paper to Dinney Huntingdon. "Is this printing familiar to you, Mrs. Huntingdon? Does it bear any resemblance to any handwriting that you know?"

"I cannot say that I have ever seen any writing that in any way resembles it, Inspector," she replied firmly.

"And you?" he asked of the maid.

"No, sir."

Knollis slid the paper and the box on the table, clasped his hands, and bent forward towards Dinney Huntingdon.

"Mrs. Huntingdon! Suppose that Dorrie wanted to sail her yacht, and wanted to sail it so badly that she slipped off alone and without telling anyone where she was going: what would have been the result if you had later found out?"

Dinney Huntingdon lifted her chin. "She would have suffered the loss of various privileges for a time. I do not believe in corporal punishment."

"So that we can assume that she would have avoided any public place in which she was likely to be recognized?"

"I—er—yes, I suppose so!" she replied uncertainly. "I'm afraid I do not grasp the implication, Inspector."

"We can assume that she would have avoided the reservoir, and the pond in the Pleasure Gardens?"

"Ye-es."

"In which case her only alternative would have been Three-Acre Dam?"

"Good heavens, but it is miles away, Inspector! She would never have thought of such an idea!"

"When a child's mind is set on doing something, Mrs. Huntingdon, there is no such thing as distance. Now I wonder if Dorrie did think of sailing her yacht on the dam?" he pondered, glancing quickly at Marie.

The maid opened her mouth, looked across at her mistress, and closed it again.

Knollis rose to his feet and looked down at Dinney Hunting-don. "May I assume that no punishment would be meted out to Dorrie—or will be meted out to her—if she had actually thought of going to Three-Acre Dam to sail her yacht, without putting the idea into commission?"

"I don't understand you, Inspector!" Dinney Huntingdon protested. "One cannot punish a child for merely *thinking*. For heaven's sake do explain yourself."

"I will," said Knollis. "The position is simply this: Marie knows exactly what Dorrie had in mind, for Dorrie confided in her. She doesn't want to tell us because she is afraid of the consequences. Now I am investigating the murder of your husband, and any question I ask has some bearing on the enquiry. I wish Marie to tell me her story, and I cannot allow either her or Dorrie to suffer as a result."

"I am not a slave-mistress," Dinney Huntingdon returned heatedly. "The girl is perfectly free to speak!"

"Fair enough!" said Knollis. "Well, Marie, had Dorrie any ideas about going to Three-Acre Dam to sail her yacht?"

The maid hesitated, and then nodded her dark head.

"She had, sir. She wanted me to take her on my day off, but I've got a young man, and my spare time was taken up. Mr. Huntingdon had promised to take her when he wasn't busy, while her mother said she hadn't time to take her at all."

Dinney Huntingdon glared, in spite of her assertion that Marie was free to speak.

Knollis said: "Go on!"

"She isn't a fool," continued Marie, "even if they tried to make her into one. She knew that her father would never have time to take her, and that her mother had no intention of taking her. I'd have helped her if me and Charlie hadn't been busy with arrangements for getting married."

"You mean that you are leaving me?" Dinney Huntingdon asked in a shocked voice.

"You'll get my notice next week-end," said Marie. "That's why I'm saying what I think. Miss Dorrie has only one idea in her mind, and that's to sail her ship. Somebody's been egging her on, and I don't know who it is. She wanted to know how much the bus fare was to the top of Coleby Rise. I made her tell me what she was thinking about, and she said she was going to play truant from the party and go down to the dam. I stopped her, because it's such a lonely place, and if she happened to fall in there wouldn't be anybody about to save her."

"When did she confide all this to you?" asked Knollis softly.

"Last Wednesday, sir, just before I was going for my day off. She had a half-holiday from school, and was back home by half-past twelve. She came down to the kitchen to talk to me. She said she wasn't thinking of going that afternoon, because her mother might be at home, and I made her promise not to go on Saturday. She usually keeps promises, so I didn't worry about her."

"And on Saturday?"

"She promised to go straight to the party, sir. When Mr. Huntingdon got the 'phone call to say she had had an accident I thought she'd broken a promise for once and had fallen in the dam and got drowned."

"Tell me, Mrs. Huntingdon," said Knollis; "on how many occasions did she mention the possibility of being taken out to sail the yacht?"

"Well," she replied ruefully, "she only asked me once, probably because she knew that I would not change my mind. I believe she badgered Richard frequently."

"She asked him three times in my hearing," interrupted Marie. "That yacht meant more to her than the rest of her toys put together, although nobody else but me seemed to see it. Even her new doll was put on one side for it."

"So that your husband would know that her desire to sail the yacht was amounting to an obsession, Mrs. Huntingdon?"

She nodded slowly and sorrowfully. "I am beginning to see that my husband's death was planned long before Dorrie's birthday, Inspector."

"I must agree with you, Mrs. Huntingdon," Knollis replied. "We are up against someone with a first-class knowledge of human nature—someone who knew the three of you inside out.

His verdict on yourself and your husband may not be flattering, but it is at any rate revealing—to me. He seems to have relied on your—er—egotism for the success of his plan. Forgive me if that sounds harsh."

Dinney Huntingdon lowered her head. "I'm afraid I am learning a bitter lesson, Inspector Knollis." She bit her lip. "I am placed in the unenviable position of having to thank my house-maid for protecting my child and looking after her welfare."

She looked up, and smiled wryly at Marie. "You may not have a very good opinion of me, Marie, but you shall not be the loser for what you have done. Oh, God, what a blind fool I've been!"

She stumbled awkwardly to the door.

"Mrs. Huntingdon," said Knollis.

She paused and half-turned.

"If I may make a suggestion, it is that you should spare the afternoon to take Dorrie to the Pleasure Gardens and the pond. A head of steam confined in a boiler, you know."

"I understand, Inspector," she murmured, and closed the door.

Marie dabbed at her eyes. "I didn't think she'd take it like that."

"Kittens open their eyes after nine days," Knollis said dryly. "It sometimes takes we humans a matter of ninety years. I wouldn't have any regrets if I were you. You have probably done both mother and daughter a good turn. Now then, I want you to tell me about Mr. Huntingdon, as you saw him. And you may as well be seated while you are doing so. Like a cigarette?"

"I would," she said frankly. After three of Ellis's matches had been poked out by the end of the cigarette she managed to light it, and Knollis returned to the questioning.

"You didn't like him?"

"He was all right," she said reluctantly, "but a bit of a wind-bag. He liked to hear himself talk. He'd walk in when he'd been speechifying somewhere, all la-di-da with his chest stuck out and his chin in the air, telling her how many reporters there'd been, and how he'd put the Bishop in his place, and what clever things he'd said until it made me sick."

"So that was it," murmured Knollis. "I did wonder."

"He wasn't so bad when he was working," Marie added. "It was after he retired and he had nothing to do but think about how wonderful he was."

"They always say that no man is a hero to his valet," said Knollis, "and it would seem that the principle applies generally. Now, his death; have you any ideas about that? You must have heard who liked him and who didn't."

"Well," Marie said bluntly, blowing a puther of smoke into Knollis's face, "from what I've heard one time and another I should say he had plenty of enemies, but I shouldn't have thought any of them would have killed him like that! He would never give way to anybody, sir, if you know what I mean. He was always right. Nobody could tell him anything."

"How long have you been working here, Marie?"

"Six years and a half, sir. I came here when I left school. I'm twenty now."

"Really!" said Knollis. "You don't look it. I took you for seventeen."

She preened herself, and touched her hair with her free hand. "If there is anything else, sir?"

"One other matter. What relatives have the Huntingdons in Coleby?"

"Only the Montagues, sir. Mr. Montague is her brother. He works for Mr. Huntingdon's firm. A nice, quiet little man he is, but she's a proper cat, claws and everything. Her and *her*"—jerking her thumb towards the door—"they can't hit it for five minutes. Both of 'em want to be *her*, if you see what I mean."

"I think I do," smiled Knollis. "Mr. Huntingdon has no relatives in the district then?"

"Comes from Oxfordshire, or somewhere that way, sir, and I remember him saying that he was the last of the family. So that's all of them, as you might say."

"Friends?" prompted Knollis as she sat back and puffed at the remains of the cigarette.

She shook her head. "None that you and me would call friends. They have dinner-parties pretty regular, but they are the sort of people they're expected to ask. She plays bridge and golf with a handful of cats, and he belonged to every club you could think of. That's what makes me say that I never want Charlie to make a lot of money. Looks to me as if you lose more than you make."

"A penetrating observation," commented Knollis. "We must see you again before your wedding!"

Ellis ushered her from the room and returned grinning to Knollis's side. "Somehow, I don't think she likes the Huntingdons!"

"Vivid sketch of an upright man," Knollis said dryly. "By the time he has been deflated a little more we shall begin to see the shape of the man as he really was. As for Dorrie, I think she's been extremely lucky. You know, Ellis, someone has been watching this family like the proverbial hawk! If Dorrie had slipped away to sail her yacht we'd be investigating her death as well as her father's. I wonder if a two-in-one murder really was planned, and the plan miscarried? Suppose he was relying on Dorrie going to the dam. Suppose he was then going to kill her? Suppose he then phoned her father, and killed him—"

"And then 'phoned the old girl?"

"And then 'phoned Mrs. Huntingdon," Knollis corrected. "Fantastic, I know, but the possibility is there. Suppose that he wasn't absolutely sure of Dorrie's reactions, so that he procured the second yacht and then rang her father? The yacht, if put into the water at the southern end of the dam, would draw her father that way, and into the cover of the bushes. Huntingdon dies. The murderer then sends a message to the mother—but she spoils things for him by bringing a friend, and, unwittingly, the police patrol car. Our man sheers off, knowing when he is beaten."

He turned back to the desk. "Let's see if we can find a copy of Huntingdon's will, Ellis. If not, the name and address of his solicitor. I don't want to ask Mrs. Huntingdon; the less she knows about our activities the better, for women will talk, and she might talk to the wrong person without realizing it."

"Hold everything," warned Ellis, "judging by the noises-off there is someone else wanting an interview."

"Let 'em in," said Knollis. "The more the merrier. I love asking questions."

A queer little man came round the door. He was no more than five feet three in height, and had badly rounded shoulders, so that his grey suit hung from him as if from a peg in a wardrobe. His eyes were of a watery grey hue, and he averted them shyly as he closed the door and came shuffling towards them, apologetically, and stroking back the wispy mouse-coloured hair from his low forehead.

"I am John William Montague, Inspector, the brother of Mrs. Huntingdon. I usually spend Sunday mornings at church, and the afternoons in the greenhouse, but I had to come along this morning. A shocking business, is it not? Dear Richard! The very flower of chivalry and righteousness! His life snapped out like—like—"

"A candle?" suggested Knollis.

Mr. Montague twisted his head so that he could look up into Knollis's face, so close had he drawn to him.

"A candle, yes. I am one of the executors, you know."

"Oh!" exclaimed Knollis.

"Shardlow and Dallas, of Brompton Chambers—in the Market Square, you know—are the solicitors. Mr. Shardlow is the other executor. You know the terms of the will?"

"I do not," said Knollis.

"His wife is the sole beneficiary. In the event of her decease—which must come some day—the estate goes to Dorrie, the child, with my wife and myself as trustees until she reaches the age of eighteen. I am personally acquainted with all their affairs, you see. Richard was worth, all told, about fifty thousand pounds."

"How recent is the will, Mr. Montague?"

"See," he pondered, pulling at his lower lip; "three years in the coming July. I distinctly remember that he approached me late in the June and asked me if I would accept the executorship. I said that if I outlived him I would most certainly accept the trust. I—er—benefit to the tune of a hundred pounds in respect of my duties, a nominal sum merely intended to defray any expenses which I may incur."

"The usual arrangement," commented Knollis with a nod.

"Yes," said little Mr. Montague. "I shall spend it all on my boy, of course. He gets so very little in comparison!"

"In comparison with whom?" Knollis asked sharply.

"Eh? Oh, yes! Yes, I see, Inspector. Why, in comparison with, say, Dorrie. He shall have a new bicycle, and new clothes, and it should help him to college if he manages to pass the scholarship. Andrew deserves so very much better than he receives."

His voice trailed away and he stared reflectively at the carpet.

"Quite a business getting a boy educated," Knollis said conversationally. "I have two of my own. Care for a cigarette, Mr. Montague?"

"Er—no!" he answered after a brief pause. "I do smoke, of course, but only in the garden or the greenhouse. Maud will not— that is, she does not like me to smoke in the house. The curtains and ceiling, you know! And yet I feel it would be discourteous of me to refuse, Inspector. This isn't Maud's house, but Dinney's, and she smokes in her house! Thank you very much!"

He ran his slim fingers up and down the cigarette and smiled shyly and happily.

"Ellis?"

The three men lit up. Mr. Montague pointed his finger at the now disordered desk. "Looking for something in particular, Inspector? Perhaps I can help you?"

Knollis shook his head. "Nothing in particular, Mr. Montague. This is the normal check on these occasions. We sometimes discover that victims of murder have private lives which they have not cared to make public. I don't suggest any such possibility with Mr. Huntingdon, of course, but the check is made just the same. Once we are sure that a certain state of affairs does not exist we are free to pursue other lines."

Mr. Montague wagged his head. "Queer! Very queer! The long arm of coincidence! But for Gloria's message no one would ever have known. Dinney will go mad if she ever learns of it. I knew, of course, because I assisted Richard from time to time, but I admired his moral courage, and so I never gave him away. Never a word has crossed my lips until this very minute."

His voice trailed away into silent retrospect, and the wagging of his head grew slower.

"I'm afraid I do not understand what you are talking about, Mr. Montague?"

Mr. Montague's head came up. "Hm? No, of course you don't, Inspector. That is really why I am here this morning. Gloria rang me this very morning, and asked me to tell you. She said you would find out sooner or later, which I suppose is true."

"Who *is* Gloria?" Knollis demanded impatiently.

"Gloria?" Little Mr. Montague chuckled. "Gloria? I am very much afraid that she was Richard's mistress. That sounds queer, doesn't it? It would to anyone who knew him. Gloria was the weakness in Richard's armour, his heel of Achilles—I remember him from my schooldays."

"Cherchez la femme!" exclaimed Ellis with great satisfaction.

Mr. Montague nodded. "Seek the woman! That is the translation, I believe. Well, I don't think she could have had anything to do with his death, but she certainly had a great deal to do with his life. Oh, dear, yes!"

"So the upright man had a mistress," said Knollis in a tone of flat understanding. "Who was she, and where does she live?"

Mr. Montague sought a chair, and from that refuge peered almost hostilely at Knollis. "I wouldn't have told you of my own free will, you understand? Not if wild horses had been used to drag the information from me. Gloria rang me this morning. Maud doesn't know anything about her—I don't think so, anyway, although she usually gets to know everything. Gloria said I was to see Inspector Bamford, but when I arrived here I was told that you were in charge of the case, and so I decided it would be all right to tell you instead. Gloria badly wants to see you!"

"Not so badly as I want to see her," Knollis returned grimly. "Where does she live?"

"On the Hedenham Road. You know where Coleby Rise turns off?"

"I do," said Knollis.

"Well, you go straight on for another mile until you come to a little gate on the right-hand side. It has a board fixed to it offering honey for sale. There are a good many similar gates, but only the one selling honey. You can't see the cottage from the road because the path goes through the wood for about two hundred yards, and winds, but Gloria's place is to be found at the end of it. Her surname is Grenson."

"A wood?" asked Knollis. "Any connection with the plantation which ends at Three-Acre Dam?"

"They back up to each other, Inspector. The wood runs along the roadside, and the plantation runs behind the wood. Perhaps you would like me to accompany you, to show you the way?"

"We'll manage, thanks," said Knollis.

He got rid of Mr. Montague, telephoned his news to Bamford, and made for the car with Ellis in his wake, *en route* to the Grenson cottage.

Chapter IV
THE EVIDENCE OF
THE PLANTATION

Miss Gloria Grenson, tall and comfortably plump, stood in the doorway of the cottage with one plucked eyebrow uplifted as Knollis and Ellis stepped from the car, apparently drawn by the sound of the engine at her gate from her preparing of dinner, for she held a wooden spoon in her right hand.

"Miss Grenson?" enquired Knollis, as he doffed his hat. She inclined her head without speaking.

"I am Inspector Knollis of New Scotland Yard. I understand that you wish to see me."

Her second eyebrow joined the superior altitude of the first. "Scotland Yard? I'm afraid I do not understand. Why should I want to see you?"

Knollis gestured his non-comprehension. "Perhaps we could talk better inside, if you are agreeable."

"By all means," she replied, "but I am afraid that I still do not understand. However—"

She led them into a comfortable room furnished in a modern style, being completely free of frills and knick-knacks. She waved a hand to the fireside chairs, disposed herself on a sea-grass stool, and laid the spoon on the table. "Now, Inspector!"

"I should explain," began Knollis, "that we are investigating the death of Mr. Richard Huntingdon. While at the Hunting-don home this morning we were informed by the dead man's brother-in-law, Mr. Montague, that you had telephoned him and requested that he should inform us that you were—well, sufficiently friendly with the deceased gentleman to make it necessary for us to interview you."

Miss Grenson's hand went slowly to her throat, and her eyes widened. She looked from Knollis to Ellis wonderingly, and then shook her head. "I don't understand, Inspector. I know Mr. Montague by sight, but certainly never 'phoned him, either this morning or any other morning."

"You have a telephone, of course?" Knollis asked sharply.

"Yes, in the next room, but I have not made a call for days. That can be checked at the exchange, can it not?"

Knollis nodded. "That puts a different complexion on matters," he muttered to himself. "Tell me, Miss Grenson; were you friendly with Richard Huntingdon?"

Reluctantly she replied: "Richard has been my very good friend, Inspector."

Knollis leaned forward. "I do not wish to embarrass you, Miss Grenson, but I am investigating a murder and cannot afford to let one fact escape me. There is one question I must ask you."

She raised her eyes hesitantly. "Yes, I know what you mean, Inspector, and thank you for your tact. Yes, I suppose that in the eyes of the world I was his—his mistress. Neither of us ever thought of it in that way," she hurried to add.

"How long has the association continued, Miss Grenson?"

She pulled her skirt over her knees, cleared her throat, and then gave him a direct stare. "It seems that we must be embarrassingly frank, Inspector. Complete honesty now may save me future discomfort?"

"I do assure you," said Knollis, "that any information you may supply will not be made public unless it has a direct bearing on the cause of his death. We do understand each other?"

"You shall have the truth, Inspector," she nodded, "but please do realize that I am not a foolish girl, but an adult woman with her head on her shoulders the right way round. Morally and ethically, I am Richard's widow. His marriage with Jean Froggatt was never consummated. I have only Richard's word for that, but he was a truthful man. There is something wrong with Jean, psychologically speaking. Her child was born as the result of—well—seduction by the man who became her first husband. She developed a fear of marriage and all it implies."

She stared into the empty grate for a moment before continuing: "Our association was born of genuine affection. At no time has he contributed a single penny to my upkeep, and by my express wish he made no provision for me in his will. We kept our love a secret, and I was prepared to swear that no one in the district knew of it—until yesterday afternoon, and then I knew that we had an enemy who wishes to defile his name."

"Yes, Miss Grenson?" Knollis asked softly.

"I had a visitor. He came to implore me to sever my friendship with Richard."

"Montague?" said Knollis.

"No, Inspector!" She rose and took a walk round the room, coming to rest at the farther side of the table. "It was the Bishop of Northcote."

Knollis jerked forward in his chair. "What!" he shouted. "The Bishop of Northcote?—So that was it!"

"He said that Richard was doing good work among the youth of the town, and that it would all be ruined if the secret of our association should leak out."

Knollis showed signs of excitement for once in his life. "At what time was this?" he demanded tensely.

"It would be about twenty past three, Inspector. He left before half-past—I ordered him from the cottage."

"He left by car?"

"No, he was on foot, Inspector. He must have left the car down the road. I assume that to be the case, anyway."

"Tell me, Miss Grenson; how near is the nearest entrance to the plantation?"

"Well," she replied, "just a few yards down the road, in the direction of Coleby. It opens on to an old bridle-path which used to run across the fields before the plantation was made, but it is supposed to be closed now that the Forestry Commission have taken over the land."

"And this bridle-path leads to?"

"Three-Acre Dam. Actually, the path forks; the right path going to the dam, and the left to the far side of the Knoll—that is the hill on the western side of the dam."

"I know it," said Knollis. "Miss Grenson, how long would it take me—or the Bishop—to walk to the dam from your door-step?"

"Oh, twenty minutes. No more, certainly."

"That gives us ten minutes to four," Knollis muttered. "Tell me one thing more; did you ascertain how the Bishop came to know of your association with Mr. Huntingdon?"

"I asked him that," she said grimly. "All he would tell me was that he had 'received certain information'. I then took the line that the insinuation was slanderous and actionable, and demanded the name of his informant so that I could take legal action. On pressing him, he admitted that his informant was not anonymous, but would say no more. It was then that I ordered him from the cottage."

"All very interesting, Miss Grenson. You have been remark-ably frank with me, and so I will not disguise my next question. Have you an alibi for the thirty minutes following the Bishop's departure?"

She smiled at him then. "I have, Inspector. My friend, Peggy Dabell, arrived by bus from Hedenham at twenty to four, and the baker called with his van at ten minutes to four. I paid the week's bill. You may have the addresses of both if you require them."

"Thank you," said Knollis. "When did you last see Richard Huntingdon?"

"Thursday evening. He left about ten o'clock."

"I see," murmured Knollis. "Do you happen to know anything about Mrs. Huntingdon's first marriage, over and above what you have already told me?"

"Only that her husband died shortly after their marriage, and that Richard met her while on holiday at Eastbourne. I believe she was living at Seaford then. Richard married her after the child was born. There was a certain amount of gossip in the district, or so Richard has told me. Evilly-disposed people said that the child was really his own, and that the first husband had been invented in order to legitimize her—or at any rate to give the appearance of legitimacy. That happens to be false; I have seen the marriage certificates."

"So have I," said Knollis. "Everything is square in that respect. Huntingdon was in no trouble as far as you knew?"

"He seemed to be singularly content with life, Inspector."

"And yet something must have been wrong, somewhere," Knollis pointed out. "There is a motive behind all such cases as this."

She came round the table and resumed her seat on the stool, clasping her hands and staring intently at Knollis.

"That is what puzzles me," she said. "I do not attempt to conceal from myself the undeniable fact that there is some cause—there must be. His business affairs were in order. He and Jean had reached a more or less amicable agreement regarding the conduct of their married life together. He was, admittedly, a little worried about her way of bringing up Doreen, but he said it was her business and he was prepared to let her go her own way, while still disapproving."

"Of what exactly did he disapprove, Miss Grenson?" asked Knollis.

"You have seen the child, Inspector?"

Knollis said that he had.

"Then the answer is obvious. Jean Huntingdon is trying to make her into an artificial and smirking doll. The child is actually rather a sweet little thing. It upset Richard a great deal. You see," she said slowly, "he always wanted a daughter of his own. Jean would not give him one, and I—well, you do see the position!"

"I understand perfectly," Knollis assured her. "Tell me, Miss Grenson; did Mrs. Huntingdon know about yourself and her husband?"

She considered the question for a few moments before answering. "She may have suspected that Richard had—well—another home, but I don't think she knew for sure, and she certainly never connected me with her suspicions, for we have met on several occasions and she has been perfectly sociable."

"Would you regard her as a clear-minded woman?"

"Oh, no!" she retorted vehemently. "Anything but that! She is so obtuse that she is unable to differentiate between friendship and the mock camaraderie that passes for such among her acquaintances. She could not appreciate genuine friendship if it was offered—and yet that is perhaps what she yearns for more than anything else. I'm sorry for her, really. She is a very lonely woman, and doesn't seem to realize it."

Knollis arose and took his hat from the table. "I must thank you for your most valuable assistance, and for your frankness. I hope I shall not find it necessary to bother you again."

He and Ellis returned to the car and were driven back to the main road. Knollis called a halt at the entrance to the bridle-path. They walked over the grass verge to a small wooden wicket-gate let into the wire fence surrounding the plantation.

"Only a hook and staple to fasten it," Ellis pointed out unnecessarily. "Anybody could go through without let or hindrance."

"The legal right to use the path probably still exists, as Montague suggested," replied Knollis, "and the Forestry Commission rely on the various warning boards to scare away would-be users. We are not intimidated, Ellis, and so we will take a walk."

"Should be about a mile, shouldn't it?" said Ellis.

"Hm?" murmured Knollis, already deep in his own thoughts and automatically scanning the path as they walked along.

"About a mile," Ellis repeated. "It's a mile from the gate to the turning down Coleby Rise, and a quarter of a mile from there to the dam, so that we've got what is approximately an isosceles triangle, and when I was at school it had two sides that were equal in length."

"They still have," said Knollis, rousing himself. "This particular path may be longer than its partner due to the winds and turns."

"I was speaking as the crow flies," Ellis replied, brushing his moustache away from his lips.

"Have you noticed how much telephones have entered into this case?" Knollis mused. "They usually do, of course, being ubiquitous instruments in this mechanical age, but it is their manner of appearing which is interesting me."

He came to a sudden halt, looking at the ground.

"Ellis, please slip back and get the bag from the car. And you may as well tell the driver to go round to the dam and wait for us there."

Ellis went without asking questions, and returned a few minutes later to find Knollis on his knees, bending over a footprint.

"Inch-tape," he said shortly. "This is the first time in my career that I have measured the footprint of a bishop."

"Looks more like a woman's to me," said Ellis.

Knollis nodded. "That is why I am taking measurements. It may be a woman's, and it may be a bishop's, and I am not at all sure. What type of footwear does a bishop favour? Certainly not the broad-toed shoe, nor yet clod-hopper boots."

"But that's neither!" protested Ellis.

Knollis sat back on his haunches and regarded Ellis patiently. "Isn't that the whole point? This print is that of a pointed-toe shoe—or boot. Further, it was worn by someone who was tiptoeing. A woman, to the best of my knowledge, walks on the ball of her foot. She has to do so in shoes having any other than flat heels. Now a woman walking through this plantation—say Miss Grenson—had no need to tiptoe, surely! The Bishop had good reason; he didn't want to soil his boots or shoes, so he went as cautiously as a cat when he came to this soft spot in the path."

"And the whole point of measuring it?" queried Ellis with a smile.

"Obvious to a detective," Knollis answered puckishly. "We have here a more or less perfect print. We can safely assume that it was made by the Bishop. Miss Grenson, being a countrywoman, would have walked straight on. The Bishop, coming to the soft spot of ground, walked round its edge, and delicately. He wasn't wanting to tiptoe for the usual reason—not to be heard. Right! Now we need the measurements for comparison reasons, my dear Ellis, in case we should find any that have behaved in a similar manner down by the water."

"A peculiar manner such as?" persisted Ellis.

Knollis sank into a sitting position on a clump of grass. "I know you are only pretending to be dense, but I'll answer your question because it will help me to clear my own mind. You once again take up the role of blackboard to my mental chalk."

"I'm so blank!" Ellis complained.

"Look, Ellis," Knollis said earnestly. "The Bishop left Miss Grenson's at half-past three, and had told his chauffeur to meet him by the gate—although he referred to it as a stile. How long would he be prepared to wait? That question is important. Remember that he is a prominent person. Take into account his mentality as a result of his eminent position. Perfectly at ease at a public dinner, or in the cathedral, he would feel self-conscious if seen waiting against a stile or a gate on a main road. He would be bound to attract the attention of any passer-by.

"Now I can't imagine him waiting longer than five minutes for the car. Accepting that surmise, then in which direction would he head? I can't see him walking along the main road towards Coleby Rise in the hope of meeting Burton and the car. He couldn't go back to Miss Grenson's cottage, firstly because he had been chased out, and secondly because Burton would not know where to find him. And so I think he would head back through the plantation to the spot where he had originally left the car. I don't know this path any better than you do, but even if Miss Grenson had not told me that it branched I would have been prepared to bet a fiver that such was the case—one branch going down to the dam, and the other to the stile or gate where Burton dropped him. See the implication?"

Ellis clicked his teeth, and nodded slowly. "He must have heard the shot that killed Huntingdon—always assuming that he was not the one who fired it. In which case we can regard him as a potential witness, and a valuable one into the bargain."

"There you have the crux of the whole thing," said Knollis. "Supposing he heard the shot? What is his immediate reaction? He could, admittedly, rush to the body, but if he knew, or learned, that it was Huntingdon, then he would be bound to pause and consider, for not many minutes before he had expressed to Miss Grenson his indignation at Huntingdon's association with her, and generally expressed sentiments which by a stretch of the imagination could be construed as a sound motive for murder. My guess is that he hurried forward, and then retreated to the cover of these trees, staying here, seeing but not seen, until Burton had explained his absence. He then emerged full of meditation and astonishment. He had already recovered from his initial shock, and probably having no experience as an actor he was unable to produce more than that well-he's-dead-and-that's-that attitude—and from what we have heard from Miss Grenson he was probably thinking it was all for the best in the long run."

"Huntingdon died about four o'clock?" Ellis asked.

"It may have been a little earlier, Ellis. The 'phone call to Mrs. Huntingdon was received at ten to four. I suggest that the one to Richard was sent a few minutes previous. As a matter of fact, it would have to be, for the murderer wouldn't know the exact whereabouts of Mrs. Huntingdon; she could have been in the club-house, you see, and he didn't want her to arrive while he was in the act of killing her husband! Say a quarter to four for the call to Richard. No sooner, certainly, because of the risk of seeing Dorrie on the main road between the bus stop and the Castle house—the risk of Richard seeing her, I mean. Now how long would it take you to drive two miles? Or nearly three miles from Red Gables? That is, if you were in the devil of a hurry?"

Ellis pondered the point for a moment. "Seven to ten minutes. Not much less than ten because he had to drive through the town, and it was market day. Ten minutes I give him."

Knollis nodded his satisfaction. "There you have the answer to your question. Medical evidence aside, I place the time of his death at five minutes to four, and that in turn gives the Bishop twenty-five minutes to walk from Miss Grenson's cottage to the dam. Allow him four minutes from the cottage to the gate, five minutes in which to wait for Burton and the car, and we are left with fourteen minutes. I can do a mile in twelve minutes if I am in a hurry, but I don't think the Old Dear could do it, so I don't think he was close to the dam when Huntingdon was killed, but he would be near enough to hear the shot, and still not near enough to be able to rush to the scene and see the killer—assuming that the killer did emerge from the cover of the trees and bushes, which I doubt. I estimate then that the Bishop was between a quarter and a third of a mile from the dam when Huntingdon was shot."

"And then?" asked Ellis.

"And then," said Knollis, his eyes narrowing as he visualized the scene, "he stood back among the trees and waited. He saw Mrs. Huntingdon and Mrs. Frampton arrive. He saw Drayton and Harrison arrive. He saw his own car arrive, and Burton join the group—and this is where I expect to find him walking up and down this path, wondering what the deuce to do. Isn't that what the psychologists call the reflective delay? There were several courses of action open to him. Which should he take? Go back and walk along the main road? Go straight forward and walk back to the car over Hampton Knoll? Or turn right and walk straight into the party? He chose the latter course, and thereby proved that he possesses moral courage—a trait in his character on which we may have to rely in the next few hours, for it will need moral courage if he is to tell us the truth about his movements. Now—" Knollis got back on his knees. "Three and five-eighths across the ball of the foot, and it is the right foot. The slight indentation of the heel of the left one gives us ten and three-quarters from heel to toe—extreme measurement. The heel is three by two and a half. And that is all we need. In case the Bishop denies that he came this way we can check from his own footwear, and that corroboration will satisfy me that Miss Grenson did not come this way."

Ellis glanced across in surprise. "You aren't accepting her alibi?"

"Yes, when we've checked it," said Knollis. He returned the inch-tape to Ellis, who pocketed it with the remark that it seemed unnecessary to lug the bag for a mile when the tape was all that was needed.

"I hope you are right," Knollis agreed, "but you never know at this game, do you?"

"True enough," admitted Ellis. "Lead on, Macduff."

They threaded their way down the winding narrow path between the miniature conifers until they came to the fork, and Knollis gave a satisfied grunt. He stepped from the path, brushing the trees aside. "You stay there," he said. "I won't have to go many yards before I know whether this path was used."

Three minutes later he was back by Ellis's side. "The Old Dear must have gone to the right after all! Now pray for another soft patch which took his prints."

A few more minutes brought them to a widening of the path. Here it was that Knollis halted again.

"I'm pleased with myself, Ellis. This was the Bishop's stamping ground."

"He certainly did some marching," said Ellis. "If he does as much in the palace while composing a sermon his carpets must be threadbare by now. Shall I look for nail-bitings?"

"A treble track," murmured Knollis. "He went down, and returned, and went back again. The prints, as you can see for yourself, aren't good ones, but they show three journeys. We'll step round them and see what else there is of interest to two curious detectives."

Twelve yards from where the plantation broke into open ground Knollis halted yet again. He stood aside so that Ellis could see for himself why he had stopped. Three cigarette-ends lay to the side of the path, two of them smoked to the last available puff, and the third one only half smoked.

He looked quizzically at Ellis. "Well, my lad?"

"The remains indicate a state of nervous tension in our man," said Ellis in a mock professorial tone. "The alarm sounded, and he dumped his third one and sheered off."

"I wonder if the Bishop smokes cigarettes?" Knollis asked of the trees.

Ellis was down on one knee, examining the butts. "He may do, but he didn't smoke these!"

"Why not?" asked Knollis, joining him.

"They are gaspers of the lowest order. Honeysuckle brand, packed in packets of five."

The normally severe and earnest Knollis laughed out loud. "I wouldn't be without you for anything. You always manage to puncture me when I'm beginning to get inflated with my own acumen. Honeysuckles, eh? Not bishops' cigarettes, certainly."

Squatting beside Ellis, he weighed the longer butt in his palm. "I wonder who else was in the wood yesterday afternoon? Was it yesterday afternoon when these were smoked? And if not, then why should anyone stand here, just nicely out of sight of the dam, and yet able to see the spot where Huntingdon made his tryst with death? It couldn't have been Huntingdon, surely? No! He would never smoke these, nor any other cheap brand. I can better imagine him having his made, and having his name printed on them; he seems to have been that kind of a man."

Ellis was staring over his shoulder into the thickness of the plantation to the right of the dam, in the direction of Coleby Rise and the main road, across the diagonal of the plantation.

"What is it?" Knollis asked without moving.

"Broken twigs. Somebody went through the trees in a hurry."

Knollis opened the murder bag and put the cigarette-ends in a small container. "Follow the trail, Ellis, while I go round the Norton Birchfield end of the dam. Meet you here in ten minutes. I'll take the bag and hand it to the driver."

Ellis vanished among the young firs, and Knollis broke out to the gorse and hawthorn-lined marge. He laid the bag on the ground, indicated that the driver was to fetch it, and he too pushed his way among the trees to the west of the dam.

Ten minutes later they met again, on the spot where Richard Huntingdon had met his death.

"There are broken twigs and branches on my side," Knollis reported in a puzzled tone. "I wonder if our man approached from the east, and made his getaway in the direction of Norton Birchfield—or what?"

"I'd like to ask the driver two questions," said Ellis mysteriously. "He was here early this morning, and we weren't."

He ambled back to the road with Knollis thoughtfully bringing up the rear. Arriving at the car, he asked: "When did rain last fall round here?"

"Oh-h! Friday night, Sergeant!"

"Look," said Ellis, handing Knollis a screwed-up envelope. "I found that among the trees."

It was a small square envelope of cheap quality, and addressed in printed capitals to *E.C. Jacland, Esq., Small Street, Coleby.*

"Who," said Knollis, "is E.C. Jacland?"

The driver's face registered astonishment. "Jacland? He's the Mayor of Coleby, sir. Socialist Mayor of Coleby. Works in Huntingdon's works. Until he was mayor he used to go to the same public-house as me—both living in the same part of the town."

"Hm! Does he smoke?"

"Heavily, sir. Like a chimney, as the saying goes."

"Any particular brand?"

"Honeysuckles, sir. Always Honeysuckles. Won't smoke anything else except for a cigar at Christmas."

Knollis looked at Ellis, and nodded. "And this isn't Christmas, is it, Ellis?"

CHAPTER V
THE EVIDENCE OF THE BISHOP

ON A SHELF in Inspector Bamford's office stood the decoy yacht which had floated on Three-Acre Dam, while on the table before him lay the pile of wrappings in which Dorrie Huntingdon's birthday present had been sent. On the other side of the table sat Knollis, resting after a late lunch. Knollis tapped his finger on the bottom of the container box which rested on his knees.

"The private marks should enable us to find the shop from which the child's present was bought. She mentioned three tradesmen who were displaying this particular model, so your men have something to work on."

Bamford made a note. "Anything else, Gordon? For heaven's sake give us some work."

"There's going to be more than you want," Knollis replied grimly. "The next point, which we both missed, was whether anyone living on the main road heard the shot. It is a mile away, but the possibility exists. Next, we must find from where the telephone calls were made, and that includes the call to Mrs. Huntingdon, and this morning's call to Mr. Montague. Now, you have the results of my morning's work, and the next round is yours. What can you tell me about E.C. Jacland?"

Bamford stoked his pipe before replying and deftly flicked the spent match into an ash-tray. "Jacland, eh?" he said at last. "Honest John type of individual. He is of slightly below medium height, has what is known in these parts as grizzled hair, has very luminous blue eyes, is fifty years of age, speaks dialect, and is proud of being a man of the people. He's done a deuce of a lot to educate himself, mainly through evening continuation classes, the W.E.A., and home reading. He's a nice fellow, but has a one-track mind. I keep clear of politics, so I shan't be accused of prejudice if I say that he could take the hobby of stamp-collecting and turn it into an argument for the abolition of capitalism. That's an exaggeration, of course, but you know what I mean!"

"Morally?"

"Stricter than a bishop," Bamford replied promptly. "One wife, two nice kids, breeds rabbits—Flemish Giants. He wouldn't be found keeping Chins or Angoras because of their aristocratic reputation; it would smell too keenly of the Right."

"You know quite a lot about him," ventured Knollis.

"Isn't that the job of a provincial crime bureau inspector?" asked Bamford. "I'm supposed to know everybody in the town. Well, I know most of 'em, and my blokes know what I don't about those I don't know. Anyway, I kid myself that I do know my town."

"Good enough. What does Jacland smoke?"

"Honeysuckles, and chain-smokes them! Uses his thumb and finger for the job, smokes them down to the limit, and the said thumb and finger are black with tobacco tar as a result. Speaking psychologically, his addiction to cheap cigarettes is another outward symbol of his acute Leftishness and his refusal to climb out of his class—God save the mark!"

"Then here is something I haven't told you about this morning's adventures," said Knollis. He pushed the envelope and the three cigarette-ends under Bamford's nose, at the same time describing the signs of activity he and Ellis had found in the plantation.

Bamford pulled at his collar. "This is getting a bit hot, Gordon! First you drag in a most respectable bishop, and now you have the mayor of the borough in tow. You know, there's something phoney about all this!"

"You say you know your town," Knollis shot at him suddenly. "Can you suggest any point or points of contact between Jacland and Huntingdon?"

Bamford considered for a moment and then raised his shoulders in a gesture of doubt. "A paradoxical connection only, inasmuch as they were at opposite ends of a diameter. Politically, they hated each other like poison. Jacland regards, or regarded, Huntingdon as the typical capitalist who treads the face of the proletarian in the mud, while Huntingdon regarded E.C. as a mean little revolutionist, which is a different thing to a revolutionary in the parlance of modern politics. I'm not trying to

insult your intelligence, but merely making my meaning perfectly clear. Both of them were damnably prejudiced, of course,
and if anything I should say that Huntingdon was the more so.
E.C. is a nice little bloke, and he does attempt to think, which is
rather more than I would try to claim for Huntingdon. Huntingdon merely accepted the standard and conventional articles of
his class—and I reach that conclusion as the result of hearing
him speak at various functions. In effect, he had been presented
with his party's list of beliefs and warned that he must observe
each and every one; he thereafter considered that it would be
traitorous to diverge by one iota. E.C., on the other hand, has
been in trouble with his own party on quite a few occasions for
daring to be an individual."

Knollis lolled in his chair and stared at the ceiling with narrowed eyes. "I'm getting Huntingdon into focus at last. I wonder
how he rationalized Gloria Grenson? And the rigid mind is
expert at rationalization; it can find an excuse for any departure
from grace which is based on self-interest. Makes you think,
Bam! A philosopher once expressed the opinion that Mayfair
was nearer to the monkey-house than was the Mile End Road. I
think he'd got something."

"It would seem," said Bamford in a dreamy voice, "that E.C.
and the Bishop were in the wood at the same time. I can see that
the Bishop had a good reason for being there, even if it was only
a fortuitous one, but why should E.C. have been present? Tell
me that, Gordon!"

"I've a hunch," replied Knollis. "The Bishop was told of
Huntingdon's irregular conduct, wasn't he? Since we have found
this envelope in the plantation we can assume, if only temporarily, that Jacland was similarly informed. And perhaps that isn't
so much a hunch as a self-evident fact. Anyway, we are going
to find out. Ellis and myself are going to interview Burton this
afternoon, and we'll try to reach his lordship afterwards. That
done, if nothing crops up, we will have a chat with Jacland."

Knollis pushed back his chair and ambled to the door.
"There is one peculiar fact which is worrying me, Bam. All three
men were due to speak at the Young Templars' meeting last

night. Now why should all three be near the dam on the same afternoon. It is remote, unfrequented, and a most unlikely spot in which to find any of 'em. It may mean nothing, but I don't believe in coincidence. Oh, well, see you later. Expect Ellis will be in the sergeants' room, champing at his bit and demanding action. Wish I possessed his fund of energy!"

The cathedral city of Linford lay to the north of the county, in the middle of a great plateau, from which the three towers rose majestically to dwarf the red-roofed and blue-slated homes of the forty-five thousand souls who made up the population of the sleepy city.

The driver twisted and turned down narrow and empty streets and at last drew up in a mews. "I've brought you to the back of the palace, sir," he explained. "You said you wanted to interview Burton first, and he lives in the domestic wing. I'll back out and wait in the street, just round the corner, if that is okay?"

Knollis nodded his agreement, and walked with Ellis the remaining twenty yards. They found Burton indulging in forty winks on his bed. He swung his legs to the floor and regarded them sleepily. "I wasn't expecting anybody, sir," he apologized.

"I merely want to ask you a few questions about yesterday afternoon, Burton."

"But I don't know anything about it, sir," he protested, "I just dropped across it, like! I don't know anything."

"I'm probably the best judge of that," said Knollis, and then, to soothe his man, he explained: "It is often the little things to which you attribute no importance that are the most useful to us. Now first of all I want to know at what time you left Linford, and what you did during the course of the afternoon."

"But that's his lordship's private business, sir! I can't discuss that with you or anyone else!" Burton was indignant.

"I am also the best judge of that," Knollis retorted firmly. "I take all responsibility for what you evidently regard as prying."

Burton glanced at him dubiously. "Well. We left here about half-past one. It's nearly three-quarters of an hour's run to Coleby—when I'm driving him, that is. He won't let me put my foot down."

"So that you arrived in Coleby at a quarter past two? And then?"

"Well, I'm a bit puzzled about the next bit because he acted a bit queer yesterday. He told me to pull into a side-street—"

"Which side-street?" interrupted Knollis.

"Durban Street, sir," replied Burton in a tone that expressed his disgust at this attention to detail.

"And then?"

"And then he got out, told me to wait, and walked off to a dead-end street a hundred yards higher up," said Burton. He looked at Knollis sarcastically and added: "That would be Grosvenor Street, sir."

"Thank you, Burton! You are most helpful!"

Burton smirked, and then shook his head sadly. "It was all wrong, sir. I mean, a man in his position isn't supposed to go frogging it all over the town. What's me and the Rolls for, anyway?"

"I see your point," said Knollis. "At what time did he come back?"

"Oh, about quarter of an hour afterwards. I just had time to smoke a fag, and was throwing it out when he came round the corner. He got in and ordered the Town Hall. I drew up in front, and he sailed up the steps to see the mayor."

"The mayor, eh?" Knollis purred contentedly. "How long did he stay there?"

"Ten minutes, roughly. He told me to drive into Norton Birchfield, but instead of pulling up anywhere we drove through the town and out towards the dam. As we were going up Hampton Knoll he told me to pull up against the stile. He was going to stroll in the plantation to think about his speech for the meeting, and I was to go forward slowly and wait for him at the gate or stile on the main road, and I wasn't to be later than half-past three."

"The time was then?"

"Five to three by the dashboard clock, sir. I backed into a gateway and went back to Norton to do a bit of shopping—razor-blades, and tooth-paste, and so on. I had a look round, an ice-cream sandwich, and then went back the same way. I was about five minutes late getting to the gate, so I hung about for five minutes more and then went back to Hampton Knoll, to the place where I'd dropped him, which is just over the crest of the hill. It got round to four o'clock, and the Old Dear hadn't turned up, so I thought I'd better do something about it, or he'd be chafing his gaiters off with waiting. It was a bit sticky in the gateway where I'd first turned, on account of Friday's rain, so I drove down to the cross-roads by the Three Crows to turn, and I was just going down the dam side of the Knoll when I saw that something was going off, and pulled in."

"What a pity you went to the cross-roads to turn!" commented Knollis. "If you had turned in the gateway you would have saved a few minutes and might have prevented the murder, or at least have seen the killer getting away!"

"You mean that he was killed while I was—cor!"

"All the evidence seems to point to it," Knollis said sorrowfully.

Burton sought for a cigarette and matches in an absent manner, and then a look of alarm came into his eyes. "Look here, sir, you aren't trying to mix *him* up in this, are you?"

"Only as a possible witness," Knollis said frankly. "I'm trying, to establish the exact position of everyone who happened to be in the vicinity of the dam when Mr. Huntingdon was killed. Now tell me, Burton; while you were dodging about between the main road and the Knoll, did you see any pedestrians, cyclists, or other motorists?"

"Not a single person, so help me!" said Burton. "But wait a minute though! While I was turning outside the Crows, there was a woman messing about on a bike down the slip road to Norton. But apart from her the road was empty. It nearly always is."

"Thanks for your story," said Knollis. "You haven't been able to tell me much that is positive evidence, but you've removed two people from the scene."

Burton rose from the bed and flicked his ash on the floor. "I only hope I haven't said anything that he wouldn't want me to have said. Still, I'm sorry I couldn't tell you more, sir."

"You can," Knollis said puckishly.

"Oh? What is it, sir?"

"How do I get to the Bishop?"

Burton gave a sigh of relief. "Oh, that!"

The Bishop of Northcote, stately, dignified, and more human than Knollis had expected, received them almost warmly.

"I was afraid that you would find it necessary to visit me, Inspector," he greeted him. "Please be seated. There is no reason why you should not be comfortable during your visit."

"I regret that I must disturb your lordship in this manner," Knollis apologized, wearing what he hoped was an expression of intense regret.

"No trouble at all, Inspector. I realize that my presence in the plantation must have appeared most suspicious in view of the tragedy which had taken place. And I appeared at such an inauspicious moment. What a terrible thing is violent death! I trust that you will be successful in bringing the culprit to justice!"

"I shall," Knollis replied grimly.

"Indeed, I hope so! Now, Inspector, I must explain my presence in the plantation. Burton informed me that a few questions were asked of him before my emergence from the—er—cover of the trees, so I assume that you are aware that I was walking with Mother Nature while meditating on the address I was to deliver later in the day—an address which was delivered, I might say, in spite of the shock which I experienced."

"Your chauffeur told us exactly what he believed to be the truth of the matter, my lord," Knollis said ambiguously.

The Bishop looked up, opened his mouth as if about to pass some remark, and then closed it again. He regarded Knollis silently for a full minute before venturing: "Am I to understand that you doubt Burton's word, Inspector?" Knollis refused to budge from the attitude he had taken up. "I repeat, my lord, that your chauffeur told us exactly what he believed to be the true circumstances. In short, he believed what he was told—by you. He believed that you were thinking out your speech for the Young Templars' meeting."

"Ah—yes!"

"What he did not know," said Knollis, "was that you intended to pay a visit to Miss Grenson's cottage."

The Bishop blinked, stared at his pink-and-white hands, and then ejaculated: "Ah, so you are aware of my visit to Miss Grenson! I had not anticipated that."

"Perhaps you would care to enlarge on the subject, my lord?" Knollis suggested politely.

The Bishop played with his thin gold watch-chain, and shook his head. "I am afraid that I cannot do that, Inspector. When a trust has been reposed in me—"

"In which case I must acquaint you with the facts," said Knollis in a more business-like mood.

"You mean?" asked the Bishop, his head coming up with a jerk.

"You called on Miss Grenson in the hope of being able to persuade her to break her friendship with Richard Huntingdon, and you did so on information received. Your meditation was a subterfuge intended to deceive Burton. Further, you did not want your car to be seen at Miss Grenson's gate in case it was recognized and caused speculation. And so you walked through the plantation, hoping that your progress from the plantation gate to Miss Grenson's cottage would not be noticed. In fact I am prepared to suggest that you waited in the plantation until the main road was clear!"

"Ah—yes, I am afraid you are correct in every detail, Inspector. I must apologize for underrating your intelligence."

"You will have anticipated my next question, my lord?" suggested Knollis.

"Yes, yes. I have, Inspector! I must tell you the truth, for the withholding of the truth is as sinful as a half-truth or a complete lie. Yes, I must acquaint you with the full facts."

"Thank you, my lord," said Knollis. "I am particularly interested in the source of your information regarding the association between Huntingdon and Miss Grenson."

The Bishop passed a pink hand over his forehead. "It is all so difficult, and so embarrassing, Inspector. I feel that I am betraying a trust. And yet a man has died, has he not, and justice must be done. The letter came by yesterday morning's post. It was marked private and confidential, and so it was not opened by my secretary. But you shall see it for yourself."

He unlocked a drawer in his ornate table and took out a small square envelope.

"Exactly similar," muttered Ellis.

Knollis warned him with a look, and took the envelope from the Bishop's hand. It was, as Ellis had said, similar to the Jacland envelope, a cheap envelope such as can be bought in twopenny packets in a back-street shop. The notepaper folded inside it matched, a greyish-white oblong of laid paper. Knollis opened it. The letter ran:

> GROSVENOR STREET,
> COLEBY,
> *5th April.*

MY LORD BISHOP,

You have often preached about whited sepulchres, but do you know that one of the worst lives in this town? Huntingdon, the man who preaches virtue to young boys and girls, has dealings with a young woman by the name of Grenson that lives in a cottage on the Hedenham Road. I'm not frightened of being taken to court for libel or whatever it is because I know it is all true and can be proved.

Your Lordship's Most Obedient Servant,

WALTER DICKENS.

"A remarkable document," said Knollis. "May I ask the nature of your reaction to this letter, my lord?"

The Bishop waved a hand. "Bewildered, Inspector! Never before have I received such a letter. I realized that if the information was true it was my bounden duty to act—but how to act? I was in a dilemma. I looked in the telephone directory and discovered that there was such a lady, there in black and white. I obtained a map of the district and realized that it would be possible to reach her cottage by walking through the plantation. She and Huntingdon must part. That was obvious. If the truth was ever known in Coleby, then every organization with which Huntingdon was connected must inevitably suffer. We differed radically on various issues, but I have to admit that he was doing very good work. I resolved to see this lady. I knew I would be wasting my time in seeing Huntingdon, mainly because his sense of honour—how ironic!—would compel him to disclaim any connection with her, but there was a slim chance that the lady might see the light. A woman will often make a sacrifice for the common good when an appeal to a man will strengthen his resolve.

"Burton has told you that he left me to wander in the plantation. I had no wish to lie to him, and so really I did meditate on my address until the moment when I left the plantation and came to the road. I saw Miss Grenson, and I think I impressed her with the urgency of my plea. I could see that I had aroused her emotions, but you probably know how a woman reacts, Inspector? Irrationally, her outburst was directed against me, and she ordered me from her dwelling! Such a snub would have been a small price to pay for Huntingdon's release from spiritual bondage, but now, of course—!"

"And after you left the cottage?" Knollis prompted in a soft voice.

"I—er—returned through the plantation, and the rest you know, Inspector," the Bishop replied, evading Knollis's eyes.

Knollis assumed a reproving manner. "You left Miss Grenson's cottage at half-past three, my lord, and it was turned half-past four when you came to us on the bank of the dam. I must ask you, with all respect, to satisfactorily account for that hour!"

The Bishop fidgeted awkwardly. "Er—yes, Inspector. I hate to confess it, but I'm afraid that I was delayed by self-consciousness."

"By self-consciousness!" Knollis exploded.

The Bishop explained, with a nod of his head here and a wave of the hand there, and all the time with the guilty manner of a little boy who has been discovered in a pantry with a pot of forbidden jam.

"I had, you see, waited for Burton by the gate. I waited for several minutes, and eventually decided that for once in a while he had met with some mechanical difficulty. I realized that it would appear incongruous if I was to be seen at a gate like some—er—well, like some lover awaiting his sweetheart, and so I decided to return through the plantation to Hampton Knoll. I had sufficient faith in Burton's intelligence to believe that he would return there if I did not appear at the gate on the main road, and I was making my way through the trees when I saw the man in the wood."

"Ah!" exclaimed Knollis, a wealth of significance in his voice. "You saw him!"

"A man, through the trees, Inspector. His back was towards me, and he was smoking a cigarette. He was on the path, standing with his legs apart and his left hand thrust deep into his trouser pocket. Again I realized the difficulty of my position—a dignitary of the Church wandering in a wood like some common poacher. I stood where I was and waited for him to go away. Several minutes elapsed, and then he dropped his cigarette, trod on it to extinguish it, and vanished among the trees to the right of the path."

"Have you any idea at what time this happened, my lord?"

"It was almost four o'clock, Inspector."

Knollis nodded at Ellis, and said: "Please proceed, my lord."

"I waited a minute or so longer to make sure that he had really moved away, and was about to walk on when I heard a shot. *Poachers* was the first thought that entered my mind, and again I experienced a strong desire not to be seen. And I was afraid that I might be attacked, for I have heard that they are very rough men, and inclined to violence."

"One point, my lord!" Knollis interrupted. "You say that you were making your way to Hampton Knoll, and yet you had taken the right-hand path instead of the left!"

The Bishop bowed his head. "I realized my mistake shortly after hearing the shot, Inspector. You must remember that I was faced with a most unusual situation. My life is normally a placid, smooth-flowing one, and in a fraction of a minute I seemed to have stepped into an adventure. I was at a loss. I had no previous experience which could serve as a guide to the way I should act! I have to admit that I was in a predicament. I walked back to a small clearing, a mere widening of the path, and paced up and down, wondering what I should do. Then a woman screamed, and that served as a stimulus and a solution at one and the same time. I hurried back to the edge of the plantation. There was a body of a man lying on the ground, and by it were standing two women and two police officers! How could I, a man in my position, walk out at such a time? I was in no doubt about being present at the discovery of a suicide.

"Still dazed by the tumbling thoughts in my mind, I peered closer. I recognized Mrs. Huntingdon. On looking again I seemed to recognize the burly figure of Huntingdon himself in the prone body. Sick at heart, I turned back yet once more to think, and I stayed among the trees until you saw me emerge. It was a most horrible experience, Inspector, and one which I hope will never be repeated. Horrible!"

He relapsed into retrospective silence.

"The writer of this letter? Have you any knowledge of him?" asked Knollis.

"Until to-day I had never heard his name, Inspector. I caused certain enquiries to be made, and I learn that while he is no churchman, he is regarded as a highly respectable towns-man—and I am thereby the more surprised by the nature of his communication."

"I see," murmured Knollis, preparing to make his departure. "And you did not recognize the man in the plantation?"

"The trees obscured my vision, Inspector. You will under-stand if you traverse the same path. I saw no more than the lower half of him."

"I must ask for the loan of this letter," said Knollis as he tucked it into his wallet.

The Bishop waved it away with a frown. "I do not wish to see it again, Inspector! It has been the cause of the most disagree-able experience of my life, and I have no wish to be reminded of it!"

"I'm grateful for the assistance you have given us, and for your willingness to place all these facts at our disposal," said

Knollis as he stood flapping his hat against his leg, "but there is one point you have not touched upon."

"Er-r?" murmured the Bishop. "And what is that?"

"You have omitted to mention that you called on Mr. Walter Dickens at Grosvenor Street on your way to Miss Grenson's cottage."

The Bishop's beringed hand went to his cheek. "You know so much, Inspector," he said after a moment, "that I am surprised that you ask so many questions."

"What did he tell you?" Knollis asked bluntly, and deliberately dropping his respectful attitude.

"This is the queerest part of the whole unfortunate business, Inspector. He denied writing the letter, and no pressure would break his denial, so I concluded that he then regretted writing it and was afraid of the results of his action. He—he was most rude to me, and demanded the return of the letter so that he could take it to the police!"

"Thank you, my lord," said Knollis. He bowed himself out, cannoning into Ellis in the doorway as the sergeant failed to negotiate the opening.

Once outside the door, Ellis wiped his brow with a large blue handkerchief. He brushed his moustache, and blew a great breath from his lungs. "Thank heaven that's over! I'm no hand at hobnobbing with bishops! Anyway, that guess of yours was about the luckiest I've seen you pull yet! So help me, it was!"

"Not so much of a guess, surely?" Knollis complained. "Burton drove him to Durban Street, and he walked to Grosvenor Street. Dickens lives in Grosvenor Street—and you call it a guess. Go on with you. Get in the car and let's get back to Coleby!"

"I've a better suggestion."

"What is this one?"

"See that cafe across the street? There's a ham in the window, and some lettuce, and fancy cakes."

So the driver was given three-quarters of an hour in which to make his own arrangements, and Ellis hurried his chief to the tea-table, smacking his lips.

Chapter VI
THE EVIDENCE OF THE LETTERS

Mr. Ernest Claude Jacland was stretched out on the settee in his living-room, minus collar and shoes, reading a translation of *Das Kapital* when Knollis and Ellis called upon him. They were shown into the mayoral presence by his wife. Jacland grinned a welcome and swung his legs to the floor, at the same time placing the book face down on the cushions in a reverent manner. "Looks as if a mayor has to work even on a Sunday, and that's bad for a trade unionist. Anyway, what can I do for you gentlemen?"

Knollis looked into his vivid blue eyes and decided that he liked the man; there was something direct and honest in his manner.

"I think I should introduce myself first, Mr. Jacland. I am Inspector Knollis of New Scotland Yard, and in charge of the investigation into the death of Mr. Richard Huntingdon."

Jacland nodded his head slowly. "Huntingdon, eh? Well, we weren't exactly friends, but I'm sorry he's gone, and sorry he had to go the way that he did. It's a bad job." And then he looked up at Knollis with puzzled eyes. "Exactly where do I come in, Inspector? How can I help?"

Knollis sized up his man, and decided on direct tactics. "I don't think I need to beat about the bush, Mr. Jacland. You were in the plantation by Three-Acre Dam on Saturday afternoon shortly before four o'clock. That is correct?"

Jacland blew away the trifle of ash that had collected on the end of his cigarette. "Yes," he admitted; "I was there all right! I wasted a deuce of a lot of time, and I think I was done—hoaxed. Why? Don't ask me. I'm still trying to sort it out."

He went to the door and took down his jacket from its hook. From the inside pocket he produced a square of greyish-white paper and handed it to Knollis. "That's the only explanation I can offer, Inspector."

Knollis read:

GROSVENOR STREET,
COLEBY,
5th April.

DEAR MR. MAYOR,

Your battle with R. Huntingdon has gone on a long time now. If you want it to finish I suggest that you might be interested in something that is going to happen by Three-Acre Dam about four o'clock to-morrow. R. Huntingdon will be there.

WALTER DICKENS.

Knollis folded the letter and inserted it in his wallet. "See anyone in the plantation, Mr. Jacland?"

"See them, no! But there was somebody else there, because I could hear them in the trees somewhere behind me. It might have been Dickens, but I don't know."

"You know the man, Mr. Jacland?"

"By sight, yes. He works up at Huntingdon's."

"Now, Mr. Jacland," said Knollis, "what did you see at the dam—if you saw anything at all?"

Jacland wiped his brow. "God help me, but I saw him shot, and I ran like a coward. I can't forgive myself that, but you never know how you're going to act until the moment, do you?"

"Tell me the whole of your adventure from the beginning," suggested Knollis. "Tell me how you got there, what you did, and what you saw."

"That'll be the best," Jacland agreed. "I left town by bus, got off at the top of Coleby Rise, and after waiting until the bus was round the corner I climbed the fence and pushed my way through the trees. You know, Inspector, I can't reckon up why I went at all! It was spying, when you've weighed it up properly, and I've never done a mean thing like that in my life. I don't understand why I went, and I don't understand why I ran away."

"One's motives are seldom obvious," Knollis comforted him. "Even when we are aware of them we tend to disguise them if the knowledge embarrasses us. I should ignore them and just continue with your story."

"I suppose you're right," nodded Jacland. "Well, I came out at a point opposite the road. There was a little white ship sailing on the water, but there didn't appear to be anyone with it. I waited, and a little while afterwards a car drew up by the bridge, and Huntingdon got out and vaulted the fence. I could see that his eyes were on the little ship, and I couldn't make out what was happening. Then he began running among the bushes, calling his little girl's name. When he was about half-way along the side of the dam he stood still, his hands on his hips, looking at the water. There was a bang and a flash among the bushes at the back of him, and he spun round and fell facing the opposite way—with his head away from the water. I went a bit swimmy then. It was all queer, like a dream I'd wandered into, and I couldn't make it out. I shook myself and was going to run to him, and then I began to wonder about the letter. I'd read about such things happening before, and I thought it might be a trap. I mean, if somebody was to turn up while I was seeing if he was dead, and the gun happened to be found among the bushes, and there were no finger-prints on it. See what I mean, Inspector?"

Knollis nodded sympathetically.

"So I ran for it," said Jacland. "Then I thought I might be heard, because I was making a good bit of row, so I forced myself to slow up. Once I was clear of the trees I walked a couple of hundred yards up the road from town, and caught a bus back. And that's all there is to it. I don't come out of it very well, do I?" he asked ruefully.

"Tell me one other thing," said Knollis. "How did you come to lose the envelope in the plantation?"

"I didn't lose it, did I?" Jacland exclaimed. "It should be in my pocket."

"Sure?" asked Knollis.

"Well—"

He took up his jacket and went through the pockets. "You're right. It's gone. Must have come out with my handkerchief or my fags. I'd never noticed it."

"Does this look like the one?" Knollis asked, producing the envelope from his wallet.

Jacland nodded. "That's the one, Inspector. Where was it found?"

"In the plantation, a few yards from where you stood smoking your Honeysuckle cigarettes—three of them!"

Jacland gave an uneasy laugh. "I'd make a rotten criminal, wouldn't I? I seem to have left notices all over the place to say where I'd been."

"So there was somebody behind you, Mr. Jacland?"

"Yes, that's true, Inspector."

"Why didn't you come straight to us with your story?" Knollis asked in a more official tone. "You could have saved us a great deal of time."

"Oh, I know!" moaned Jacland. "Look, Inspector! Have you ever been on the wrong side of a murder? Imagine how I felt. I'm mayor of this borough. I was spying on another man. I'd no right to be there. Wouldn't my story have sounded lame?"

"Very well," sighed Knollis. "Good afternoon, Mr. Jacland."

"Now for Dickens," said Ellis as they re-entered the car. "He didn't write those letters, of course," said Knollis. "If he did, then he is using the old device of turning the attention away by drawing it to himself. A paradox, but it has been known to work. If he really did write those letters, then he must have been cognizant of the projected attack on Huntingdon, and was therefore either the killer or an accessory before the fact."

Ellis whistled. "Yes, of course! We can expect a denial from him—or can we?"

"I'm quite expecting it," replied Knollis.

Mr. Dickens did present them with a denial, and an indignant one. He was a towny-looking fellow, with a bow-tie and an air of conscious smartness. The whole of his physical appearance could be summed up as 'natty'. He spoke in a sharp, clipped manner which became noticeably sharper as Knollis stated his errand and posed his first question. "You are aware that two letters of an unusual nature, and bearing your name, have been received by prominent people in the district?"

"Two now?" he snapped. "I've had a row about one of them. Who got the other?"

"The Mayor of Coleby. You deny all knowledge of them?" asked Knollis.

"I deny writing them, if that is what you mean," barked Dickens. "The Bishop came round here about the one he'd received. I told him where to get off after he refused to let me have the one he'd received."

Knollis showed him the two letters, and waited for the reaction. It was almost instantaneous.

"They can't even be called forgeries," shouted Dickens. "My name's at the bottom all right, but it isn't my signature, and it isn't an attempt to copy my writing. This stuff is illiterate in comparison. Look here! I'll do you a sample!"

With a crafty smile he added: "It will save you the trouble of fishing round for one."

He threw himself into a chair. "There!" he said after a minute. "Is there any resemblance?"

"There is no resemblance whatever," Knollis admitted. The writing of the letter was dull and uninteresting in comparison with Dickens' ornate and elaborate script.

"Quite apart from the writing," Dickens went on excitedly, "I didn't know that Huntingdon was anything but what he pretended to be—a sober-living married man. And if I had known of it, what advantage would I have gained by informing the Bishop of Northcote and the Mayor of Coleby? Tell me that?"

"I wouldn't know. I couldn't even guess," said Knollis. "All I know is that someone wrote them, and my job is to find out who it was. Having assumed, we'll say, that you are not responsible, we are then faced with the incontrovertible fact that the killer wanted those two eminent gentlemen near the scene of the crime at the time of its commission, and also wanted to connect you with the affair."

"But why on earth?" Dickens demanded in a voice that rose almost to a scream.

"There'll be a link somewhere," Knollis said in a tone of quiet assurance; "there always is. At the moment I can't see anything that will lead us to it, but I will, of course, in due time. Look, you know the Huntingdons?"

"Well, yes, I'm a sort of uncle to young Dorrie. I visit the house occasionally."

Knollis raised his head from the sample he was still quietly studying. "You do, eh? And you are a sort of uncle? What kind of relationship is that, if I might ask?"

"Well, I *am* her uncle if you really want to know!"

"I do want to know," said Knollis. "I take it that you are Mrs. Huntingdon's brother? No, that can't be right," he corrected himself. "Her name was Montague before she married. And you can't be Froggatt's brother, nor yet Huntingdon's brother. Look, Mr. Dickens, I know it is Sunday, and that I'm not very bright except on weekdays, but do you mind explaining how you come to be Dorrie's uncle? There must be something in the laws of consanguinity that I haven't been told about. I mean, it doesn't make sense, and I have a mania for wanting to understand the correspondences between people and events."

Dickens fiddled with his green polka-dot bow-tie. "I am her first husband's brother if you want to know!"

Knollis cocked his head. "His name was Froggatt, surely, Mr. Dickens!"

Dickens tried to avoid Knollis's accusing eyes, but was brought back to them by the sheer force of their wilful persistence.

"Oh, lord," he exclaimed, "have we got to dig up the past again! I thought all that was over and done with!"

"Did you?" murmured Knollis. "I'm only asking you a straightforward question," he said with the air of a man making a reasonable request.

"My name is Froggatt!"

Knollis smiled innocently. "You've changed your name by deed poll, eh? All very simple, you see, and it can be checked without any embarrassment to yourself!"

"I didn't change it by deed poll!" snapped Dickens. "My full name is Walter Dickens Froggatt, and I dropped my surname when my brother died."

Knollis continued to smile. "His name was Walter Froggatt, too! What confusion it must have caused in the family circle!"

Dickens pushed the chair back from the table and mopped his neck and forehead with a large green handkerchief. "Phew! You don't seem able to understand, Inspector! The whole thing is perfectly clear if you'll only think about it!"

"I must try to think," said Knollis. "Meanwhile, you will perhaps help me to comprehension by explaining the matter in simple English—words of not more than, say, two syllables."

"Now look," said Dickens heatedly; "it has nothing whatsoever to do with these letters nor with Richard's death, but my brother was always known as Walter, and myself as Dick. He—well, he committed suicide, so I dropped the surname and left town."

"That was Eastbourne?"

Dickens gave him a suspicious glance. "I lived there with Walter. He was managing a shoe shop, and I was working up at Lewes as a motor mechanic."

"Tell me how he died," Knollis said flatly.

"He fell from the cliffs between Eastbourne and Seaford—the Seven Sisters."

"Anybody see him fall?"

"Yes, two people who were about half a mile beyond Birling Gap."

"An inquest was held?"

"Yes. His hat was found on the cliff. The body was pretty badly smashed about and was almost unrecognizable. The coroner said that he had done it while the balance of his mind was disturbed."

"After which you left the district?"

Dickens nodded.

"We've established the fact that you knew Huntingdon quite well, and also that you were related to his wife by her first marriage. May we take it as fact that she found the job for you in the works?"

"Well," Dickens admitted reluctantly, "she did. That is, she broached the subject to Dick, and he interviewed me at the works. I did a probationary three months, and then moved into the office with the permanent staff. I may have had Dinney's influence to get me in, but what I've done since has been on merit. I'm a worker, although I say it myself!"

"I'm sure you are," Knollis said smoothly.

Dickens was showing more confidence by now, and asked, almost jauntily: "Anything else I can do for you?"

"I don't think so, thank you," said Knollis as he examined his notebook. "You have made the whole position admirably clear—so clear that even I can understand it, and relieved my doubts on a number of points."

Dickens beamed, and toyed with his bow-tie.

"There is just one small point" said Knollis, wearing a worried frown.

"Anything I can do, Inspector!" Dickens offered airily.

"Tell me, Mr. Dickens; where were you at four o'clock yesterday afternoon, Saturday the sixth of April?"

Dickens' jaw dropped. "I—"

"Yes, Mr. Dickens? Where do you say you were?"

Dickens regarded him blackly. "That's the game, eh? Trying to win my confidence, and then attempting to trick me! For two pins I wouldn't answer your question. As it happens, I have nothing to conceal. I was here, in my own home! See?"

"In that case you have certainly nothing to fear by answering the question, have you?" said Knollis. "Your wife can doubtless corroborate your statement."

"I'm not married."

Knollis shrugged. "Your housekeeper then."

Dickens looked from one to the other, and gulped. "She—she left at two o'clock, Inspector. She always does on Saturdays. I'm at home from noon, you see."

"I notice that you have a telephone, Mr. Dickens. Someone must have called you during the afternoon!"

Dickens licked his lips uneasily. "They didn't."

"Hm!" muttered Knollis, flicking over the pages of his notebook with a business-like air. "No wife. Housekeeper not present. No 'phone calls."

"So what!" Dickens demanded in a panicky voice. "Because I can't prove that I was in the house all afternoon, does that prove that I—oh, yes, I know what you are trying to do! Well, I didn't have anything to do with it, see! And you can't pin it on to me, either!"

"Come, come!" Knollis chided him patiently. "You completely mistake my motives, Mr. Dickens. Please try to see it from my angle. I am investigating a murder. Two letters appear which bear your name. Both of them were intended to take prominent people to the scene of the crime—and to incriminate you. As it happens, the evidence of those other two men clears them both—each clears the other, I am trying to say. That being so, I need not waste further time on them. Now, if only I can clear you as easily I am instantly relieved of the task of chasing red herrings. You do see my point? I am actually wanting you to be able to provide an alibi, and not trying to burst any alibi you can produce. The trouble is that I am so inept at making myself understood."

"Yes, I see, Inspector," said Dickens. He locked his hands round his bent right knee and stared at the table. When at last he looked up he shook his head. "I can't do it, Inspector. Heaven help me, I can't! In fact it looks worse with every minute that passes. This house is the end house in the street—and I can get out of the house via the service lane without anyone seeing me do so. I can't establish an alibi! If anybody was to say that I was round Three-Acre Dam at four o'clock yesterday afternoon I just couldn't prove otherwise."

"What did you do during the afternoon?" asked Knollis. "Don't omit anything, no matter how trivial it may appear to you. It is the apparent trivialities that count in these cases."

Dickens gave a grim grunt. "I shaved, bathed, changed my undergarments, smoked, read for an hour, and got my own tea ready. I then packed the pots in the kitchen for my housekeeper to deal with this morning, and read again until it was time to go out for a game or two of billiards and my nightly drink."

"Good enough," smiled Knollis. "I think we are getting somewhere—and don't be alarmed if I call to see you again. It looks to me as if you were picked for the scapegoat, or sucker in modern parlance. Oh, and please don't repeat anything that has been said at this interview!"

"I understand," said Dickens glumly. "Oh, what a rotten mess to be in!"

"I wouldn't worry," smiled Knollis. "Good evening to you, Mr. Dickens."

The driver flicked his cigarette-end overboard as they returned to the car. "Where next, sir?"

"Red Gables, the Huntingdon home. That will be the last call of the day in case you are interested."

"It seems to be warming up slightly," remarked Ellis as he slammed the car door. "Think we can cross off the Old Dear and Jacland?"

"Not yet," said Knollis with a shake of the head. "They may be red herrings, but they have crossed the trail, you know, and therefore are important—potentially."

"What have you got in your mind?" Ellis asked curiously.

Knollis turned to smile at him in the half-light. "If I am right, our friend Dickens—a Dickens who does not write fiction—has given me a clue to the whole thing. It may take ages for us to get down to the basic material, but we shall be really starting the chase from the moment we begin this interview with Mrs. Huntingdon. Have a mental run back to our interview with Dickens, and tell me where you see light."

Ellis grunted. "It needs you to turn up the gas."

"The light will come on when the penny drops," said Knollis, and was thereafter silent until they reached Red Gables, in Chestnut Road.

Mrs. Dinney Huntingdon received them sadly; her mood matched her dress of sombre grey. "You have news?" she asked.

"Not at the moment," Knollis replied, "but the trail has taken us back to an unfortunate affair that happened some years ago, and I regret that I must ask you for certain details which perhaps you alone can supply."

"You mean?" she said, and suddenly looked alarmed.

"Your first husband had a brother. Is that correct?"

"Ye-es. Why yes! Yes, he had a brother," she said with unusual emphasis.

"And his name was?"

"Froggatt, of course. Walter Dickens Froggatt."

"The same person who is now living in Coleby as Walter Dickens, Mrs. Huntingdon?"

"Yes, Inspector," she said simply.

"Now you were married on the sixth of August, nineteen-thirty-four? Is that correct?"

She inclined her head. Her hand was now at her throat in an unconscious attitude of defence.

"I am sorry if my questions disturb you, but would you mind telling me the date of your first husband's death?"

"Why—it was the thirteenth of September."

"A month and a week after your marriage?"

"Yes. Yes, that is correct."

"You were married at Eastbourne?"

"At a registry office in Streatham."

"I see," Knollis said non-committally. "Your husband fell to his death from Beachy Head?"

"Oh, no, Inspector! It was—"

The maid interrupted to say that Mrs. Huntingdon was wanted on the telephone.

She hurried away with a muttered excuse. Knollis beckoned to the maid as she was closing the door. She glanced behind her, and hurried in.

"Who is it, Marie?"

"Mr. Dickens, sir. He said it was important, and I was to find her if at all possible."

"Thanks. Now hurry away. I'll see you again later."

"See it coming out, Ellis?" Knollis asked in a self-satisfied manner.

"Hanged if I do. I can't even see the cage door opening as yet," Ellis replied.

"Then watch a little closer."

Dinney Huntingdon returned four minutes later. "I must apologize for the interruption," she apologized, watching Knollis circumspectly.

"Please do not apologize, Mrs. Huntingdon," smiled Knollis. "It is only natural for your brother-in-law to want to tell you what has transpired."

Dinney Huntingdon's eyes narrowed, and the hands by her side slowly clenched into small tight fists. "It is false, Inspector Knollis! Walter did not write those notes, and my husband did not have a mistress. He was an upright man! A moral man!"

"Quite so," murmured Knollis. "See, I was asking you about the death of your first husband, was I not? You were surely saying that he did not fall to his death from Beachy Head. Am I correct?"

"It was the Seven Sisters, about half a mile from Birling Gap, in the early morning."

"And two witnesses half a mile away saw the tragic fall. That too is correct, Mrs. Huntingdon?"

She bowed her head. "It is, Inspector."

"You met Richard Huntingdon the same year?"

"Late in the September," she explained. "I had been living in Seaford before my marriage, and I went back there after Walter's death. Dick—that is the living brother—left the district rather than face the scandal, and I was left alone with, well, Dorrie was on the way. I met Richard and we were unofficially engaged a month after Walter's death. We thought it would look—well, you know!—if we married before the baby was born. Dorrie was born in the following March, and Richard and I were married in the August of the same year."

"That would be nineteen-thirty-five?"

She nodded.

"Thank you, Mrs. Huntingdon," said Knollis with a smile. "You make the whole circumstances admirably clear."

She took a cigarette from a box on the table, and lit it. "I suppose you have come across the gossip that circulated round town at the time Richard and I were married?"

Knollis blinked, and then quickly agreed.

"There were people in town who said that Dorrie was Richard's child, and that Walter Froggatt was invented by us to explain the presence of Dorrie before our marriage. That was quashed when Walter—Dick—came to Coleby. Richard knew his real relationship to me, and knew why he had changed his name. He agreed that he should be a cousin who had known the whole story, and in this disguise he was able to tell Coleby that he had been present at my wedding to Walter Froggatt."

"I really must thank you for your frankness," said Knollis, "and I regret that it has been necessary to pain you by resurrecting the past. I think, however, that you understand."

She gave a wan smile. "I do understand! I really do, and I appreciate the tactful manner in which you approach your task. You are going? I will show you out myself; Marie is now off duty."

The door closed behind them with slightly too much passion, so that Knollis smiled as they walked back to the car.

"Notice her outburst when she came back from the 'phone, Ellis. Walter did not write those notes, and her husband did not have a mistress. Walter came first. I know your argument before you state it. You will say that it is a trick of rhetoric, and that the emphasis is thereby placed on her husband, but she was in no mood for considered rhetorical tricks. The woman was angry. We were abusing Walter—and there is your clue. Now back to headquarters, an interview with Bamford and the Super, and then I'm looking for a thirst-quencher."

"I still don't get it," complained Ellis. "Perhaps I need a drink, too!"

"You'll see it to-morrow," Knollis said dryly, "for you are going to Eastbourne to investigate the death of Walter Froggatt, late of that parish. I want every fact connected with the case, complete with dates and times, and all corroborative evidence. Got it?"

Ellis sniffed. "I knows my job."

Chapter VII
THE EVIDENCE OF THE SHOPKEEPERS

A TELEPHONE MESSAGE was received by Inspector Bamford shortly after half-past ten on the following morning, as a result of which he went through to the office in which Knollis was making out his reports and generally speculating on the slightness of the evidence on which he had to work.

"Got something interesting for you, old man!" Bamford announced triumphantly. "One of my blokes, Sergeant Hall, has rung to say that he's found who bought the yacht that was used as the decoy. He thought he'd better inform us before taking the enquiry any further."

Knollis bounced from his seat. "Let's go. I was just silently bewailing the lack of evidence. You're coming?"

"How true!" said Bamford.

"Which of the shops is it?" Knollis asked as they hurried down the steps from police headquarters. "I suppose it is one of the three mentioned by Dorrie Huntingdon?"

"Yes, Franklin's in Carter Gate. Old-established shop run by a genial old lady of sixty or so who knows everybody in town, and knew their fathers and grandfathers before them. She's a bright and observant old darling with a memory that I envy."

"Your sergeant didn't waste any time!" Knollis remarked gratefully. "Must be a live wire."

"Hall will go places," Bamford replied. "He's as ambitious as you and I were in those early days, and a first-class ferret."

The car drew up before a double-fronted shop, the windows of which were crammed with toys, games, and children's books so that barely an inch of space remained for the solitary fly that buzzed miserably around in search of living-room.

They were shown to an office behind the shop, where Hall, a tall weather-tanned fellow, was chatting with a little old lady with jet-black hair and smiling blue eyes. She bade Bamford a good morning and smiled a welcome to Knollis.

"Now let's have the facts," said Bamford with ill-concealed impatience when once the courtesies had been exchanged. "The yacht was really sold from your shop, Miss Franklin?"

She pointed to the model which lay on the table beside her. "I'm sure of it, Mr. Bamford, for the simple reason that I put it together in order to display it in my window. They are packed flat when despatched, you know, and children do like to see the completed object they are going to possess, so I put this together myself—or should I say that I rigged it? At all events, I can recognize it by the knots I used."

Knollis took up the yacht and examined it closely. "You have used the thieves' knot, Miss Franklin! Where on earth did you learn that, if I may ask?"

"My only brother was a sailor, Inspector," she replied smilingly. "An old type of sailor who learned his trade in sail—or is it under sail? I never can remember which it is. He taught me all the knots when once I was very ill and confined to my bed for several weeks. He said that this one was used by sailors to tie up their kit-bags—or was it ditty-bags? He said that by using it one could tell whether anyone had interfered with it during one's absence. It looks like a reef-knot, but it isn't. I have used it for years now on all the parcels I send from the shop—in fact I've used it for so many years that I doubt if I could tie a reef without thinking very carefully about it."

"I see," said Knollis, "and you distinctly remember selling this particular ship?"

"Most certainly, Inspector!" she said emphatically. "I sold it to Mrs. Montague of Chestnut Road. She wanted it as a present for her little niece—Mr. Huntingdon's little daughter. She insisted on taking the one from the window for the very reason that it was made up. I said that it would be difficult to pack for the post, but she said that she only lived at the other end of the road, and would hand it in."

"The price of it, Miss Franklin?"

"Twenty-four and eleven, Inspector."

"Miss Franklin," said Knollis, "you are aware that we are investigating the death of Mr. Huntingdon, and having read the morning newspaper you will also be aware that another model yacht comes into this affair. I think we have established the fact that this present one was bought from you; now can you, from the private marks on the container box, say whether or not the other one was also purchased from you?"

Miss Franklin nodded brightly. "I think so, Inspector. What were the marks, please?"

Knollis wrote them down on the back of an envelope: NA/W and OT/NN.

Miss Franklin replied almost immediately, shaking her head. "They could not possibly be mine. I use the first ten letters of the alphabet, from A to J, but in reverse order. A represents nought, B represents nine, C represents eight, and so on. I have no N, W, T, nor O in my price code."

"Shall I get moving, sir?" asked Sergeant Hall.

"On your way," said Knollis.

"I'll 'phone in, sir," said Hall, and strode from the office with a purposeful stride.

"I was thinking," said Miss Franklin; "if this yacht was priced in my code it would be marked IG/JJ."

"I see that," Knollis said thoughtfully. "Anyway, you are prepared to swear—if necessary—that you sold this particular ship to Mrs. Montague?"

"Unless there is another tradesman in town who uses my knot, the answer is a definite yes, Inspector."

"Can you remember how you wrapped it for her?"

"In a large folded sheet of corrugated cardboard, and then in a large sheet of brown paper. It wasn't my usual kraft—you know, the usual brown stuff—but some almost black and very thick paper that had come round some goods from the warehouse. It was a very large sheet, you see. Oh, and my name and address would probably be on it!"

"You are an admirable witness," Knollis said happily. "Our best thanks for your assistance, Miss Franklin." With the yacht under his arm he led the way from the shop. "We'd better see Mrs. Montague straight away, Bam. What can you tell me about her on the way?"

"Before we come to that," said Bamford, wrinkling his brows, "I'm wondering about the possibility of her having shot—but it's impossible!"

"Nothing is impossible," Knollis said suavely as he followed Bamford into the car. "Women have shot men before yesterday, and they will be shooting them after to-morrow. At the same time it seems a little too good to be true. A woman who does a shooting usually does it on the spur of the moment. If her crime is premeditated, as this one undoubtedly was, then she has a habit of descending to poison. Again, assuming her to be a thinking woman, she surely would not make her purchase so open? There's a catch in it somewhere, Bam, a catch that will most likely come to light as we interview her. Looping the loop again, what motive has she for the shooting?"

"Now I come to think about her," Bamford said earnestly, "I know quite a lot about her. There is something of a rivalry between her and Mrs. Huntingdon. Both of them want to be Queen of the May—metaphorically speaking—and Mrs. Montague can't get nearer than second place. The Huntingdon woman has had far more practice at pushing herself to the front and getting what she wants. Both the urge and the capability are there with Mrs. Huntingdon. Mrs. Montague only has the urge. See, you've met her husband, haven't you?"

"Yes, I've met him," said Knollis. "He's the mousy little man who came to me at Red Gables."

"Perfect example of the hen-pecked husband. He just crawls round the earth, letting everybody use him as a door-mat. Heavens, what an existence!"

"I judged that," said Knollis. "He let it slip that he was only allowed to smoke in the garden or the greenhouse."

"And he's a perfect wizard with flowers," Bamford replied enthusiastically. "You can guarantee that he'll sweep off the first prizes at our chrysanthemum shows later in the year, and he's just as good with picotees, dahlias, and roses. He must live in his greenhouse. Oh, and he was a keen naturalist at one time, too. He has a super collection of birds' eggs—they are on loan to our museum, mainly, I think, because Mrs. Montague wouldn't have them taking up room in the house."

"Seems to be a bit of a tartar," commented Knollis. "If I had a wife like that I'd do something about her. By the way, how did she and Richard Huntingdon get along together?"

Bamford shrugged. "Can't tell you that. My knowledge of them is only superficial. They have never come within the survey of my department until now. Still, knowing your aptitude for questioning I am prepared to believe you'll find out all you want!"

They turned into Chestnut Road, and Bamford indicated a modest detached villa on the right. "That's the place."

Mrs. Maud Montague was small, brisk, and shrewish, with a queer-shaped face; it was tiny and seemed to have been pulled forward a full inch, giving her an inquisitive and peering manner. Her nose was a perfect triangle whether seen from the front or in profile. Her neck was thin and stringy; it shot up like a capstan from the collar of her pastel-blue blouse. Her long white hands smoothed down her pleated grey skirt nervously as she faced them in the doorway, and her pointed tongue searched her narrow upper lip as they introduced themselves. She remarked in a hopeful voice that she was afraid there was little she could do for them—"But do come inside, please."

Knollis waited until she closed the door behind them and then pushed the yacht at her. "Can you say whether you have seen this before, Mrs. Montague—or one like it?"

"As soon as I saw it under your arm I knew why you had called," she said with something of a whine in her voice. "I have seen it before, or one like it. I wondered whether to notify you, and then I could not see how it could possibly have had anything to do with Richard's death. I bought one like it from Miss Franklin's. It cost twenty-five shillings, all but a penny."

"Very interesting," said Knollis. "Do you mind telling us what you did with it?"

"I sold it again," she replied, and Knollis's eyebrows went up an inch.

"Sold it!" Bamford exclaimed. "Why on earth?"

"The whole thing is simple," she said bluntly. "There is nothing mysterious about it, and anyone else would have done the same. I bought it, of course, for Dorrie's birthday. On the morning of her birthday the child rang me up shortly after breakfast to tell me what presents she had received, and of course she mentioned the yacht—which you will know all about by now. I naturally didn't want to duplicate a present, and so I took it out and sold it, and bought a miniature sewing-machine instead."

"Telephoned you from higher up the street?" asked Bamford incredulously.

Maud Montague shrugged carelessly. "You know how children like to use the telephone when they get the chance!"

"That's true enough," Bamford replied.

"Where did you sell it?" Knollis asked.

"There is a little shop on the Hedenham Road, recently opened by an ex-Service man. I don't know his name, for there is no name over the shop. Anyway, I sold it to him for a pound."

"But why on earth didn't you take it back to Miss Franklin?" interrupted Bamford. "Surely she would have exchanged it for a sewing-machine, and you wouldn't have lost any money!"

"Oh, I know!" Maud Montague said awkwardly. "I could have done so, but it would have looked so foolish, and I hate looking foolish."

"Tell me," said Knollis; "did you take it back as it is now, or did you dismantle the mast and sail?"

"I took it as I bought it, Inspector, and in the original wrappings. You see, the man did not know me, and so it caused me no embarrassment to explain that a present had been duplicated."

"The sewing-machine, Mrs. Montague; you bought that from the same shop?"

"Oh, dear, no! We always buy from Miss Franklin. Anyone who is anyone buys from her. We've done so since we were children. She has a little rhyming slogan, you know, which we learned in the prep school—her father had the business before her. *When we were boys we bought our toys from Franklin's. Now we are men we'll go again—to Franklin's.* That is literally true. The Franklins have always sold toys to the best families in town, and we wouldn't dream of deserting her!"

"So that you bought the sewing-machine from there?" Knollis said dryly. "I see. Thank you, Mrs. Montague."

On the way out, Knollis noticed two telephones in the hall; one a standard instrument, and the other an ex-army field telephone known as Type F.

"You have a house telephone, Mrs. Montague?" he asked conversationally.

"Oh, that is to the greenhouse, Inspector!" she replied. "My husband practically lives there, and in the workshop attached. He arranged this second telephone to save me the trouble of going down the garden to tell him when meals are ready. Actually, my son arranged it. He is only eleven but has a *most* remarkable mind for mechanical things. I want him to be an architect, but I'm afraid that I shall lose the fight; he is so set on being an electrical engineer, you know!"

"An interesting and profitable profession, I believe," said Knollis. "Oh, well, thanks again, Mrs. Montague, and good morning."

"So what?" asked Bamford as they drove to the Hedenham Road.

Knollis grimaced. "So nothing. Her story is perfectly straightforward and understandable. There's nothing there. But wait a minute," he said, his eyes narrowing. "There's nothing there—unless our man knew that she had bought the yacht! Bam, we've forgotten something. Back to Miss Franklin's for one more question."

Bamford was driving, so he obligingly turned right instead of left on reaching the Market Square, and Knollis was out of the car almost before it had drawn to the kerb outside Miss Franklin's shop. He returned two minutes later. "Bought on the eighteenth of March, three days before Dorrie's birthday. That doesn't mean anything at the moment, but we will file the information. Miss Franklin has the carbon of the receipt, and a very neat hand she has for a lady of her years!"

The nameless shopkeeper on the Hedenham Road proved to be a Mr. Samuel Loseby, late of the Lancashire Fusiliers, and holder of the D.C.M., and a horrible bayonet scar on his left cheek. He remembered the lady selling the yacht, and he thought he could trace the date because his purchase represented Money Paid Out, and he kept books.

"Twenty-first of March, gentlemen," he said after a search. "I sold it later the same day, and I remember that it was just before I closed the shop."

"It was then dark?" Knollis asked sharply.

"Dunno? Was it?" wondered Loseby. "I suppose it would be. I closed at half-past six, and she was the last customer of the day. I remember that I was just going round the counter to close the door and lock it."

"Was it on display on the counter or in the window?"

"In the window, sir."

"And the window was unlighted?" continued Knollis.

"Well, yes, apart from the bit that gets over the back partition."

"And you say that it was bought by a woman?"

"Oh, yes, it was a woman all right."

"Can you describe her, or give us any idea whatsoever about her build?"

Loseby shook his head. "'Fraid not, sir! I'd turned off my lights, leaving only one at the back of the shop."

"And you don't think you'd recognize her again?"

Mr. Loseby was certain that he would not—"Not to be honest about it."

"I see," said Knollis. "Now, roughly, how long did the ship remain in your window?"

"Well, the woman brought it in during the morning, about an hour before dinner as far as I remember, and as I say, it went just before half-past six."

"You've never stocked this type of yacht, Mr. Loseby?"

"No, sir. I've only been in business a few weeks, and well—money has been scarce. I'm working on my savings, my gratuity, and credit."

"Well, thanks, and good luck to your venture," said Knollis. He touched Bamford on the arm and they left the shop.

"Nothing there!" Bamford said sourly.

"Only one point," agreed Knollis. "If he had but that one model yacht in his shop it means that Dorrie must have seen it on her birthday—and that doesn't mean anything at all, does it?"

"Sweet Fanny Adams," said Bamford. "Where do we go from here?"

Knollis consulted his notebook. "The Harrow Road seems to be indicated, surely."

Bamford's eyebrows went up in surprise. "Why there?"

"Dorrie mentioned three shops, didn't she? We've been to Franklin's, and we've just interviewed Loseby, so Hall must have struck lucky at Spencer's in Harrow Road. If he hasn't, then we are sunk on this particular line of investigation."

Bamford slid under the wheel and started the engine. "Look, Gordon, what do you make of the case up to now?"

"We are up against a very clever man or woman, Bam, and I don't mean perhaps. He's thrown a nice kettle of red herrings across the track. The Bishop, Jacland, Dickens, Mrs. Montague, and Miss Grenson have all been thrown under our feet, and most of them are obviously innocent of any connection with Huntingdon's death, and yet we daren't neglect them just in case! It's as tricky a problem as I've come up against."

He was silent for a minute, and then asked: "You've got a man working on the telephone calls?"

"Of course," said Bamford. "He should be down at the exchange this morning. I rang the supervisor in advance, and she promised to assist in every possible way. Not that there is much she can do!"

"Don't get despondent," smiled Knollis. "You know—but never mind; it won't work out that way!"

"What's on your mind?" Bamford asked curiously.

"I had an idea about the telephone lines, that's all. It was just a crazy and momentary jump at a thousand to one chance. Forget it! This Harrow Road?"

"The shop is a few yards farther along. Kept by two brothers. They are sports outfitters and run toys as a sideline."

"Jacland," Knollis said absently. "He works at the Huntingdon place when he's not mayoring, doesn't he? What's his job at the works?"

"No idea," Bamford replied.

"Been in engineering all his life?"

"No, I believe he worked for the post office for a time—oh, yes, he was in the engineering department! I'd forgotten that."

"Interesting," nodded Knollis. "And before that?"

"I haven't the foggiest, Gordon," said Bamford. "Anyway, are you going to get out, or do we stay here all day?"

"Come on," Knollis smiled. "Sorry if I'm acting a wee bit absently. This case is getting under my skin, and making me irritable. We have just reached that darned stage where everything seems to be standing still—and probably isn't once we see straight."

"Well," said Bamford, excusing both himself and Knollis, "the man hasn't been dead forty-eight hours yet."

Both the Spencer brothers waited upon them, and both eagerly examined the yacht.

"Has Sergeant Hall been to visit you?" asked Bamford. They shook their heads in concert. "We sell this type of yacht. Popular line, too!"

"You didn't sell this one," Knollis assured them, "but you probably sold another exactly similar. The only clue we have to its source is the private price-code on the bottom of the box. There are two sets of letters—"

"Wholesale and retail prices," interrupted the younger Spencer. "Our code is *North Wales*. The wholesale price of the yacht is seventeen and six, and we sell at twenty-four and eleven."

Knollis flicked over the pages of his notebook. "So that NA/W and OT/NN indicate that the yacht was purchased from you, eh? This is splendid. We are getting somewhere at last!"

"That is correct," said the elder Spencer.

"Now we come to the main point," said Knollis, "and I am prepared for disappointment. Can you trace the purchaser of a yacht sold by you before the twenty-first of March, this year? The possible dates are the eighteenth, nineteenth, and twentieth."

The Spencers looked at each other, and shook their heads. "Not a hope! We have two young girls behind the counter, and I don't suppose either of them know a soul in town outside their own street. They are not very bright, I'm afraid."

"You do not go behind the counter yourselves?" Knollis asked despondently.

The elder shook his head again. "If the shop gets very busy, yes, but the majority of our work is done in this back room. I mean, if you get Randolph of the County Eleven wanting to buy a dozen bats, well, you'd hardly attend to him over the counter, would you? Just isn't done. See?"

"I see, to my sorrow," said Knollis. "It works out that your patronage falls into two distinct classes, and the girls handle the general small sales?"

"Exactly!" said the elder brother.

Knollis grimaced at Bamford. "We're up against a brick wall, my friend. Let's go to lunch and see if the fog will clear."

A report was waiting for them on their return from lunch, compiled by the detective officer who had been working on the calls.

"Interesting stuff," commented Bamford. "One inward call for Red Gables during the afternoon, and that from Coleby 1438. No outward call from Red Gables. The Sunday morning call to Mr. Montague from Grenson can't be traced. The call to Mrs. Huntingdon may be among the dozen or so calls to the golf club, and there was one from Coleby 1438."

"And 1438 is whose number?" Knollis asked impatiently.

"Wait for it! Wait for it!" chided Bamford. "It is Miss Grenson's number, my friend."

"It is, eh?"

"Further to the point," added Bamford, "both the calls—to Richard at home, and to Mrs. Huntingdon at golf—were made *after* Miss Grenson's friend arrived from Hedenham!"

"Now what does that add up to?" Knollis pondered.

"That's what we both want to know," Bamford replied. "Suppose we go up to her cottage and ask a few awkward questions? That should be right up your street, shouldn't it, old-timer?"

Sergeant Hall trudged in on them before they left, a rueful smile on his face. "Seems I've been following you round," he groaned. "Sorry if I got off on the wrong foot as it were."

"If you've followed us round you seem to have been on the right foot, Hall," Bamford assured him. "Go and eat and don't worry so much. There'll be more work for you later."

In one respect, Knollis and Bamford were lucky at the cottage, for Miss Dabell was present with her friend. Both Knollis and Bamford put forward every question they could devise in the hope of trapping either one of the ladies into an admission that the telephone had been used, but both persisted that no calls had been made from the cottage, and none received. Miss Dabell put forward an item of feminine logic which Knollis recognized as unassailable: "We were too busy chatting!"

"Oh, well," said Knollis. "That would seem to be that, but tell me, Miss Grenson, do you have any trouble with the telephone? Many wrong numbers? Inability to raise the exchange?"

She did not. "Only during the very wet weather, when the bell sometimes tinkles lightly. It is not disturbing, and so I have not reported it."

"I see," said Knollis, although he saw nothing whatsoever that was likely to be of interest.

On leaving the cottage he traced the wires back to the main road. Owing to the building being set back so far from the normal building line, a pole had been erected on the boundary between Miss Grenson's garden and the wood. The wires ran parallel with the boundary fence, and in places were almost invisible owing to the ambitious poplars which made an avenue of the winding drive.

"Well?" murmured Bamford wearily, following Knollis's gaze. "What is it this time?"

"Those wires set me thinking, Bam. Drive to the engineering department of the post office. I want a chat with the Chief Engineer. I've still got a notion that the calls were made from the

R.A.C. box along the road, and that some neat jiggery-pokery made it appear that they came from Miss Grenson."

Twenty minutes later he explained his theory to the engineer, but that gentleman shook his head dubiously. "I can't see anything like that managing to work, but I'll have the box tested if it will help."

"Thanks," said Knollis. "By the way, didn't the Mayor of Coleby once work under you?"

"Mr. Jacland? Not during my time, Inspector. Mind you, I've only been in Coleby for seven years, being promoted from Hedenham, and he may have been here before then."

Knollis took the lead back to the street and the car.

"What was the point about Jacland?" demanded Bamford. "You surely don't think that he was responsible for the calls, do you?"

Knollis tipped his trilby back from his forehead, and planted his hands on his hips. "Bamford, I don't know what to think, and that is the honest truth—but I'll crack this case wide open if it takes me a year!"

CHAPTER VIII
THE EVIDENCE OF
THE MONTAGUES

KNOLLIS STALKED ABOUT police headquarters in a thoughtful mood for the remainder of the day. From time to time he returned to the sheaf of statements, examining, checking, comparing; all to no purpose. He was reaching a state of despondency when a laconic message from Ellis arrived via the teleprinter, and was borne to him by a puzzled Bamford.

"There's a message from your sergeant, Gordon," he said, "and I'm hanged if I can make head or tail of it. It reads: *Walter Froggatt married August sixth. Died July sixth same year. Ellis.*"

Knollis's expression matched Bamford's own for perhaps half a minute, and then he suddenly jumped to his side. "Let's see, Bam! Died July—married August. Now I wonder?"

"Wonder what? If it's a mistake?" Bamford ventured uncertainly. "Looks screwy, doesn't it?"

"It isn't a mistake if it's from Ellis. He doesn't make mistakes. No, he's picked up something vitally important and we'll just have to wait until he's got it sorted out."

"Going to join him in Eastbourne?"

Knollis shook his head. "No need to do that. Ellis and the Eastbourne police are quite capable of handling it. No, we'll think it out and see if we can work on it from this end in any way."

He scratched his ear. "It's the most unusual twist I've yet met. The fellow died before he was married. Now it may be possible to fool a parson who has never seen the couple before, but it's more difficult to fool a coroner who has the body before his eyes. Any idea where we can get hold of Mr. Montague?"

"Should be at the works," Bamford replied shortly.

He lifted the telephone receiver. "Get Mr. John William Montague at the Huntingdon works, please."

They stared silently at the teleprinted message until the P.B.X. operator called back, and then Bamford said: "He's got a few days off to attend to Huntingdon's affairs. He's the executor in case you didn't know."

"Yes, so he told me," Knollis nodded.

"Shall we try his home?"

"We'll go along and seek him out."

Mr. Montague was busy in his greenhouse when they arrived. His wife suggested fetching him to the house, but Knollis said they could talk as well in the greenhouse as anywhere else, and so they were shown into Mr. Montague's second home, where he was contentedly puffing away at his pipe. He welcomed them with as much ceremony as if he was in the drawing-room, and pulled out boxes for them to sit on.

He looked shyly over his pipe, seeming more mouseish than ever. "I was wondering if you made anything of the call on Miss Grenson," he ventured hesitantly.

"Nice little place you've got here," Knollis said conversationally. His gaze wandered round the greenhouse, taking in the newly-painted stands, the heating system, the hanks of bass that hung from a nail behind the door, and the long banana box that lay under the stand on the north side.

"It's in a bit of a mess at present," Montague said in a deprecatory voice as he watched Knollis's eyes on tour.

"I'm getting ready for my tomato plants, you know, and then there are the seedlings—they'll soon have to be moved out to the cold frames for hardening-off. It does look quite nice in here though when the tomatoes are growing, and the vine is in leaf."

He trotted down the aisle and returned with a large pot.

"I'm trying to rear a peach. Looks quite healthy, doesn't it? It's an experiment—hortomone rooting, you know! Have you tried this new setting solution? It makes a wonderful difference to the fruit crops."

"How long have you been interested in horticulture?" asked Bamford, apropos of nothing in particular, and wondering when Knollis intended to start his session of questioning.

"Oh, several years now," Montague replied with rising enthusiasm. "I have always been a nature enthusiast, you know. In my younger days I went in for birds' eggs, and pressed flowers, and leaves, but your ideas change, you know; all that was dead nature, as you might say, and I wanted to create something—you know, to make something grow better than it had ever been done before. And again, I'm not so young as I was, and the garden is right outside the back door, so that when I'm tired I haven't far to go to the easy chair. My old nature walks used to be in the nature of expeditions, with lots of preparation, and often I would be tired out when it was time to come home—you know what I mean. Did I tell you about my birds' egg collection? It is rather a good one, and has a willow-wren at the smaller end as we might say, and a golden eagle at the other. I have lent the whole collection to the museum. It was rather difficult to find room for it in the house. Twelve large cases all told, and the curator was very pleased to have it. Oh, and there are six cases of butterflies, and three of moths. I'm rather proud of it, you know!"

"This the private telephone to the house?" asked Knollis, indicating the oblong instrument that stood on the stand behind the door.

"Andrew's work," smiled Montague. "My boy, you know! He's only eleven but a perfect genius with mechanics. I let him do all his experiments in here and in the workshop farther up the garden. You can see it from here, beyond the laburnum. His mother doesn't like him to litter the house, you know. Women are like that, aren't they? Still, I see her point, because I like my greenhouse to look nice. A garden isn't anything really without some glass in it."

"Talking of telephones," said Knollis; "you took the message from Miss Grenson, or did your wife?"

"Oh, I did!" Montague said quickly.

"From the house?"

Montague looked from one to the other with a sheepish smile. "Er—well, actually, I took it in here. I'll get into trouble, I suppose, if the post office people find out, but Andrew invented a switching device that enables my wife to put me on to the post office telephone. Miss Grenson probably asked for me, and Maud switched her through—or it may have been Andrew. I never thought to ask."

"You did recognize her voice, Mr. Montague?"

"Why, yes! I mean, it sounded like her, and I had no reason to believe that it was anybody else." He blinked at Knollis. "You mean that it might not have been her? But that's impossible!"

"I'm not suggesting anything of the kind," said Knollis. "I am only asking for confirmation of the statement you made to me yesterday morning."

"Oh, yes, I see," murmured Montague. "Well, either Maud or Andrew will be able to verify her identity, I suppose."

"How?" Knollis asked laconically.

Montague blinked again, and shrank into himself as if the question was in the nature of a snub. "What I meant was the caller—Miss Grenson—must have announced her name when she rang up? She would, wouldn't she?"

Knollis conceded the possibility. "Most likely, Mr. Montague. By the way, were you present at your sister's wedding?"

Montague twisted his head in a bird-like manner. "Me? Why, of course!"

"Her first wedding, I mean," said Knollis.

An elusive shiftiness came into Montague's eyes. "Her first wedding! Oh, yes, I was there, Inspector," he said, and unaccountably sniggered.

"Your wife, too?"

"Er—no!" Montague replied.

"She was married at a registry office, I believe?"

"Streatham, Inspector. She moved there after—well, you know! After the tragedy."

"After the tragedy, Mr. Montague? You sound very uncertain. Now did she move to Streatham after the tragedy or before it?"

Montague ran a loosening finger round his collar and looked horribly embarrassed.

"Well, Mr. Montague?" asked Knollis.

Montague coughed his confusion. "The—er—plain and unfortunate truth of the matter is that Dinney was—er—well, pregnant before her marriage. She could not face up to a church marriage, so she left Seaford and went to Streatham, where she was not known, and there achieved the necessary residential qualification—residence in the parish in which she was to be married, you know! Froggatt got a week's holiday, and they married and honeymooned in London."

"I see," said Knollis. "Now her second marriage? Did you and your wife attend that wedding?"

Montague shook his head and avoided Knollis's eyes. "My wife did not. I'm afraid she did not approve of what she regarded as a marriage in haste, and consequently refused to attend. She was wrong, of course, because there was no haste, and she had merely judged Dinney from the first unfortunate affair. I did attend it; as a matter of fact I gave her away."

"Where was that marriage solemnized, Mr. Montague?" asked Knollis, knowing the answer. "In Coleby?"

"Oh, no! Marylebone, Inspector!"

"Froggatt died about a month after his marriage to your sister, did he not?"

"September, Inspector. I think it was the tenth," Montague replied. "A most horrible affair! He went back alone to Eastbourne, intending to resign his job and move back with Dinney nearer to us. He was out for an early morning walk, it seems, and somehow fell over the cliff. Considering how Dinney was placed," he added dryly, "it was a good thing that he did not make the mistake before they were married."

"Very fortunate," Knollis agreed. "By the way, I suppose you know his brother quite well?"

Montague looked up sharply. "You know? Walter Dickens, of course. His real identity is a family secret, you know, because none of us wish the truth about Froggatt's death to become public property."

"How could it become public property by the mere exposure of Dickens' identity?" Knollis asked curiously.

Montague wriggled, changing his weight from foot to foot like an uneasy and guilty child. "Well, I mean, you never know, do you?"

Knollis shook his head wonderingly. "I'm hanged if I do. With regard to Froggatt's death; you mention what you call the truth of the matter? Can I consider that he committed suicide?"

Montague laughed uneasily. "Well, he did, didn't he! The thing as we see it is that the fewer people know anything about Froggatt and his connections the better. They are always so anxious to rake up the unsavoury past, you know! Dickens turned up some two years or more after his brother's death, and Richard found him a job in the works. He goes to Red Gables from time to time, but he isn't encouraged."

"You wouldn't be suggesting that he got the job at the Huntingdon works by using what is generally known as polite blackmail?" Knollis asked with great deliberation.

"I can't say from personal experience," Montague replied with a nervous snigger, "but no one can stop me thinking, can they? Thought doesn't constitute evidence, does it, you know?"

"It does not," said Knollis. "There are times when I almost wish that it did."

He and Bamford walked back to the house. Maud Montague was heading them for the front door and the road, but Knollis had different ideas and ignored her unspoken invitation to leave and be gone.

"I take it that you were at home on Sunday morning, Mrs. Montague?" he asked lightly.

"Of course!"

"So that it would be you who switched through the call to your husband?"

Her eyebrows lifted. "He did have a call, and I did switch it through. Surely it was of no importance? I mean, he has said nothing about it."

"You informed him that there was a call for him?" Knollis went on, ignoring her query.

"No, I did not. There was no need to do so. I merely rang the bell of the house telephone and switched him through—a device invented by my son. Then I returned to the kitchen and carried on with my preparations for lunch."

"The lady announced her identity?"

"She said her name was Grenson," Maud Montague replied sharply, "and said it was necessary that she should speak with my husband. She refused to leave a message with me, and so I got off the line."

"Tell me, Mrs. Montague," said Knollis; "did you glean the impression that she was speaking from a kiosk?"

"She was not," Maud Montague replied instantly. "If she had been speaking from a kiosk there would have been the usual delay while she pressed the button. She was waiting on the line when I answered the ring."

"I see," said Knollis. "Did any calls come in during Saturday afternoon—say about the time that Mr. Huntingdon was killed."

"I cannot say, Inspector. I was out. I went down town on my cycle to do a little shopping. Andrew was playing in a cricket match at his school, and as John was spending the afternoon in the greenhouse I switched through to him before I left the house."

"He was in the greenhouse before you went out?" said Knollis. "He was aware that you were out? And would be aware that the telephone was switched through?"

"Oh, yes, of course!" she replied. "The cycle is kept in the shed at the bottom of the garden. I called in at the greenhouse and then took the cycle through the back gate."

"There is a tradesmen's service lane behind the house?"

"Yes. It leads into The Avenue, which leads back to the road."

"So that your husband is the only person who can say whether there was a call between three and four?" said Knollis, adding: "I may take it that you were absent during that hour?"

Maud Montague laid a reflective hand on her sallow cheek. "I think it was earlier than three when I left the house, Inspector. Good heavens, yes, it was shortly after two o'clock. I got back about half-past four. I was later than I intended being, but I met Mrs. Brownson in town, and she would insist on having a chat, and she is one of those people who talk, and talk, and talk—you know the type. She never says anything, really, but just—well—she just talks, and one cannot get away."

"I see," murmured Knollis idly. His eyes roved to the two telephones and the small switchboard that was attached to the wall.

"Er—this question is rather a delicate one, Mrs. Montague, but perhaps you won't mind saying whether you suspected that your brother-in-law had a mistress?"

She screwed up her small eyes with distaste. "I had more than a suspicion, Inspector; I knew it! Richard Huntingdon was using John as a kind of alibi. Whenever he was missing from home he would tell Dinney that he had been here in the greenhouse with John—allegedly learning how to become a gardener. I disapprove of such hypocrisy, and told Richard so repeatedly, but John seemed to be hypnotized by Richard's rather—I am afraid—stronger personality, and there was nothing I could do about it."

She shrugged her narrow shoulders in a gesture of feminine helplessness.

"See," Knollis murmured softly, "I believe your husband told us that you did not attend your sister-in-law's first marriage?"

"Nor her second one!" Maud Montague snapped back.

"There was a certain amount of gossip in town regarding the paternity of her child, Mrs. Montague?"

"Hm-mm! No one could clear up the matter but Dinney herself—and no one could expect her to be intellectually honest. The child *could* have been her first husband's, of course. One cannot deny the possibility!"

"I think I understand," said Knollis, interpreting the attitude which represented the unspoken thought. "You are fond of cycling, Mrs. Montague?" he asked surprisingly.

She gaped at the question, so unrelated as it was to the subject of conversation. "Why no! Not particularly. I'd rather have a car, but John never seemed keen, preferring to jog along on his cycle. The cycle is handy for running into town, of course"

"Your husband gave away his sister on the occasions of both weddings, did he not?" asked Knollis. He added: "I am merely trying to learn something about the Huntingdon background, so please do not think that I am being vulgarly curious about your personal affairs, Mrs. Montague."

"I see your point," she nodded. "The Huntingdon background? You mean you want to know all about Richard?"

"Why, yes, of course," Knollis assured her with an easy laugh. "You see, I came to Coleby with a complete ignorance of the man whose death I am investigating."

She nodded again. "I appreciate that, and of course Richard was not the easiest person on earth to understand. For years he would have no dealings with women—even in his business he was antagonistic to women clerks and typists. He was determined to make a success of himself, and believed that women were brakes on a man's progress. He would often quote those lines of Kipling's. You know them?"

"It depends," said Knollis. "I know something of Kipling's work."

"Something about going down to Gehenna or up to the throne, he travelled faster who travelled alone."

"Sounds more like Shaw than Kipling, but I expect you are correct," smiled Knollis. "So he believed that a wife would act as a drag-anchor?"

"I don't know what a drag-anchor is, but its name indicates its possible use," she replied sharply. "I often told Richard that a good wife would help rather than hinder, but he only laughed at me in a superior manner—Richard was superior, you know! And then he went to Eastbourne during the late summer of thirty-four, and the moment he got back I could see that something had happened to him. He never said anything to any of us, and it was months later when we learned that he had fallen in love with John's own sister. John had been south on business for the firm shortly before Richard took his holiday. He had met his sister, and it seemed then that she was resigned to a state of dignified widowhood. No one was more surprised than John when Richard announced that he intended to marry her!"

"I take it that Richard Huntingdon did know of your sister-in-law's existence before going on holiday, and also knew where she was living?" asked Knollis.

Mrs. Montague played with her wedding ring as she answered. "John says that he had talked about her to Richard, and thinking it over afterwards we decided that Richard must have been stirred by her tragic history and had deliberately sought her out. He was of a chivalrous nature, was Richard!"

"By the way," said Knollis, going off at a tangent once more, "we traced the yacht which you sold!"

"You have discovered who bought it?" she asked in a surprised tone.

"No, not quite that," laughed Knollis, "but we have learned that it was sold the same day to a woman."

"Oh," she murmured, and seemed to be waiting for Knollis to take the matter further. He did not, but thanked her, and left with Bamford.

"Where does Mrs. Brownson live?" he asked casually as the car slid down Chestnut Road.

"If it's the one I think she means, we can be at her house in about four minutes," said Bamford. "What bee have you got in your bonnet now? Want to call on her?" Knollis nodded without replying verbally.

"How are we doing?" Bamford asked anxiously. "I'm still in a fog, and I must admit it."

"I'll tell you better when we've seen Mrs. Brownson," Knollis replied slowly. "You are correct when you say a bee is buzzing round my head. It is a remarkable idea, and if I'm correct, then we are going to draw back the curtains from the most fantastic story either of us have yet encountered. And that means something to people like you and I!"

Bamford slumped back in the seat. "I can wait," he said with a deep sigh. "I know all the signs by now. Go on with the thinking, old man."

Knollis's approach to Mrs. Brownson's knowledge was evasive, casual, and haphazard—or so it seemed to Bamford, who, in spite of having known Knollis for a number of years, was still unacquainted with his methods.

"I should explain," he began circuitously, "that Mrs. Montague received a telephone call on Saturday afternoon, which we are trying to trace. She is not at all sure of the time it was received, but she tells us that while in town she had the pleasure of a fairly long chat with you, and then returned home; the call was received some few minutes after her arrival. Now if we can place the time she left you, it will be a simple matter to estimate the time it took her to get home, and consequently the approximate time of the call. You do see what I mean, Mrs. Brownson?"

Mrs. Brownson tipped back her head, rubbed her hands briskly over her outsize in bosoms, and stared at a spot some two feet above Knollis's head.

"Chat, eh?" she chuckled. "Mrs. Montague is still capable of exaggerating, it seems. Chat is hardly the word. She was on her bike going up Brookdale Road, and I was walking back into town after visiting my married daughter. She pulled up and asked me if I was going to the Young Templars' meeting. I told her that I was not. The meeting was for the young people—obviously—and Geoffrey, my boy, was old enough to find the way there and back. My husband was taking me into Hedenham, to the theatre. She seemed to regard that as a snub, for she threw up her pointed chin and rode off. I can't give the exact time, but I should say it would be about twenty past to half-past three. And in any case she couldn't have gone straight home, Inspector, because she was biking the opposite way."

"Thank you so much," smiled Knollis. "You have been most helpful."

They returned to the car.

"Why looking so pleased?" demanded Bamford.

"Well, wasn't she biking away from her home?" asked Knollis. "Where is this Brookdale Road, anyway?"

"I'll take you," sighed Bamford. "Lord, what a man you are!"

The road forked a quarter of a mile before reaching Bamford's house, and they turned right. A few minutes later they left the houses behind them and emerged in open country. A mile farther on they turned left on to a second-class road, and here it was that Bamford called a halt.

"That was Brookdale Road, Gordon," he explained. "If we had turned to the right—behind us there—we should have gone into Norton Birchfield. If we go straight forward now we reach the cross-roads by the Three Crows. The right turn there goes to Norton, straight on takes us to the main Hedenham Road, and the left takes us—"

"To Three-Acre Dam?"

"Right first time!"

"Now listen," said Knollis. "Assuming that Mrs. Montague cycled home via Norton Birchfield, and made no calls on the way, how long would it take her to reach Chestnut Road?"

"Sounds like one of those old school problems about a pipe filling a cistern in two hours and all that," Bamford grinned. "However, the probable answer is half an hour to forty minutes on a push-bike."

Knollis tipped his trilby hack on his head and stared thoughtfully at the road. "Okay, Bam! Let's get back to the station."

Arriving back at police headquarters they learned that the county superintendent was awaiting them. Bamford led the way to his own office where the superintendent was reading through the very incomplete dossier so far compiled.

He glanced up and pushed the dossier aside. "Any further progress, or are we still struggling with Satan?"

"Satan seems to be doing his worst, but I'm hopeful, sir," said Knollis. "It's a fantastic case, but I'm one hundred per cent certain that I'm going to solve it."

"Oh-ho!" said the superintendent. "That sounds good to me. Let's hear what's in your mind."

"I didn't think you were quite so satisfied with our progress," Bamford said in a surprised tone. "What has happened that I've missed?"

"Ellis's message," Knollis said bluntly. "He said—or the message suggests—that Jean Huntingdon's first husband was married a month after he died. That is impossible, and we know it. Right! Now I'm working on the old axiom that when the impossible has been removed, then whatever remains, however improbable, must be the truth! We know that the axiom, *vide* the definition of an axiom, is a self-evident truth. Our past experience confirms that it should be necessary. Therefore we are faced with the following alternatives: that Walter Dickens Froggatt did not meet his death from the Seven Sisters, and four; or that he did die, and that Jean Montague married Jean Montague on the sixth of August nineteen thirty-four; or that he did die, and that Jean Montague married someone else who temporarily assumed the name of Walter Dickens Froggatt!"

"But that's preposterous!" exclaimed the superintendent.

"So is the assertion that he married her a month after he fell to his death from the Seven Sisters," retorted Knollis.

"Fantastic," mumbled Bamford.

Knollis extended his hands, the palms upwards. "Don't say I didn't warn you. Anyway, which of the three possibilities is the most fantastic? One of my two theories, or the story facing us—that Froggatt was married a full month after a coroner had brought in a verdict as to cause of death? And, mark you, a full month after a doctor had performed an autopsy on his body! Isn't that fantastic?"

"Horribly so," grunted Bamford.

"The second axiom we have to take into consideration," Knollis went on, "is the one stating that the more complicated and bizarre a case appears to be, then the easier it is to solve. A screwy case like this bristles with difficulties—and with leads, and by following each one in turn until we have exhausted its possibilities we are bound, in time, to get the right man or woman!"

"Or woman?" ejaculated the superintendent.

"Or woman," nodded Knollis. "I'll explain. The whole case at the moment, rests on two factors: the faked telephone calls, and the two letters signed with Dickens' name. I haven't even a bad guess at the motive for Huntingdon's death, and I'll admit that frankly, but I have ideas about the 'phone calls. They were made from Miss Grenson's home, or perhaps I should say that they were made to appear as if they came from there. Now how can that be done? I can suggest but one method—by the tapping of wires between her home and the exchange. The person who killed Huntingdon tapped the wires and sent two messages before he killed him. Before, mark you! And also mark that it was he or she! Now I have pondered on the possibility of Jacland being the culprit, for it has been stated that he once worked in the post office engineering department—public telephones. He would at least have the necessary technical knowledge."

"Still in the realms of fantasy," Bamford muttered through his teeth.

"Admitted. It is. Especially as we have not the slightest clue or hint that will provide a link between Jacland and Huntingdon, other than the fact that they were political enemies—and murder is not committed for political motives in England. The last recorded case was the conspiracy to kill Lloyd George in the first war. And so I have taken Jacland from my list."

"Leaving whom?" asked the superintendent sharply.

"Mrs. Maud Montague," Knollis answered quietly.

"Why on earth?"

"Bamford has seen the set-up in the Montague entrance hall," explained Knollis. "There is the usual public telephone, and there is also a private line running to the greenhouse, the greenhouse where Mr. Montague, hereinafter referred to as John Willie because he looks like one, seems to spend all his spare time. Now, he's a bit of a bug-collector! Used to collect eggs, wild flowers, leaves, and otherwise indulge in nature study. Getting too old for rampaging about the countryside chasing butterflies, he has rusticated in his greenhouse. See the point? There's nothing mechanical about his mind. Nothing whatsoever! Now the son is responsible for various mechanical and electrical tricks and devices—"

"Now look!" protested Bamford. "You're surely not going to drag in an eleven-year-old lad!"

"No—his mother!" Knollis shot back. "I'm suggesting, and only suggesting, that she took advantage of her son's mechanically-inclined brain."

"Inspector!"

"Yes, sir?" Knollis asked smoothly and unruffled.

"Mrs. Montague is a well-respected woman hereabouts!"

"So was Crippen a well-respected man in his own neighbourhood!" Knollis retaliated. "So was Richard Huntingdon—the pure knight without reproach; but he had a chink in his armour. It isn't what a person says that defines his or her character, but what they *do*! And what Mrs. Montague did on Sunday morning stamps her as a nasty-minded woman."

"And what on earth did she do?" demanded Bamford. "This is getting a worse mystery than the primary one. Lord help me, it is!"

Knollis took a deep breath, and shook his head sadly at Bamford as he went on to make his theory clearer. "The John Willie man got a call from Miss Grenson on Sunday morning. He must go to the police and tell them that she was the late Richard Huntingdon's mistress. Correct?"

"Correct!" both his listeners agreed.

"Your men were unable to trace any call going into the Montague house on Sunday, Bamford! Therefore, no matter how the two calls of the previous day were arranged, the Sunday morning call to John Willie *did not* originate outside the house. You've seen the switching device in the hall."

"Good heavens, yes!" shouted Bamford excitedly. "So that Mrs. Montague—"

"Mrs. Montague rang her husband from the entrance hall," interrupted Knollis. "She disguised her voice, and made belief that she was Gloria Grenson. The post office telephone was never used! Maud relied—correctly—on John Willie jumping to the conclusion that he had been switched through. You're darn well right, Bamford!"

"It's you who are darn well right," said Bamford. "I hadn't got a hint of it."

"You see," said Knollis, "the psychology of the thing was all right as far as John Willie was concerned. She knew he would jump to the conclusion I've just stated, but she was completely out on Gloria Grenson, and I knew there was something wrong as soon as we interviewed Grenson. Why should she, having kept her association with Huntingdon quiet for so very long, suddenly want to draw attention to herself? Of her own admission she does not benefit by his death, and in her own interests she would want to keep the thing quiet. No, Mrs. Montague was responsible!"

"And you follow that up by thinking that if she was responsible for that she might be equally capable of bumping off Huntingdon?" said Bamford.

"The possibility is there," Knollis admitted grudgingly. "The whole secret of the case, as I see it, is to be found wrapped up in the thirteen or so months between Dinney Huntingdon's first and second marriages, or between Froggatt's death and her marriage to Huntingdon."

"And your next move?" murmured the superintendent.

"I've changed my mind. I'm going to Eastbourne tonight to help Ellis ferret out the true facts."

"One point, Inspector!"

"Sir?"

"Why should Mrs. Montague ring her husband as Miss Grenson and ask him to inform us that she was Huntingdon's mistress?"

Knollis shook his head. "There's some spite in it, sir."

"Jealousy," echoed Bamford. "Maud has tried hard to be something in Coleby, but she can't compete against Dinney Huntingdon. Further, I think you'll find that she is jealous of Dorrie. Dorrie is her mamma's Angel Child, much made-of in these parts. Young Montague, well, apart from knowing that they have a son I don't know a thing about him. Can it be that Maud wants to drag the Huntingdon name in the mud so that she can hoist young Andrew to first place?"

"While I'm away there is a job for your blokes," said Knollis. "Find out where those two envelopes were bought, or from where they could be bought—in what part of the town. I suggest you try a long way from Chestnut Road and Maud Montague. The motive behind those letters seems to match the one behind the faked Grenson call."

Bamford ran his tongue over his lip. "You know, Gordon, there is one other possibility."

"And that is?"

"They could have been written by Jacland—sending himself one as a blind."

Knollis regarded him through half-closed eyes. "I've got that on the agenda, my friend. I haven't overlooked it."

"Hang you!" said Bamford, and laughed.

CHAPTER IX
THE EVIDENCE OF EASTBOURNE

KNOLLIS TRAVELLED SOUTH during the night, and early the next morning sat in conference with the Eastbourne superintendent and Ellis, placing the full details of the case before them.

"There you are," he said when the recital was finished, "and if you can think up anything crazier than that I'll raise my hat to you. The whole thing is crazy, but frankly I can't see any other solution for it. Either Froggatt did not die, or his fiancée produced a husband in order to legitimize her child—for knowing something of the world she must have known what she would otherwise be up against in the way of intolerance."

"The whole thing was before my time here," said Superintendent Peters, "but the files should tell a story, and there are bound to be men on the Force who remember the affair—although I have to admit that at the time it wouldn't appear to be any more important than the usual suicide case. Where do you want us to start?"

"I'd like to know whether a motor mechanic by the name of Walter Dickens Froggatt ever worked in Lewes; that is, round about the year thirty-four. If we find that he did, then we have to start thinking again. If no such person existed, then we can get right on Froggatt's trail. The second point to settle is whether any resident of Eastbourne, or Seaford, or visitor to either town, vanished on the morning of Froggatt's alleged death."

"You're suggesting a substitution!" Superintendent Peters said slowly.

"Just that, sir. I'm suggesting the possibility that Froggatt witnessed a successful suicide, and took advantage of it for his own benefit."

"It has been done before," the superintendent admitted. He lifted the telephone receiver. "Send in Sergeant Dell and Sergeant Forsythe, please."

When the two sergeants arrived the superintendent passed on Knollis's orders. Both men nodded their complete understanding.

"Now for the two witnesses," said Knollis. "If we can trace them through the files—"

"You can have the files, Inspector."

"If we can learn exactly what they saw," said Knollis, and then broke off to explain himself. "You see, sir, it is the interpretation that matters."

The superintendent nodded. "I see what you mean, but please do remember that it all happened twelve years ago, and that a witness's memory for detail isn't always reliable for more than twelve hours."

"I've a worse job than this coming up, considering the time lapse," Knollis retorted grimly.

The superintendent studied him closely for a moment or so, and then gaped. "You surely aren't suggesting an exhumation, Inspector Knollis!"

"That's it!" said Knollis. "I'm afraid we'll have to do it, sir. Meanwhile, if we can see the files we can get working on the other aspects of the case."

He and Ellis spent the morning going over the evidence of the coroner's court with a small-tooth comb. At half-past twelve the ever-hungry Ellis suggested a meal.

"You know," said Knollis, looking up and tapping the documents with his pencil, "this inquest gives away the whole thing. There can be no mistake. Dickens is Froggatt's brother. Froggatt did fall over the cliff. The body was identified by Dinney—and heaven knows that she had no reason to assist Froggatt in a phoney suicide! The question now arises: whom did she marry—as if we didn't know!"

Ellis nodded his understanding. "Yes, we know all right!"

"She married her own brother, John Willie," Knollis said quietly. "He was away for a spell, and attended her wedding before returning to Coleby. In short, he married her as Walter Dickens Froggatt, although the good Lord alone knows how I'll prove it. See, Streatham is Z Division, isn't it? I want you to get a doings off to them to-day, requesting a search for a Walter Froggatt who lived there during July and August, nineteen thirty-four, and who was married at a registry office—I suppose there's only one, but I'm not sure."

He pushed back his chair. "I'll now take you to eat. On the way back we'll call at the shoe shop where Froggatt used to work."

Ellis brushed back his moustache with an anticipatory movement, reached for his bowler hat, and opened the door.

"You called at Jean Montague's old digs?" Knollis asked as they walked along to the restaurant.

"She was there until the fourth of August that year," Ellis replied. "She gave no explanation and no address. The old girl who had housed her was upset about her manner of leaving. She had taken a fancy to her, but offered the information gratuitously that she wasn't the same girl after she met Froggatt. Jean was living in Seaford, you know, and not Eastbourne."

Knollis nodded. "Yes, I know that, Ellis. She left on the fourth, eh? That means that John Willie was the partner who satisfied the residential qualification. She did take Froggatt to her digs then?"

"Apparently, yes. She was terrifically proud of having a man, and wanted to show him. Mrs. Helpman, the landlady, says that she had no use for Froggatt herself, but added that a young girl in love can see more in a man than can anybody else, and more than there is in him anyway. She says he was Jean's own choice, and so she tried to be sociable."

"This Mrs. Helpman; she knew about Froggatt's death? Or didn't she?"

"She did," replied Ellis. "She went along to the inquest with Jean, and generally nursed her through the period of shock. Which is why she felt hurt when Jean scarpered without a word of explanation."

"It all ties up very nicely," Knollis purred. "This your restaurant?"

He was silent throughout the meal, and Ellis was too interested in food to want to talk about the case. Back on the pavement an hour later they made their way to the shop where Froggatt had worked as manager. Knollis got right down to work when he had introduced himself to the present manager.

"I take it that you were not working here when Mr. Froggatt was the manager?"

"No, sir," the fellow replied. "I was then assistant in the Seaford branch."

"Ah!" exclaimed Knollis. "Then you may have known Froggatt's fiancée, Miss Montague!"

"I knew her pretty well, sir. As a matter of fact Froggatt first saw her from our windows. He was on the half-yearly stock check when he saw her pass the shop. He wanted to know all about her. I told him that she went to the local dances—"

"You've a remarkably good memory," Knollis said suspiciously. "I hope you are not pressing it for our benefit."

"My memory has been trained," the manager replied earnestly. "In any case, I had half an eye on her myself, and was consequently interested in Froggatt's reaction. I didn't want to antagonize him, because he was really in charge of the six branches, and my promotion depended on him to a certain degree. At any rate, I was hoping that he would forget her, because he would see a good many more girls, having what you might call a roving commission."

"And a roving eye?" suggested Knollis.

The manager shook his head. "No-o! He was a one-woman dog to the best of my belief. A careful and thoughtful sort of chap he was, with one eye on his money most of the time. That was why I realized that he had it bad when he started dancing, because that meant spending money, and he didn't like doing it."

Knollis turned to Ellis. "I'm beginning to see why he went over the cliff, or vanished; whichever he did. That type don't usually like the responsibilities of married life."

To the manager he said: "I don't suppose you have a photograph of him?"

"Afraid not, sir," he replied. He then held up a hand. "Wait a minute! He should be on the old groups! We have a staff outing every year, and usually have a photo taken as a souvenir. There must be a dozen of them in the old stock room upstairs. Miss James! Can you get me the staff group for the year—"

"Nineteen thirty-three or thirty-four," supplied Knollis.

The photograph was produced, complete with dust and cobwebs. After a duster had been applied to it the manager pointed out the person he had known as Walter Froggatt.

Knollis nodded happily. "May I borrow this for a few days? I'd like to have it copied and enlarged."

"It's yours for as long as you want it, Inspector," said the manager. Hopefully, he added: "I don't suppose I'm expected to ask you why you are making these enquiries?"

"You can ask, but I'm afraid I can't give you an answer just yet," Knollis said regretfully. "You'll read about it in due course;

in the meantime please accept my assurance that you have helped me a great deal this afternoon."

"Looks like him," said Ellis as he walked back to police head-quarters with the framed photograph under his arm.

"This messes us up once more," Knollis replied in a grim voice. "The inquest evidence had just about convinced me that Froggatt really did die, and now this! It looks so much like Dickens that he and Froggatt must be identical twins. It's no good, Ellis; it'll be a messy job, but we must have that body exhumed. I'll get into a ton of trouble if it does prove to be Froggatt, but I'll wager my inspectorship against a pair of old boots that it isn't. This photograph has turned me upside down again. Heavens! What a case!"

The list of missing persons was waiting for them when they reached headquarters, and Knollis tapped it with an impatient forefinger as he faced the superintendent across the table. "You know, sir, we can't do much with this until we've had the corpse on the table for measurement and general examination."

"Why on earth not?" complained the superintendent. "There is your man right on the very day. See it, second on the list? Frederick Telsen; went for an early morning swim from East Dene. Left his digs at half-past six and was never seen again. Single man, too, which is helpful for your man. Came on holiday alone with the intention of tramping the Downs. Knew no one in the district. Just vanished! Height, about five feet eight, moderately broad, dark hair, pale complexion. Disappearance reported to patrol constable by his landlady. Never a trace of him found."

"He has possibilities," Knollis admitted.

"Must be him!" protested the superintendent. "The previous missing person was a fellow who vanished a week before, and you can read that his body was washed up at Hastings. The next one after Telsen was a girl, and she died on the Downs as the result of taking a bottle of aspirins—unlucky love-affair. Telsen's the only one for it, or I'll eat my hat."

"Where did Telsen come from?" asked Knollis.

"Woolwich, isn't it? Clerk in an insurance office. Full description supplied by mother and father."

"Now pray for some distinguishing feature which might have defied decomposition," Knollis said through his teeth. "Some dental work, or fractured bone."

"You're determined to dig him up, Inspector?"

"I must do it, sir!"

The superintendent nodded. "Then up he comes. I'll make the application to-day."

Knollis settled down with the Missing Persons list and the inquest reports. Ten minutes later he bustled into the superintendent's room.

"You can kick me," he exclaimed. "I missed one point in three readings of the inquest reports. We need one fact and we are made! Jean Montague was asked if she was aware that the big toe of his right foot was missing. She replied that she was not aware of it—explain that how you like! We'll ignore the implication which arises in view of her pregnancy, but surely she must have known whether he had ten toes or nine! What we now need is information regarding Telsen's feet!"

The superintendent smiled. "Eager beaver! All right, Inspector; let's get down to composing a batch of messages, shall we? I do admire your enthusiasm and tenacity!"

"I'm on to something," said Knollis. "I feel it, and I know it. There should be forty-eight hours in the day when I feel like this. By the way, the photograph is being looked after?"

"They are working on it now. A wet print should be available within the next few minutes, and dry ones twenty minutes hence."

"Thanks. Thanks. This is first-class co-operation!"

A slice of rare luck came Knollis's way later in the afternoon when it was reported that the couple who had witnessed Froggatt's fall from the cliffs were now resident in Eastbourne, having decided five years previously to make their home in the town in which they had spent their honeymoon. Knollis and Ellis hurried into a waiting car and were whipped to the northern outskirts of the town.

Mr. Albert Fox had arrived home from work, and he and his wife regarded Knollis nervously as he put his questions to them faster than they could answer them.

"Don't let my visit perturb you," he said. "I am merely seeking information regarding an accident you witnessed while on your honeymoon."

"Froggatt!" exclaimed Mr. Fox.

"Exactly," said Knollis. "Just tell me what you saw and in your own words. I'm sorry to rake up the matter again, but I do assure you that it is absolutely necessary that I should hear your story."

"Well," said Fox, "we were up early that morning and thought we'd have a stroll along the cliffs before breakfast. We walked a fairish distance—some miles as a matter of fact—and were standing on the cliffs looking out to sea when Janet pointed to a small dark figure about half a mile away. He was standing on the edge of the cliff and seemed to have his hands above his head—as if he was diving. He leaned forward, seemed to sway for a few seconds, and then down he went! He somersaulted a few times, and then we didn't see any more of him because there was a spur in between us and him. So we didn't see him hit the beach."

"That was all?" Knollis asked in a disappointed voice. Fox looked across the room at his wife.

"Going to tell about the dog, Albert?" she ventured timidly.

"Dog?" murmured Knollis. "Surely I am correct in saying that no dog was mentioned at the inquest."

"Well," Fox said hesitantly, "we didn't mention it at the inquest because we didn't see that it could matter. It looked like a dog, although of course it was only quite a speck at that distance. Low to the ground it was, and dark in colour. It seemed to creep to the edge, look over, and then walk away. It vanished in a hollow, and we hurried back here to tell the police."

"This dog was there when you first looked?"

"Oh, yes, but some distance away. It seemed to be going towards him while he was getting ready to jump. That's right, isn't it, Janet?"

His wife nodded mutely.

"You went with the police when they searched for the body, Mr. Fox?"

"I did, sir. The wife stayed at the boarding-house. She was upset about it all. We found him at the foot of the cliff, and it looked as if he had fallen on his face, because it was all smashed in and unrecognizable. The sergeant said it looked as if he had hit the rocks on the way down and then bounced off again."

"I see" said Knollis, staring into space.

"I made a statement at the police station, and a sergeant and a constable came later and took one from my wife. We went to the inquest, but they read out the statements and only asked me a few questions. It was a rotten thing to happen on our honeymoon, and we were months getting it out of our minds."

"I'm sure it was," Knollis said soothingly, "and I regret the necessity of raising it again. I don't think I'll have to bother you again, although I take it that you won't object to making a supplementary statement with regard to the dog?"

"No," said Fox. "That will be all right, sir. We won't get into any trouble for not mentioning it at first?"

"Heavens, no!" laughed Knollis. "It couldn't have helped at the time, anyway."

The superintendent nodded gravely when Knollis reported the result of his visit. "So you think he was helped over the cliff, eh? Interesting."

"Don't you?" challenged Knollis.

"We aren't supposed to theorize without having something to work on, are we?" the superintendent murmured. "Nevertheless, I agree now that you are justified in asking for an exhumation. As you see it, the dog was Froggatt, eh? Lying there on the cliff he sees this stranger happen along, and sees his chance of getting clear of the girl. He lures him to his side for a chat, and trips him over. He then crawls along, goes down the cliff, bashes his face in, and changes clothes. It's a reasonable proposition, really."

Late that night Sergeant Forsythe reported that he and two detective officers had made a thorough check-up in Lewes with the help of the Lewes police, and all were satisfied that no mechanic of the name of Froggatt—or Dickens—had ever worked in the town.

"Another link forged," smiled Knollis. "A negative one, but important."

Sergeant Dell had taken the trail of the missing Telsen, and turned up the next morning in a temper, having clashed with a detective officer from the Yard while in Woolwich. They had compared notes, and Dell now produced positive evidence with regard to the missing toe; Telsen's big toe of the right foot had been amputated following a pillion accident.

"So that's that!" Knollis said happily. "Hard work and enthusiasm can break down any case on earth."

"And what about the exhumation?" the superintendent asked anxiously. "Don't you think we can cancel it now?"

"Yes," Knollis agreed, "I think we can take the risk. He can always be fetched up at a later date if that should be necessary. Well, that seems to be about all we can do here, so we'll return to Coleby and leave you to forward any other information you may acquire. And thanks for everything, sir!"

He and Ellis returned to Coleby by the night train, and walked in on Bamford and the Hedenham superintendent at ten the next morning. Knollis slammed his reports down on the table, and smiled.

"Never mind these for now," said the superintendent. "Let's have your story."

Knollis told it with some relish, concluding: "So up to now it reads as if a fellow by the name of Telsen was pushed over the cliff by Walter Dickens Froggatt, who then vanished."

"That's awkward," muttered Bamford. "It means that she might have married Froggatt after all—and that would mean that she committed bigamy!"

Knollis sat with open mouth for a moment, and then gave a groan. "Don't hit me with such things, Bamford! Yes, I'm afraid it is on the list of possibilities. John Willie could have been in town on legitimate business. It could have been Froggatt who was living in Streatham, and who married Jean. But why in the name of all that's screwy did he murder Telsen if he intended to marry her? There was no other reason in his life why he should bump off Telsen and vanish? His job was a good one, and safe. He wasn't a drinking or betting man—in fact all the evidence points to a steadiness that is abnormal. And if he did clear out and leave her to play the widow—no, it won't work, Bam!"

"It doesn't appear to make sense, does it?" Bamford admitted miserably.

"The case hasn't made sense since it opened," growled the superintendent. "It's a heck of a case!"

Knollis opened his despatch-case. "Here is a photo of the alleged dead man, Walter Froggatt, taken in the year of his death."

Bamford opened a drawer in the table. "Here is my present to you, a photo of Walter Dickens, taken two years after he came to town."

The four men bent over the table, comparing the photographs.

"It's him," said Ellis.

"They're him," the superintendent grunted.

"It's Dickens," said Bamford.

"Froggatt, you mean," said Knollis.

"And now we know how he got himself that nice little berth in the Huntingdon works," said Bamford. "Blacked Dinney Huntingdon. Threatened to expose her fake marriage if she didn't persuade Richard to take him in."

"Well, we've established the fact that Froggatt is alive," said Knollis. "If not actually established it soon can be if we make Dickens give an account of his movements since the death of his alleged brother, and until coming to Coleby. It will mean a lot of work otherwise, but it can be done, and then he's trapped as neatly as can be."

"We also have to trap John Willie," said Bamford. "How is that going to be done? We can't ask Dinney, because she's sure to warn him. We can't go direct to him and demand an explanation of his London visit, and any evidence we get from Streatham is going to suffer from the tarnish of twelve odd years. So what?"

"Put a good bloke on the factory end to find out whether or not he went on the firm's business as Maud alleges," suggested

Knollis. "If he went on the firm's business, then find out whether anyone else could have gone in his stead, or whether he was the only possible for the particular job. If the former whether he wangled it. If he proves to have been on private business, then we can tackle him directly."

He broke off and stared across the table.

"What is it?" asked the superintendent.

"I deserve kicking," replied Knollis. "It isn't often I slip up so easily—and the thing is so obvious!"

"What is?" asked Bamford.

"The whole thing can be solved in half an hour!"

"Sounds interesting," said the superintendent, "but how do you propose to do it?"

"Compare Dickens' and John Willie's handwriting with the register at Streatham."

"Heavens, yes!"

"If John Willie was actually there to give her away, then Froggatt's signature must be there as the groom's signature. Otherwise, John Willie must have signed as groom, and the odds are that the clerks in the office acted as witnesses."

"We have the signed statements of both," Bamford reminded him.

"Then get 'em photographed and send them to the Yard to-night. Meanwhile, I am going to have a chat with Dickens, a gentle conversation during which I can lull him into a false sense of security and at the same time learn something. Let's get moving, Ellis."

"Very good, sir," Ellis said respectfully. Once through the door his attitude changed. "You haven't the slightest consideration for my dogs."

"Dogs?" Knollis asked absently.

"Plates!"

"Oh, your feet!" smiled Knollis. "Sorry, old man, but duty is duty, you know, and you are going by car. You know, this is a most fascinating case. You should be proud to work on it."

"Which of them are we going to hang?"

"Dickens for killing Telsen, probably. Who knows? We might even hang him again for killing Huntingdon. He has no alibi. As Dinney's late fiancé and/or husband he couldn't feel friendly disposed towards Huntingdon. And don't forget that Dorrie is his child! Not Richard Huntingdon's, but Froggatt's. That may mean a lot in the long run. Yes, I think that from now on we must pay more attention to Mr. Dickens. Seems to me that he can tell almost as good a tale as his more famous name-sake."

He paused to light a cigarette before entering the police car. He smiled down his nose at Ellis. "There is still a great deal we don't know about the Huntingdon *ménage*, my lad. He and his wife lived in the same house, and were legally married, but that was as far as the marriage went. Who knows what currents may have been working beneath the surface? Huntingdon may have been giving Dinney a bad break—and what a motive that would be for Walter Dickens Froggatt's intervention! *Somebody* was obviously trying to make mud of Huntingdon's name, and there may have been two people concerned, which means conspiracy. They wanted the whole town to know of his association with the Grenson woman. The best people were informed of it so that it would reach all circles: Jacland as his chief political opponent; the Bishop of Northcote representing the Church; the faked message via Montague to us, representing the Law. It was a most comprehensive programme, and missed nothing out."

"As Maud faked the Grenson message she could have written the two letters," mused Ellis.

"So could either Dickens or Jacland. Remember that whichever way we look at it we find it easy to suggest an attempt at creating an alibi. We've stated Jacland's—sending one to himself. Dickens could have written them in a disguised hand, and then disowned them in order to gain sympathy and be regarded as an injured party."

He sniffed, and slammed the door of the car.

"It's a pity that the ingenuity exercised in the commission of crime cannot be employed for lawful purposes. We should then be very near the millennium, and there'd be no work for detectives. The Huntingdon works, please!"

Chapter X
THE EVIDENCE OF DICKENS

They discovered Dickens, or Froggatt as he was now known to be, in a small office partitioned from the grinding shop. He looked up with surprise as they came upon him so unexpectedly, and a momentary flash of alarm came into his eyes, as a result of which Knollis changed his plans. Then Dickens was smiling, and inviting them to be seated.

"Didn't expect you to-day, Inspector. Anything I can do for you, or are you just taking a look round the works?"

"I don't know whether you can help us or not," Knollis replied doubtfully. "We've come upon what seems to be a very peculiar state of affairs, and there is the odd chance that you may be the one man who can straighten it out for us."

"Anything I can do" Dickens said uneasily.

"It concerns your—er—brother, known as Walter Froggatt," Knollis said ambiguously.

Dickens shot him a sharp glance. "Oh! My brother!"

"Your brother," Knollis repeated, as if relishing the word. "It would seem that a ghastly mistake was made in identifying the body which was found at the foot of the Seven Sisters."

Dickens winced, and hurried to make an explanation.

"Jean identified the body, Inspector," he protested. "I don't see how any mistake could have been made. I mean, the coroner was satisfied!"

"Yes, that is the peculiar part of the business," said Knollis. "It is queer that Jean Montague should have recognized the remains as those of her—husband."

"I'm afraid I don't see what you are driving at, Inspector," Dickens shrugged.

"A clerk by the name of Telsen vanished on the same day, Mr. Dickens."

Dickens drew in his breath sharply.

"Never heard of him, of course, Mr. Dickens?"

"What, me?" Dickens jerked out. "Not me. Never heard the name in my life—except as the name of a famous researcher in electrical history."

"Ah! I was afraid of that," said Knollis. "Now your brother, Mr. Dickens; did he carry any scars or other mutilations?"

"He was badly battered, Inspector. They think he must have caught several jagged rocks on the way down."

"I am referring to operation or accident scars," Knollis said patiently. "He never had any accidents?"

Dickens shook his head. "No, I'm certain of that. His body was as whole as my own."

"And you can really swear to that?" asked Knollis as if with great relief.

"Well, I should know the state of my own brother's body, Inspector!"

Knollis grunted. "That rather settles the matter, doesn't it, Ellis? Telsen was minus one big toe, and Froggatt had no scars or mutilations. The body found at the foot of the cliffs was complete but for one toe. Now once the body is exhumed the Home Office pathologist can—"

Dickens rose slowly from his chair, both hands tightly clutching the edge of the table. "Exhumed!" he shouted. "You mean that you are going to dig him up? You can't do it without my permission, and I refuse to allow my brother's grave to be desecrated. I definitely refuse to allow it!"

"Tell me, Mr. Dickens," Knollis said quietly; "why were you absent from the inquest?"

"I wasn't absent. I was there!"

"Then you must have heard the coroner ask Jean Montague about the toe, and also have heard her reply. In which case why didn't you protest that they were holding an inquest on the body of a stranger?"

"I—I—"

"Well?" said Knollis.

"I—well, I wasn't there. I was unable to attend owing to pressure of work," Dickens faltered lamely.

"At the garage in Lewes?"

Dickens jumped eagerly at the explanation. "Yes, of course! At the garage!"

"Most unchivalrous of you," commented Knollis, "leaving the poor bereaved girl to identify your brother's remains. Surely your employer was not so hard-hearted as to refuse you a few hours' leave of absence for the purpose of attending your own brother's inquest?"

Dickens licked his lips and stared through the small window into the grinding shop.

"Suppose we have all the cards on the table?" suggested Knollis. The soothing tone had gone from his voice, and his features were severe and tense.

"The cards?"

"I'll play mine first," said Knollis. "At no time did you or anyone of your name work in a garage at Lewes—at any garage. That fact has been established. Secondly, Walter Dickens Froggatt lived alone in a boarding-house in Eastbourne, and no brother ever lived with him. Thirdly, the girl concerned was pregnant before Froggatt was alleged to have died. Fourthly, she worked a miracle by marrying in August a man on whom a coroner's court had sat a month previous. Now I enjoyed fairy-stories when I was a little boy, Mr. Dickens, but I seem to have got more materialistic since then, and I no longer believe in fairy-stories or miracles."

"It's—it's an extraordinary story you are suggesting, Inspector. I knew nothing of all this. I cleared out of Eastbourne when my brother died, and I never went back again. I sometimes think I will go back."

"You can go back to-day," smiled Knollis artlessly.

"To-day? What for?"

"An identification parade, Mr. Dickens," said Knollis, still smiling. "I think several people in that town may be able to identify you. If they decide that you are Walter's brother, well and good. If they have any different idea—well, that won't be so hot for you, will it?"

"I—I won't go!"

Knollis toyed happily with the brim of his trilby, bending it back and flicking it over again with his thumb.

"You know, Mr. Dickens, I don't think you are going to have any choice. I think you should return with us to police headquarters. I shall there charge you with the murder of a gentleman by the name of Telsen, and I must therefore give you the usual warning that anything you may say will be taken down and may be used in evidence."

Dickens flopped back and pulled at his collar. He suddenly paled, groaned, and slid from the chair to the floor.

"Water, Ellis!" snapped Knollis. At the same time he knelt beside Dickens and loosened his collar and tie. With one heave he restored him to the chair, and then pushed his head between his knees. "I think we hit you in the solar plexus that time, Mr. Dickens," he muttered grimly.

Ellis reappeared with the works nurse and several excited would-be onlookers. Ellis closed the door in the faces of the latter. The nurse went to work on Dickens, after which Knollis thanked her and invited her to leave, which she did reluctantly.

He sat watching Dickens as he endeavoured to regather his wits. His gaze kept rising to meet Knollis's own, and dropping away again. "I didn't kill the fellow," he muttered. "I didn't kill him! He was over the edge before I could stop him!"

Knollis said quietly: "Remember my warning. You are not bound to say a word."

"You are going to charge me?" Dickens mumbled.

"At the moment, no," Knollis said frankly, "because I have no evidence on which I can make an arrest. I'm seeking the truth of this most remarkable masquerade, and I intend to get it. I can get it, you know, but it will save valuable time if it comes from you. I repeat that you are not obliged to say a word, but if you walk out now you haven't an earthly chance of making a getaway, because you will be watched day and night until I have the evidence I need, whether it clears you or further implicates you. You may be an important witness in this Huntingdon affair, and I have no intention of mislaying you. The rest is up to you."

Dickens stared at each of his finger-nails in turn, and then raised his head. "All right. You win. What do you want to know?"

"First, why you faked the suicide act."

Dickens wriggled uncomfortably. "I—well—I wanted to get clear of Jean. She fascinated me when I first met her, but later I knew that while she was in love with me it didn't go down very far in my own case, and that it would be a mistake to marry her. I daren't attempt to throw her over because—well, she had a certain hold over me, and could have made it awkward. I was casting about for a means of cutting clear, and she was pestering me to marry her."

"Dorrie Huntingdon is your child?"

"I guess that is right, Inspector."

"Go on."

"Well, I hadn't slept for nights, and that morning I went for a walk along the cliffs to clear my head and see if I could think something up. You've guessed why she was pestering me; Dorrie was on the way," he said grudgingly. "I was walking along when I saw this Telsen fellow behaving queerly on the edge of the cliff. He was emptying his pockets and generally making preparations for a header. I knew it was no good running at him because he would have heard or seen me before I was within reach. There was a depression in the ground, and the slope ran upwards to the edge of the cliffs, so I crawled along it in the hope of getting near to him without being seen. Then I was going to make a dash for him. Just as I crawled out of the hollow he put his hands above his head and dived over. I came over horribly sick, and I hadn't the nerve to walk to the edge, so I crawled to it and saw him lying at the foot of the cliff. I backed away, took a minute or so to recover my nerve, and it was then that the idea came to me."

He paused to take a drink of water.

"Go on!" said Knollis.

"I pocketed his belongings and screwed his hat into my pocket as well, and crawled clear of the edge. I did that because I didn't want to be seen by anybody who might happen to be around. The only way down the cliff was a fair distance away, in the direction of Seaford. I don't like to think about the next bit. I had to clench my teeth and force myself to go through with it, but I changed clothes with him, and I never realized before what an awkward thing a body can be to handle. I managed it after a time, and then went away."

"After bashing in his face so that it would be unrecognizable!"

Dickens covered his eyes. "God help me, I did just that! I must have been more desperate than I realized at the time. It all seems so needless now!"

"You did not change his boots for yours?"

"No, he was about my own size, but his feet were smaller, and I knew I couldn't cram mine into his boots."

"And so you never knew that he only had nine toes?" Dickens gave a grim smile. "It was perhaps as well that I didn't know at the time. I wouldn't have known what to do. As it was, I cleared out after leaving a short suicide note in his pocket. Telsen had a post-office savings book in his pocket, and I hung on to that. I had to have money from somewhere. I didn't know the first thing about forging a signature, and I had more sense than to try it, so I bandaged my head and my right hand, and apologized to the girl at the counter for inability to sign my usual signature. I had Telsen's papers with me, of course, and I offered them as proof of identity. The girl was sympathetic regarding the accident, and I drew three pounds. During the following month I managed to milk his account of thirty pounds, and had my address changed in the book. The girl suggested that it would save trouble to apply for a lump sum. I told her that my signature would be suspect as long as my hand was in bandages, but the thing went through and I drew out a hundred. Incidentally, I can replace it all. I had to leave my own account untouched, and there is still three hundred to my name with an Eastbourne branch of the Southern Counties."

"He left an aged father and mother," Knollis said quietly. "Anyway, do you want to tell us more?"

"You may as well have the whole thing while I am telling it," shrugged Dickens. "I got myself a job in a London warehouse, and meanwhile hunted for news of Jean. I wanted to know what happened to her, but did not want to be recognized, so I grew a moustache, altered the manner of wearing my hair, bought a flash suit as a contrast to the quiet ones I have always worn, and went on the trail during my week-ends. Enquiries proved that she was busying herself with a man from Coleby, so I kept an eye on her until he married her, and then relaxed. I got myself a job in a north London shop under an assumed name, and was eventually transferred to Birmingham as a branch manager."

Dickens gave a rueful smile.

"I'd made a bad mistake when I thought I didn't want her. I can see now that I panicked because I thought that marriage would tie me down too much. Well, perhaps it would have done so, but I began to miss her. I'd wronged her, and Huntingdon had stepped into my shoes and cared for her, and I had no intention of trying to force my way between them—but I had to be near her! I resigned my job, shaved off my moustache, and reassumed my old appearance. I dropped off the surname, and came up to Coleby, living on my savings until I had made enquiries about Jean and Huntingdon. Then I went round to see her when I knew he was out. She'd had more than a hunch that it wasn't my body that fell over the cliffs, so she wasn't shocked to see me. She treated me with all the contempt I deserved, and said that for old times' sake she would persuade Richard to give me a trial at the works.

"I was later introduced to him as her first husband's cousin, and Huntingdon reluctantly agreed to give me a chance. He was no believer in favourites, and if I hadn't possessed the necessary ability he would most certainly have turfed me out. However, I've been conscientious and worked hard, and here I am! I've been able to keep one eye on Jean and Dorrie, and there has been no reason why I should interfere with the Huntingdon family life. I know you half suspect me of killing Huntingdon, but let me ask you a question: what would be the point in it? I'm comfortable; Jean is comfortable; Dorrie is being educated. It wouldn't make sense, would it?"

"A remarkable story, Mr. Dickens," said Knollis. "We will use your new name to avoid confusion, and for the time being your story will not be published. You are supposed to be dead, and Mrs. Huntingdon will be placed in a very awkward position if the story becomes public property. There is one point on which I need information. Who married Jean in your name?"

Dickens unfastened his tie and began to straighten his loosened neckwear. "That's what I want to know, Inspector. I didn't marry her, and that's certain. I'm aware that she actually was married to someone assuming my name, because I've seen a copy of the certificate."

"You've never seen the original at the registrars' office?"

"No," replied Dickens. "What puzzles me is why she went to all that trouble. She could have told Huntingdon that she was married, and that I was dead, couldn't she? It would have been no more of a lie than this marriage farce!"

"Well, she had two people to think about, surely," suggested Knollis. "She hadn't met Huntingdon then, as far as we know, but what man is going to accept a woman's word in such circumstances? A youngish woman bearing another man's child? Surely your knowledge of the world can lead you to the inference, Mr. Dickens! And again, there was the child to consider. You know, I'm no judge of morals, but you behaved rather badly!"

"Yes," nodded Dickens, "I realize that now. Twelve years gives one time to think. Anyway, how do I stand now, Inspector? Am I indictable for any felony?"

Knollis shrugged his shoulders. "It is not my place to advise you on that matter. I suggest that you consult a solicitor. I merely report the facts in these cases, and the rest is left to the Director of Public Prosecutions. Quite frankly, and speaking off the record, I think you will be lucky to dodge a murder charge—and I do warn you that you will stand in jeopardy if some adequate reason for Telsen's suicide is not forthcoming!"

"He had a most adequate reason for jumping over," said Dickens. "He left a note in his pocket. He had borrowed money from the firm's safe and couldn't put it back. It was nearing the half-year audit—mid-July—and he got the wind up."

"You still have the note?" Knollis asked quickly.

Dickens gave a grim laugh. "Don't you worry! It's in safe custody at my bank!"

Knollis grabbed his hat. "Put on your jacket and let's go."

"I'll have to return home for the receipt."

"We'll take you!"

Half an hour later they were in the bank manager's office. The envelope was brought from the vaults, and opened. A ribbon-tied wad fell from it into Knollis's hand.

"His bank-book and a few letters," said Dickens.

"Written by Telsen?"

"I judge so. They are sealed exactly as I found them, and apparently addressed to his parents."

"You might have posted them," Knollis said reproachfully.

Dickens shrugged. "Not me! I wanted all the evidence I could lay hands on in case a situation like this should ever arise! The letters will verify the fact that he wrote the suicide note."

"You thought of everything," said Knollis. "He had two hundred and forty-three pounds in the post office bank before you started drawing, eh? Phew! He must have tapped the safe to some extent if he couldn't meet the amount. Well, the handwriting seems to tally, so we'll have the experts work on them and their findings should either clear you or incriminate you. Now, we'll take you back to the works."

Dickens glanced at his watch. "There's no point in going back now. I'll go home."

"Then we'll run you round," said Knollis. "There are a few minor points to be cleared up before we leave you."

They left the bank and escorted Dickens to his home in Grosvenor Street.

"Now," said Knollis, "do you think that Huntingdon guessed the truth? Did he suspect that you were Dinney's first husband?"

Dickens' jaw tightened stubbornly. "I've cleared up the Telsen business, Inspector, and I'm saying no more. Neither Jean nor myself had anything to do with Huntingdon's death, and I'm not interested in it. I shall wait my time now, and then see if I can persuade Jean to marry me so that I can look after young Dorrie."

Knollis flashed a quick look at him. "That could be interpreted as a motive!"

"Don't be so darn silly!" snapped Dickens. "You spend your time looking for motives! I thought detectives were supposed to use inductive reasoning and not deductive! You are stuck with the business, that is the truth of it. Well, if you want a scapegoat, don't pick on me, because I'll give you the fight of your life—and I don't mean maybe!"

"Very good," sighed Knollis, preparing to leave with Ellis. "Your statement will be submitted to you when typed. If you agree that it is a correct version you will be asked to sign it. I promised you that none of it would be made public unless it proves to have some direct bearing on Huntingdon's death, and that promise will be kept. I do assure you that I shall find the culprit, and that I have no need to seek a scapegoat. Good day, Mr. Dickens."

They returned to headquarters, and handed Telsen's effects to Bamford, who would turn them over to the Eastbourne police. The Froggatt-Telsen suicide case would have to be re-opened despite Knollis's assurances to Dickens, but the case was no longer the concern of the Coleby police or Scotland Yard.

"And now what?" asked Bamford.

"I must slip along to Red Gables and collect those marriage certificates. I don't know why I didn't do so when Ellis and I were there—oh, yes, I do! John Willie disturbed my routine with his news of the Grenson message. Anyway, it will be an excuse to get into the house and lure Dinney Huntingdon into conversation. You know," he said wistfully, "I'm sorry I wasn't able to pull Dickens in on some charge or other, because you can bet your boots that he'll have been on the 'phone to her by now."

"There's one point worrying me," Bamford said slowly. Knollis grinned. "In which event you are lucky. I've more than one problem chasing round my mind."

"Huntingdon was a clever man, Gordon. He was a good business man with a clear head for detail, and almost a passion for clearing up loose ends, dotting his i's and crossing his t's. Now then; he was in possession of his wife's marriage certificates, wasn't he?"

"True enough."

"Did you see anything of the Froggatt death certificate when you were turning out his papers?"

Knollis glanced sharply at him. "No, I didn't, now you come to mention it. What are you suggesting?"

"A simple but perplexing point," replied Bamford. "Huntingdon was not the man to take anything for granted. He would want to know the whole of Froggatt's history, and therefore, in my opinion, he must have been aware of the fact that she was married after his death."

"Yes?" Knollis murmured encouragingly.

"Well," continued Bamford, "in that case he was either a partner in the business, or else was aware of it and condoned it, and I'm hanged if I can understand that. It isn't like him. He wouldn't be acting in character, as they say. Again, if he had charge of his wife's papers, why wasn't the death certificate among them?"

Knollis fingered his ear. "You know, I think you've missed a point, Bam. Surely the most consistent trait in Huntingdon's character was the streak of almost medieval chivalry. It was the major tenet in his code, and as inviolable as the laws of the Medes and the Persians. Can you, from what you know of him, imagine him reading his wife's letters, or prying into her handbag?"

"No-o, I can't," Bamford admitted. "Such actions would be foreign to his nature."

"Well, there you have the key to the whole thing," said Knollis. "It worried me too until I thought it out. Dinney was sensitive about the whole affair. Huntingdon, as an intelligent man, would notice her discomfort, but misinterpret the cause. He was intelligent, but superficial, and consequently inclined to snatch at the most obvious solution—that Dinney was wounded by the harsh way in which life had treated her. Huntingdon, chivalrous and considerate, would steer away from the subject. You've admitted yourself that he wasn't the man to pry, and my best bet is that he repressed the whole thing in his own mind and never referred to it directly or indirectly."

"That could be," Bamford said reluctantly; "in which case the death certificate will be in Dinney's personal possession!"

"I'm taking that for granted, Bam. I'm not so much bothered about her copy of the certificate as about the Streatham marriage certificate. We know now that Froggatt did not die, and that his death certificate is virtually Telsen's. The point at issue is whether Dinney married Froggatt or John Willie."

"Or Huntingdon," Bamford said softly.

Knollis stared uncomprehendingly at Bamford for a full minute. "What did you say?" he demanded.

"Or Huntingdon," repeated Bamford. "Why not?" Knollis perched himself on the corner of the table and regarded Bamford keenly. "Go on! Get it off your chest. The idea had never entered my head."

"Well," Bamford said hesitantly, "it could have happened that way, you know!"

"Go on!" said Knollis as Bamford stared at him as if waiting encouragement.

"Well, look at it this way, Gordon. Suppose that Huntingdon went on holiday and met Dinney. Suppose she told him the whole tragic story—because it was tragic, wasn't it?"

"It has been said that tragedy is not what people do, but what happens to them," agreed Knollis.

"Then suppose that Richard, his chivalrous streak working full blast; suppose that he decided to rescue this poor girl and protect her for evermore from the outrageous slings of fortune and all that. Suppose that he said to her, in effect, that he wanted to marry her, and would marry her, but that the child-to-be-born must be satisfactorily accounted for. Suppose that he himself married her as Froggatt?"

"They were married on a common licence," protested Knollis, "and the residential qualification would still have to be satisfied."

"Yes, but he could have paid someone to stand-in, and then have taken over Froggatt's identity at the registry office! In fact he could have paid John Willie to do it! Who was in a better position to account satisfactorily for John Willie's absence from Coleby? Who could better invent some plausible business that would take John Willie to London for a month? I've hesitated to suggest this theory to you before, but I think it has possibilities."

Knollis slid from the corner of the table and took a turn round the room, returning to face Bamford squarely.

"Bam," he said, "I raise my hat to you, and a yard high. It is both probable and possible. As I see it, if Huntingdon was capable of rationalizing his association with Miss Grenson then he was capable of finding excuses for the line of conduct you have outlined."

"Anyway, sleep on it," said Bamford. "While you are thinking about it you can mull on an item of news brought in by Hall. He has traced the envelope and paper. At present it would seem that Loseby is the only tradesman in town retailing that particularly vile form of notepaper. He admitted that it was darned cheap, and explained, as he did to us, that he was having to sing small on expenditure until such time as he had built up the business. Further to the point, the Jacland envelope bears out Hall's statement; it must have been the bottom one in the pack, and the price was pencilled on the top right-hand corner of the flap; as Loseby marked his stock in that manner, the odds are all in favour of the stuff being sold by him."

"That would make sense," Knollis said cautiously. "The bloke who bought the yacht"

"Or the woman who sold the yacht," Ellis broke in for the first time.

Knollis glanced at him. "That is also on the cards."

"The lab people report an incongruity," said Bamford. "The notepaper, as we know, is of a very low grade. The ink is first-class quality. Of course we have arrived at the conclusion that both letters were fakes, but it does help to receive expert corroboration. They also state that the letters were written with a broad-pointed fountain-pen—an ordinary dip-in-the-inkwell nib being inclined to spray."

"And the average person who buys such foul notepaper doesn't usually possess a fountain-pen!"

Knollis cast his mind back to the occasion of his first visit to Dickens' home, when he had gratuitously supplied a specimen of his handwriting. "Dickens uses bright blue ink. This stuff was blue-black. You know, Bamford, I'm beginning to see Dickens crawling out of this case scot-free, and he doesn't deserve to do so. The luck is with him all the way. Still, we'd better forget that and get to Red Gables."

"Not to-day," smiled Bamford. "Why not pack in and take a rest? You could have had little or no sleep on the train. Let me take you both to the theatre at Hedenham where you can relax."

"That's the second brainwave in one hour," smiled Knollis. "We'll accept, eh, Ellis?"

CHAPTER XI
THE EVIDENCE OF REFLECTION

KNOLLIS STROLLED SLOWLY along the Hedenham Road towards the crest of Coleby Rise. It was a fine April morning, but he was oblivious of the warm sun, the burgeoning hedgerows, and the passing motorists who cast curious glances at him. His mind was too fully occupied with the twists and turns of the line of investigation. Traced on paper, it might well have been taken for the path of an outer planet; progressing, becoming stationary, retrogressing, and again progressing to its logical destiny. Forwards, backwards, forwards; with mutations that defied his power of prophecy when attempting to forecast the direction of the next movement.

Truth to tell, he was tired, both physically and mentally. During the past few days he had crammed facts into his brain, tossed and turned them as if he was making hay, until they now lay scattered over the whole of the mental field in disordered heaps, with odd ends sticking out of each heap at every conceivable angle.

Understanding his mental processes as far as is possible to any man, he knew that he had to get away from the case for a time, away from everyone connected with it; he had to go out into the wilderness, as it were, there to meditate rather than concentrate on the facts involved. He had to give both intuition and reason their opportunity to create order from chaos. As a result of years of experience, Knollis was convinced that some queer department of the human mind, or some mysterious complex of processes, was always at the disposal of man, working silently and unseen to speed him towards his destiny, and that the process, entity, machinery, whichever it might he, was as much concerned with the microcosm as the macrocosm, as much concerned with the details of mentation as with the details of digestion, circulation, and glandular activity—all of which it seemed to manage very well if left to its own devices.

There were rules which must be observed; so much he had learned by close observation. He must have all the available facts to hand. He must have them marshalled and classified in their due order. And then he must leave them alone. It was advisable to occupy himself with some manual occupation, but failing that he must at least occupy his mind with some subject far removed from the problem on which he wished his mind to work. His last case had been solved, virtually, by spending an afternoon in a news cinema and engaging his conscious attention with the antics of Donald Duck. This one would be solved by taking a country walk, or so he hoped, and Knollis was nothing if not confident and optimistic.

Whether he could dismiss the problem from his consciousness at this time was doubtful, for his mind was afire, but he could at least do something in the way of marshalling and classifying the evidence. A man had died, and died by violence. That was the primary fact, and from it rose three questions: who had killed him, why had he or she killed him, and how had he or she managed to evade detection?

Knollis had a vivid power of visualization, and he saw Huntingdon as the focus of a circle. Round him, at specific points of the circumference, were the people who had, fortuitously or otherwise, been drawn into his orbit. There were nine of them all told: Dinney Huntingdon, Dorrie Huntingdon, John

Willie Montague, Maud Montague, Gloria Grenson, Walter Dickens Froggatt, E. C. Jacland, the Bishop of Northcote, and the long-dead Telsen.

Telsen could be dismissed immediately. He had served his purpose in the tale. His tragedy was his own, and only by chance had he been drawn into the Huntingdon sphere of attraction. Jacland and the Bishop could be dismissed as stale red herrings, not worthy of further attention. And those three dismissals reduced the list to those who were members of Huntingdon's family.

Dinney Huntingdon had a perfect alibi, and unless she was capable of some metaphysical duplication of her body she could not have been responsible for her husband's death. Knollis was no believer in astral projection or any other form of occult meandering, and so Dinney was tossed forth from the circle. For similar reasons, if no other, Dorrie also made a graceful exit from the case.

Gloria Grenson? Knollis wasted no more than a few seconds on her. She had no logical motive as far as he could see. Capability did not come into the reckoning, for her alibi wiped out the more vital consideration, that of opportunity. Her alibi was simple, and yet one of the soundest he had encountered, and so she went with a flick of his thumb and finger.

That left him with Dickens, John Willie and Maud.

Dickens had an alibi, and the worst possible kind of alibi, an alibi that was as difficult to disprove as to prove. He was in his own home, alone; pottering round the house in bachelor style, reading, bathing, and eating his tea. Who could prove that he was not doing all those things? It was necessary that he should bath, shave, change his clothes, and prepare and eat his own tea before sallying out for a bachelor's evening at the bar and the billiards-table. Was it likely that he should spend the afternoon in an unpleasant game of murder, and then arrive at his local in an unshaven state, complaining of hunger? Dickens as a suspect was impossible.

Knollis lit a cigarette, and shot the spent match into the hedgerow.

Even Dickens' motive, his possible motive for the crime was not worth thinking about. His child was being brought up by Huntingdon, and in a far better state than he himself would be able to afford. Cuckoo-like, he had planted his fledgling in another's nest, and the result was satisfactory to at least three of the four people concerned. His love for Dinney? Well, by now it was doubtless modified beyond all recognition; a burning passion reduced to a mere proprietary interest. Even supposing that the old passion did still exist between the two, there was ample opportunity for them to satisfy it illicitly. It was certain that neither Dinney nor Dickens would embrace the great risk entailed in murdering Huntingdon so that they might marry and live together; suspicion inevitably attached itself to any woman who lost two husbands by violence and married a third. Dinney might be some kinds of a fool, but she was not that kind, while Dickens was the smart type who would revel more in fooling Richard Huntingdon alive than in sneering at his grave. Dickens as a suspect was completely impossible.

And that left Maud and John Willie!

Maud and John Willie. The shrewish small-town would-be socialite, and the timid hen-pecked husband. Suspicion automatically attached itself to Maud as the result of her action in 'phoning her husband in Grenson's name, for there was not a doubt about her responsibility for the call. Regarded casually, that action might be construed as an attempt to blacken Grenson's name, and only Grenson's name. Regarded more carefully, it could be seen as a monstrous attempt to cast odium on Huntingdon and Grenson, and ridicule on Dinney Huntingdon— for who are regarded with such contempt in English society as the male cuckold and the woman whose husband seeks another woman for his pleasure, and directly under her nose? Maud had good cause to hate the Huntingdons. Maud had been seen near the Three Crows. Maud bought the yacht and sold it again, which would seem to clear all suspicion from her, but what if she bought it again, mildly disguised? A complicated method, but then some people have tortuous minds and cannot conceive the simplest forms of action. Maud, Maud, Maud. Always Maud.

She wove her way through the case like a persistent slug in a lettuce patch.

Knollis came to the crest of Coleby Rise, stood for a minute to take in the view, and then began the descent. He lit a new cigarette from the stub of the first, and threw away the stub.

Why should Maud want to kill Richard Huntingdon? Even frustrated ambitions could not produce a motive that would lead her to the capital crime. Or could they?

Knollis came to a sudden halt in the middle of the road, and blinked.

So that was it! Maud was not working for herself and her ego's demand to be important. She was working for her son, for Andrew, the ultra-brainy child who had to creep along in the shadow of the gorgeous Dorrie, exactly as his mother had to walk behind Dinney! Dorrie had everything; personality, opportunity, and financial backing. Andrew—according to his parents—had brains, but little chance of developing them. Envy of Dorrie, added to hate of Dinney and Richard, provided an ample motive. Maud had every possible reason to hate the Huntingdons, as the position was seen from her angle; her temperament was the type that could feed hate until it became an obsession and had to be expressed in positive action. Maud *did* make the faked Grenson call to John Willie, and she *could* have written the letters which similarly aimed at discrediting Grenson and the Huntingdons!

Knollis swung into a brisk walk. He passed the scene of the murder without a glance. He pressed up Hampton Knoll and once more came to a halt. The whole of the country to the farther boundaries of Norton Birchfield lay before him, spread out like an aerial map. His eyes became thin slits as he took in the scene. Directly before him, half a mile away, lay the cross-roads with the Three Crows on the nearer right-hand corner. From the inn ran the shorter route to Norton Birchfield, and from it, back towards Coleby, ran the Brookdale Road, along which Bamford had taken him the previous day.

And then Knollis noticed that from the Brookdale Road to the continuation of the one upon which he was standing ran a narrow connecting lane, hedge-lined, and from this angle almost mistakable for a dividing hedge between the two fields which bordered it. It appeared to join the Knoll road half-way between the point where he stood, and the inn.

Four minutes later he reached the end of the lane. Directly opposite was a stile, and to this he went first. Satisfied that this was the way taken by the Bishop, he returned to the beginning of the lane. Its surface was of dusty gravel. Knollis searched his memory. Rain last fell on the Friday, the day before Huntingdon's death. There was, then, just an odd chance.

The strip of gravel was no more than two feet wide. On either side ran deep ruts which ventured in and out of the wild herbaceous verges of grass and hogweed, sorrel and striving meadow-sweet. The unpleached hawthorn hedges reared ten feet to the sky and overflowed the lane in cascades of spring-green leaf.

Knollis moved along the right-hand verge, his eyes shifting continuously from the gravelled surface to the green walls, until at last he gave a satisfied smile and sank down on one knee to examine the tyre tracks which showed faintly in the dust. There were two sets of them, in a depression probably dust-filled by a flurry of wind. They were narrow tracks with a V-patterned tread. At a point they became fainter and were mixed with indefinite footprints. Knollis looked across at the farther hedge, noting a few broken twigs hanging limply by their skins of brown bark.

He nodded silently. There was still no proof, but he was prepared to wager that Maud Montague had cycled as far as this point, and had then pushed the cycle into the cover of the overhanging hedge while she—what? While, obviously, she walked the remaining few yards to the road, climbed the stile, and vanished among the close-set trees of the plantation.

Knollis's meditative mood had vanished. He was once more the man of action. He got to his feet and walked quickly down the lane, his eyes following the evasive tracks of the cycle tyres as they vanished on hard patches of the surface, reappeared in occasional pools of dust, and vanished again. They led him to the Brookdale Road, and here he paused while his eyes scanned the landscape. At last he saw what he was looking for, and strode towards the Norton Birchfield road and the red-domed telephone kiosk. A minute after entering the box he was speaking to Bamford.

"Sorry I couldn't let you know where I was going," he said softly. A smile crept into his voice. "I didn't know where I was going. I wanted to get away to think."

"I may take it that you've thought," replied Bamford.

"I've done just that, and now there is a great deal of work ahead of us. That being so, I'd like you to come along here with a photographer."

"Pleased to oblige," said Bamford, "but where the heck are you, anyway? That information is rather necessary, you know!"

"Finicky, eh?" Knollis retaliated. "As a detective you should be able to trace me. I happen to be on the Brookdale Road, at a point where a narrow lane runs up to Hampton Knoll. I shall be, anyway, by the time you arrive."

"I'll be with you in no time," said Bamford. "Cheerio!"

"Just a minute!" Knollis called anxiously. "Is there a detective officer attached to Norton Birchfield section?"

"Of course, but why bother with him when my own men are available?"

"I want somebody with a good knowledge of local conditions, and you can't beat the local man. Can you get them to send him up here?"

"You're the boss," said Bamford, and rang off.

Bamford and his man were the first to arrive. Knollis painstakingly outlined his theory, and pointed out the meagre evidence which seemed to justify the line of reasoning.

"You may have got something," Bamford admitted. "I've had a sneaking suspicion of her all along, but I'm blessed if I could think up a motive. So you want photos of the tyre tracks, eh? That's about the only thing we can do to get a record of them, isn't it? Even the redoubtable Professor Hans Gross couldn't rake up a suggestion for taking casts in these circumstances. The next point that arises seems to be the difficulty of getting samples of Maud's tyre tracks without making her curious."

"Simple," grunted Knollis. "Any of your staff happen to possess a boy of near school-leaving age?"

"Yes, Fardon has one. What's in your mind?"

"John Willie is at work all day. Tradesmen use the rear gate on the service lane. We find the butcher or grocer who supplies Maud, and we borrow one of their trade cycles. We ask them or him to let our boy deliver some commodity to the house, and he asks Maud if he can borrow a pump. She isn't likely to accompany him to the cycle-shed, and will probably tell him to help himself, return the pump, and close the door again. Once he's inside the shed with a lump of plasticine—well, that is that!"

Bamford was enthusiastic. "Good scheme. Quite cute. It's quick and workable."

"If she won't lend a pump, or doesn't give him an opportunity to take an impression, then we must indulge in a spot of breaking-in one night. A cast we must have!"

"I'll organize that as soon as we get back to town," said Bamford. "Here is your man, by the look of the car."

A rickety car drew in at the end of the lane, and a tall bulky fellow padded along towards them. He flicked a salute and announced himself as Simson, Detective Officer Simson.

"You know this district well, Simson?" said Knollis.

"Should do by now, sir," he nodded.

"There's a job for you. A lady cycled along the road from Coleby about half-past three on Saturday afternoon. I want you to find someone who saw her and who can describe her. It's a bit early in the year, but some farmworker may have seen her."

"Any description, sir?" asked Simson.

Knollis shook his head, and smiled. "That's the whole point. I'm not giving you a description of our suspect. If a woman was cycling this way, and we describe her to anyone who saw her, they will jump at our description—you know how they do! So we'll get the descriptions first and then see if they tally with that of our suspect."

"Y'know," protested Bamford, "I see your theory clearly enough, but she said she was home by half-past four, and she couldn't have hiked from the dam to—"

"To where she lives?" interrupted Knollis, anxious lest any clue to her identity should be given to the detective officer.

"Yes, to where she lives."

"Any corroboration of her statement yet in our possession?" Knollis asked mildly.

Bamford looked up and fingered his chin. "No, hang it, there isn't. Have it your own way. Now, the photographing of these patches."

Knollis caused several areas of the gravel surface to be photographed, together with the section of hedge against which he considered the cycle had been leaned. "She pushed it as far under as she could," he explained to Bamford.

"Yes, I do see that, and you've almost convinced me," Bamford agreed; "nevertheless you do seem to have overlooked one point, or perhaps you've minimized its importance."

"Oh? What is that?"

"The pistol. You haven't asked a single question about it since the case opened."

"Now look here," said Knollis severely. "You can get search warrants and search the houses of everyone concerned in the case. You can find the pistol—probably—and you can have comparison tests made. You can have absolute proof from the gunsmith that the bullet that killed Huntingdon was fired from that self-same pistol, but you still can't prove that the owner fired it! I'll readily grant the importance of scientific evidence, but in the end the success of the investigation will rest on motive, capability, opportunity, and the breaking down of whatever alibi may be advanced by the culprit. Scientific evidence regarding the pistol will help to cook the hare, but we must remember the advice given in the cookery book: first catch the hare!"

Bamford turned away, laughing. "You're both incorrigible and unorthodox!"

"Unorthodox my foot!" exclaimed Knollis angrily. "We have three major suspects, and three or four other people we can pull in to make up a team. Now why go chasing all of them for a pistol when we have only to reduce the team to one by the process of elimination and then concentrate on discovering where that one hid the weapon—for it will be hidden, and there are no doubts about that."

Bamford raised his hands in self-defence. "All right! Granted! I grant every ounce of your logic, but I still want that weapon, whether it be a revolver, automatic, or even an arquebus!"

"Well, why not set about it?" challenged Knollis.

"That's fair enough. I will."

"Good! By the way, what was Ellis doing this morning when you came away?"

"Having an interesting chat with someone at the Yard," replied Bamford. "He had then been on the 'phone for a quarter of an hour."

Knollis nodded happily. "Which means that news will be waiting for us when we get back."

Knollis was correct. The Yard were satisfied, subject to expert confirmation, that the signature of the groom at the Jean Montague—Walter Froggatt wedding was identical with the signature of John William Montague, and that no attempt had been made to disguise the handwriting.

"So that's another link forged," said Bamford. "We aren't doing bad, considering all things."

"I only hope we don't have to rely on the evidence of the signature in court," mused Knollis.

"It's good food and not red herring," Bamford said with some surprise at Knollis's remark.

"Yes, I agree, but if we take the matter into court we'll have at least two handwriting experts contradicting us, acting for the defence."

"We'll also have our own experts!"

Knollis nodded cynically. "That is the whole point. They'll contradict each other until they are blue in the face. They think up such remarkable arguments. The defence will say—to coin an example—that Montague always put the dot a fraction of an inch before the i, and the prosecution will say that it was bound to follow the letter if he was in a hurry, as he might be in this instance. They'll think up something equally absurd! Bamford, I don't like expert witnesses, and never did. I prefer evidence which is not dependent on opinion in any way. The expert can only get up in court and say that in his opinion this is this and that is that. When you and I give evidence we can say that the accused was seen by such and such a person in such and such a place at such and such a time. That is evidence! There is no opinion about it. Further to the point, were you or I to get on our hind legs and attempt to express an opinion we should be ruled out of order by the judge. Facts, my lad! You can't beat facts, and facts are what I am seeking. To the lions with opinion!"

Bamford heaved a sigh. "It's a waste of time arguing with you to-day. I'll go and organize the clay-modelling class. What are you going to do?"

"Hanged if I know," Knollis admitted reluctantly. "Walk and think again probably. Which reminds me! There is a wee point here over which you and Ellis can mull in your spare time."

"Which is when?" Ellis asked glibly.

"The remainder of the day as far as I'm concerned. John Willie told us that he was aware of the Huntingdon-Grenson link-up, didn't he? Years ago he went to a deal of trouble to help Dinney out of a jam. Right! So why should he now deceive his sister instead of helping her? Both he and Maud have told us that he consented to act as Richard's alibi. That doesn't make sense to me. Anyway, it is all yours to play with in your spare time. You may see light where I can't see it."

He strolled to the door, and there paused. "On second thoughts, you'd better come with me, Ellis. We'll take a run to the Huntingdon works. There is a question which needs an answer—one concerning Huntingdon."

On arrival at the works he sought an interview with the secretary and made known his chief need of the moment. "I want a chat with someone who was working in close contact with Mr. Huntingdon thirteen years ago. Have you a suggestion?"

"Mr. Palmer, one of his co-directors, will be your best man, Inspector. He and Mr. Huntingdon were the sole partners in the original firm."

Mr. Palmer, a comfortable-looking man of fifty or so, nodded when Knollis repeated his request through the cigar smoke which befouled the atmosphere.

"Dick and I were the original firm, Inspector. We started in a disused garage at the other end of the town. We worked like stink, and here we are to-day—or perhaps I should say here *I* am," he added bitterly. "It was a foul day's work on somebody's part last Saturday. Dick should have been enjoying the fruits of his labours for at least another twenty years."

"How long has Montague been working with the firm?" asked Knollis, trying to steer Palmer from a detailed history of the firm's progress.

"Almost from the beginning, Inspector. We moved from the garage to an old factory, and Montague came in then as clerk, secretary, and general factotum. I don't know what we'd have done without him in those days. This may be not quite fair on him, but the fact remains that his usefulness declined as the firm grew, and much as we should have liked to repay his loyalty by giving him the secretaryship of the new company we reluctantly had to demote him. We did it as tactfully as possible, but I'm afraid he did resent it to some extent. I don't blame him. I'd have felt the same in his place."

"He has managed to put a lot of business in your way in his time?" Knollis asked artlessly.

"Clever man at business negotiation," said Palmer. "I have to give him that. It wasn't so much that he put business in our way as that he was expert at clinching opportunities when they presented themselves."

"Ah!" sighed Knollis. "Mr. Palmer, some years ago—it was the year before Huntingdon married—Montague went to Streatham for a month. Can you tell me whether he went on private business, or for the firm?"

Palmer glanced suspiciously over his cigar. "That was over twelve years ago!—What are you getting at, Inspector?"

Knollis shook his head. "I can't tell you that, not at the moment, anyway. Still, I can't expect your memory to take you so far back. It is asking too much."

"My memory is a darned good one," Palmer said indignantly. "I most certainly can remember Montague going to Streatham! If you enquire, you will learn that there was at that time a Great-end Engineering Company operating in Streatham. They were on a point of balance, like so," he said, see-sawing a hand. "They were as likely to go up as they were to go flat, and Montague had heard that they were going flat. He suggested that we might be able to step in and buy some of the plant before they went into voluntary liquidation. Candidly, I thought the whole idea a bit far-fetched, but he'd pulled off a few fast moves, and Dick was behind him, so he vanished for a month or so. It happened to be his one big flop. Nothing came of it, despite his long absence and the bill for expenses he sent in."

"What happened to the Streatham firm, Mr. Palmer?"

"Pulled round," he said shortly. "They are in Essex to-day, operating one of the biggest plants in the country. They are also our toughest rivals!"

"Nothing there," said Knollis as they left the works. "It looks as if Montague did a spot of engineering for a change—engineering an excuse to go south. As far as I can see it might just as easily have been Streatham or any other place."

"Now what do we do?" ventured Ellis.

"There's only one thing we can do, my lad, and that is attempt to reconstruct the manner in which Maud organized the death of Huntingdon and threw so many red herrings across the path. It was well thought out, and I've got to give her that. See, she left home at two o'clock, and was seen by Mrs. Brownson at twenty past three. Why did she allow herself to be seen going that way? Probably bluff. She must have felt pretty confident of the success of her plan. You know, Ellis, if she took the route I've suggested she must have been right in the Bishop's tracks for most of the way through the plantation, and during the actual shooting she had Jacland and the Bishop almost facing her. That's nerve for you!"

He dropped Ellis in town, advising him to lose himself for a few hours and take a rest. "As for me, I'm going to see Mrs.

Huntingdon again. It will look too much like an official interview if the two of us are present. See you later!"

Chapter XII
THE EVIDENCE OF DINNEY HUNTINGDON

"Mrs. Huntingdon," said Knollis, "I am compelled by the urgency of the problem of your husband's death to delve into the most personal aspects of your family life."

Dinney Huntingdon, dressed in flannel slacks and a sober brown sweater, nodded and waited.

"I am particularly interested in the relationships which have existed between yourself and certain members of your family."

Dinney Huntingdon nodded again.

"Primarily," Knollis went on, "I am interested in the relationship existing between yourself and your sister-in-law, Mrs. Montague."

Dinney Huntingdon gave a dry laugh. "I wondered when you would get round to her, Inspector, but why approach me so circumspectly? I have told you previously that I am prepared to go to any lengths to help you to find my husband's—yes, my husband's murderer. Some words are frightening, but they have no synonyms."

Knollis flashed her a quick glance. "I am almost inclined to take you up on that offer, Mrs. Huntingdon."

She gestured eloquently with the beringed hand that held her cigarette. "Why not, Inspector? What could there be that I could possibly wish to conceal?"

Knollis eyed her for the space of a few seconds, and then made up his mind. "The truth, the whole truth, and nothing but the truth about your first marriage, Mrs. Huntingdon. Perhaps I should say wedding, since there was no marriage within the meaning of the word."

The expression of some emotion flickered across her face and was gone. She regarded Knollis sphinx-like as she asked: "Wasn't it Pilate who asked what was truth?"

"Pilate received no reply," Knollis replied.

Dinney Huntingdon stared through him as if she was staring through an infinity of space and an eternity of years. "What is truth?" she whispered.

"I have a suspicion," said Knollis, "but you know the truth."

"What is right and what is wrong?" she asked. "What is moral, what is immoral, and what is amoral? *All things are lawful, but not all things are expedient.* And yet expediency was my sole justification."

She looked up and gave a direct question. "How much do you know, Inspector?"

"I know that Walter Dickens Froggatt was supposed to have fallen to his death in the July of thirty-four, and that he did not die. I know that he was alive when you were married in Streatham in the August of the same year. I know that your brother assumed Froggatt's identity and that you went through a form of marriage with him. I know that your husband had a mistress, that your brother was shielding him, and I suspect that your sister-in-law hated both you and your husband—and the child!"

"Then you know everything," she said. She took a turn round the room, returned to face Knollis, and sat heavily on the edge of the settee. She took a great breath of smoke and blew it down her nostrils. "You are wondering about me, aren't you, Inspector? I've changed in a matter of days."

She rose again, walked to the fireplace, and threw the remains of the cigarette into the grate. "All passion spent. That is the answer. All that remains of Mrs. Richard Huntingdon is what you see before you. An empty shell!"

"I thought," Knollis ventured slowly, "that—well, that you and your husband were living a mere play of married life. Pardon the suggestion!"

"We were," she nodded slowly. She rested one sandalled foot on the fender and looked at Knollis under lowered eyebrows.

"We were. That is the whole point. You see, Inspector, now it is too late, I've discovered that I loved him—and I sent him away, to Gloria Grenson."

"You knew about her, Mrs. Huntingdon?"

"Oh, yes. Oh, dear, yes! Richard told me about her. You never knew Richard when he was alive, did you? He was the most honourable man who ever lived—and like a fool I despised him for it. Queer, isn't it?" she asked with a shaky laugh.

Knollis considered the implications of her statement, and bent forward incredulously. "He told you about it?"

"You find that difficult to believe, Inspector? That is because you never knew Richard. Even while taking a mistress he was honest with me."

"But the Montagues both assert that he was deceiving you and that John Willie—pardon, Mr. Montague—was aiding in the deception."

Dinney removed her foot from the fender and walked briskly back to the settee. "You're a married man, Inspector?"

"With two sons, Mrs. Huntingdon," he nodded.

"Let's clear the decks for action, shall we?" she asked intensely. "I am beginning to see light. You suspect Maud of murdering Richard, don't you?"

Knollis hesitated, and did so for a fraction of a second too long.

"You do!" snapped Dinney Huntingdon. "As a man, you have reason behind your suspicion. As a woman, I have my intuition, and I *feel* that no one but a woman could have killed him in such a cowardly manner. That woman was Maud! You'll ask for a reason, but I can't give you one. I just know!"

"Please do go on, Mrs. Huntingdon," Knollis murmured.

"There's a lot of talk about psychology these days, isn't there?" she asked rhetorically. "I don't know anything about it. That's Maud's line. It seems to me to be just human nature with a fancy name. And, you know, that's what puzzles me! It almost frightens me at times. Do you ever get wondering about yourself, and why you do things? Do you ever stop and wonder why you did things in the past? Then, they seemed the most obvious thing to do, and later you see that you did the very worst thing possible. It's almost as if we aren't in control of ourselves, but as if we were some kind of machines and were being driven from inside. Can you understand me, Inspector, or do you think I am just talking?"

"I seem to remember that D.H. Lawrence expounded some such theory," said Knollis non-committally.

"The man who wrote those books?" she asked. "Well, that is how I sometimes feel. I mean, why should I have treated Richard as I did if I was in control of myself? You see, Inspector—and this is why I asked if you were a married man—it all started in those early days when Walter Froggatt was courting me. Two little sparks are drawn together, and suddenly there is a great blinding flash. It was like that with Walter and myself. Dorrie was the result. Then the police came to tell me that Walter had fallen or thrown himself over the cliffs. There was a short note in his pocket saying that he could not face marriage. They took me along to the inquest, and they showed me the body. I knew straight away that it was not Walter lying there, but I knew I had seen the last of him, and that he was already dead as far as I was concerned, and I found myself telling them that I recognized the remains as Walter's. The man had only nine toes. Walter had ten. I said it was Walter, and I couldn't help myself. The falsehood came from me as if I had no control over what I said.

"Later, when the inquest was over, I began to think about Dorrie and the fact that she would be illegitimate when born. I sent for Willie, and explained the plan that had come from somewhere inside me. He didn't want to help me, but Willie was always like putty and I made him promise. He said that it would not work, and that anyone who knew me would know that Walter had died before the time I married. I told him that it would work if I got away from the district where I was known, because I could then tell people that Walter had died in the September instead of the July. He saw the reason in that, and we went ahead with the plan. It was obvious that I could not marry in the Eastbourne district, and equally obvious that it would be difficult for me to live somewhere for a month while we satisfied the needs of the licence—"

"The residential qualification?" murmured Knollis.

"Yes. And we couldn't decide where to arrange the marriage until Willie wrote to say that he could find a reason for spending a month in Streatham. That, of course, was where we were married. Willie lived at a small hotel as Walter Froggatt, and I married him in that name. The next thing I had to think about was Dorrie's future. Willie had told me about his employer, and what a fine man he was, and that he was taking a holiday at Eastbourne later that month, so I slowly pumped him and found where he would be staying—after which I made sure that he came to know me. The rest of that story doesn't matter. Sufficient to say that Richard was sensitive about getting married in Coleby, so I lived in Marylebone for a time, and we were married there."

She paused and stared bleakly at her sandalled foot.

"The marriage with Richard was never consummated. It was my fault. Something inside me coupled the idea of marriage with the idea of desertion—Walter's desertion. It seemed to me that Richard would leave me if I once gave myself to him, and—and—oh, God, what makes us think such destroying thoughts, Inspector Knollis?"

"It's a mystery," said Knollis.

"A mystery indeed. It couldn't go on, and even I could see that, but I couldn't see a way out of it. Every minute of my time was spent in worrying about it, until I realized that if I didn't get out I would go mad. I had to *do* something! I took up golf. I joined clubs and societies. I never gave myself a minute in which to think. And then Richard came to my room one night and told me frankly and without embarrassment that he had found someone he loved and who loved him. Did I want a divorce? I didn't want a divorce. I still loved him, but there was a barrier I could not break down. It was like an iron bar or a door placed between two halves of me. I think I could have dissolved it with tears, but I could not weep. I can never remember weeping, even as a child. I told Richard that I did not want a divorce. I told him to go and be happy, knowing that I would not resent it and that I would not pry. He bowed, and looked so absurd at that moment that I laughed. I saw the pain that laugh caused him, and then something inside me told me that I had snapped the last link between us, and that it was better that way, better for him, better for me, and better for Gloria Grenson. From that day we lived in the house together as strangers. Previously we had lived as brother and sister, and now it was as strangers."

She gave a wistful smile.

"I had thrown away my last chance, so I plunged headlong into my social activities. I've been accused of being an exhibitionist, a climber, and a snob. That is where Maud comes into the story. Maud was all of those things, and she resented my appearance in the arena. I began to feel the confidence of power, and I took on every position that came my way, and almost more than I could chew. I saw Maud as the symbol of everything that stood in my way, and I—well, I'm afraid I swept her aside.

"There was Dorrie, too. I wanted her to be something, and it wasn't until after Richard's death that I saw what a mess I was making of her life. Richard had remonstrated with me on a good many occasions, but I ignored him. Well, I see it now, and it isn't too late in her case. I can spend my time straightening her out again. But Maud—well, she never did like me, and I think she suspected the truth of the Streatham marriage and resented the way I had handled Willie, despite the fact that she has always treated him in the same way. Further to the point, despite the fact that the evidence has been literally pushed under her nose, she regarded Dorrie as being Richard's child and self-righteously held us both in contempt."

"All this is very enlightening," commented Knollis, "but I still haven't got what I am looking for. Why did she hate your husband?"

"Do you know anything of Richard's early history?"

"A little," Knollis replied. "I have had an interview with Mr. Palmer this morning."

"He and Richard laid the foundations of the present Huntingdon and Palmer Engineering Company, Inspector. They invested their meagre savings, and starved themselves of food and the necessities of life in order to build a big business. Willie joined the firm in its third year. He became a valuable asset, but although he is my own brother I am bound to admit that he never deserved the reward which Maud expected. She expected him to share in the glory—and the profits—which came to Richard and Palmer. But why should he? He never invested as much as a pound in the business. Willie was always too cautious for that. He was a conscientious worker, and they always paid him well, but Maud seemed to expect him to be promoted to the board. She continually accused Richard of climbing to success on Willie's back, and that is all nonsense, of course. Furthermore, I believe that she compared Richard and his confident manner with Willie's peace-at-any-price attitude towards the world. Willie is right in his own way, and so was Richard. Each of them acted according to his temperament, but in spite of all her psychology you could not expect Maud to see that! She sees only what she wants to see."

"And their son, Andrew?" said Knollis, still anxious for Dinney Huntingdon to do all the talking.

"A grand boy, Inspector, and a clever one if Maud will only let him alone. Dorrie, who is a year younger—almost—is the bone of contention there. Dorrie is by no means brainy, but even at her age she is a good little tennis player, a good horsewoman, and a remarkably good little dancer. Andy is none of these. Andy runs to brains, and has the making of a fine engineer—I am quoting Richard's opinion now. Maud wants him to shine socially. She wants him to vie with Dorrie at tennis and dancing, and horse-riding, and the rest of it. She can't see that it is opposed to the boy's natural inclinations, and she blames us—Richard and myself—for deliberately encouraging Dorrie to put him in the shade. In fact she *hates* us for it!"

"And Willie? Where does he come in?"

"Willie comes in just where and when Maud gives him the cue. Willie cannot smoke in the house. Willie has to change into slippers before he comes in from the garden. Willie has to come-hither and go-thither when Maud gives the word. Oh, I could hit him for his peacefulness! If I was a man I'd take Maud into the bedroom and give her a good thrashing with the back of a hairbrush so that she wouldn't be able to sit down for a week. I beg your pardon, Inspector Knollis! I forgot myself!"

She rose in confusion. "Perhaps you would like a drink, Inspector?"

Knollis smiled. "I don't think so, thank you, Mrs. Huntingdon. I'm supposed to be on duty, you know!"

"Oh, but you must have one!" she said, and hurried from the room.

Knollis, still smiling, got to his feet and wandered round the room. He eventually arrived before the bookcase and noted that it was mainly filled with engineering manuals. And then he looked again and saw that lying on its side on the other books was a well-known book on popular psychology.

"I thought she knew nothing about the subject," he mused. He opened the bookcase and took out the book. *Maud Montague* was scrawled across the fly-leaf. He flicked the pages. A passage half-way through had been underscored in red ink:

> *The human mind is analogous to a boiler in which a great head of steam has been confined. Providing that the stop-cocks are open the steam will dissipate harmlessly, either doing useful work or escaping through the safety valve provided, but if the cocks and valves are closed and the fire is continually stoked, then something is bound to blow up. So it is with the emotions. They must have outlets. There must be ways of escape, either through useful work or through recreational activities. You must act! You must do something about your problem! Or you will blow up!*

The last two sentences were doubly underscored, and a large exclamation mark brandished itself like a bludgeon in the margin.

Knollis turned guiltily as Dinney re-entered the room, carrying a tray on which stood a decanter, a siphon of soda, and a glass.

"I'm afraid I was taking the liberty of looking at your books, Mrs. Huntingdon," he apologized.

"Why not?" she smiled sadly. "I doubt if any other person will ever read them now Richard has gone. Oh! I see! You have got Maud's book. She lent it to me months ago. Lent it? I should say she forced it upon me and told me it would do me good to read it. I'm afraid I never did like anything that was likely to do me good, and I have never glanced at it. Is it readable?"

"The author apparently bought exclamation marks by the thousand," Knollis replied. "The book is scattered with them. Your sister-in-law has spent a considerable amount of time in underscoring passages and making marginal notes. A passage here interests me greatly, and you may care to read it."

He held the book so that she could read it by standing beside him and looking over his horizontal forearm.

"Are you," she asked after a minute; "are you considering the possibility that Maud—oh, you know what I mean, Inspector!"

He closed the book and slipped it into his pocket. "With your permission I would like to borrow it, Mrs. Huntingdon. Meanwhile, allow me to relieve you of the tray."

He poured himself two fingers and added a dash of soda. Then he wished Dinney Huntingdon good health and put down the glass.

"Mrs. Huntingdon, I am going to break a lifelong rule by telling you what is in my mind. I am brutally frank in saying that I am fully aware that it would be impossible for you to have shot your husband last Saturday—otherwise I wouldn't have told you a thing."

She inclined her head. "I'll take that as a doubtful compliment, Inspector, and I will respect your confidence."

"On Sunday morning last," said Knollis, "your brother was working in his greenhouse when a telephone message was received from Miss Grenson. She asked or instructed him to inform the police that she had been your husband's mistress. He came along here while I was going through your husband's papers and passed on the message."

Dinney Huntingdon's hand went to the throat of her polo-necked sweater. "Incredible! Why should she?"

Knollis raised a hand. "Just a minute, please! Do you know the telephone system that is installed in your brother's house?"

"Why, yes, of course. Andy made it, or fixed it up, or whatever you may call it."

"So that you are aware that it is possible to speak direct to the greenhouse from the entrance hall, or alternatively to switch the post office telephone to the greenhouse?"

"Yes, I know all that because Andy explained it to me one evening. As a matter of fact he gave a demonstration."

"Then you will be interested to know that no call was made to the house on Sunday morning. That is confirmed by the telephone exchange."

"And Willie was in the greenhouse?"

"Willie received the message in the greenhouse!"

Dinney Huntingdon screwed up her eyes. "But that means that—"

"Yes, Mrs. Huntingdon?"

"That *Maud* impersonated Gloria Grenson!"

Knollis lifted his shoulders. "I have found no other possible explanation. I can now return your question. Why on earth should Gloria Grenson want us—the police—to know that she was your husband's mistress?"

"She couldn't have a reason in the world," Dinney Huntingdon whispered softly. "No woman would want the police—or anyone else—to know that—"

"So that, as a woman, you agree that it was not likely to be Gloria Grenson who telephoned?"

She stared at him in amazement. "Why, of course! It must have been Maud. But why should *she* want the police to know, and why trick Willie into acting as the informer?"

Knollis lifted his glass. "I am leaving you to think that out for yourself, Mrs. Huntingdon."

Dinney Huntingdon looked straight before her with incredulity written across her sallow features. "God, how that woman must hate us!"

"There were two witnesses of your husband's death, Mrs. Huntingdon. One was the Bishop of Northcote, and the other was the Mayor of Coleby. The names of neither have appeared in the press reports of the case. Both were there as the result of letters sent to them."

He opened his wallet, and folded each of the letters so that neither the address nor the signature could be seen. Then he handed them to her without comment.

"I—I didn't know about all this," she faltered. "What in heaven's name is behind it?"

"Do you happen to recognize the writing?"

"No. I should say it is a woman's writing, but I do not recognize it. It is not Maud's; I must admit that."

Knollis gently took the letters from her, unfolded them, and handed them back. "Now . . ."

She stared unbelievingly at the signatures. "Walter?" she asked tremulously. "But this isn't Walter's writing! Walter has a flowery hand. What purpose could be served by anyone signing his name on such letters?"

Knollis sighed. "I had hoped that it would be more obvious, Mrs. Huntingdon. Don't you think that whoever was responsible for your husband's death was trying to discredit the whole Jean Montague circle? Yourself, your first lover, your husband, and your brother? The letters are signed with Dickens' name and the police become interested in him—and we usually dig deep when we dig, so that his faked suicide would be unearthed. That leads us to the peculiar fact that he was married to you a month after his death. That leads us to you. Your brother is placed in the role of an informer, and we generally take a great interest in the history of informers, so that his participation in your first marriage is unearthed. And so it goes, clue leading to clue, until every member of your immediate family circle is discredited. That includes Dorrie, too, for she is revealed—forgive me for this—as an illegitimate child. And, the final point, if the duplicity of your first marriage is not revealed, and the living existence of Dickens *is*, then you are once again placed in jeopardy as a bigamist! Now do you see what I am getting at, Mrs. Huntingdon?"

"No! No!" she answered dully. "Please tell me, Inspector. I cannot see anything at the moment."

"You suspect Maud Montague of being responsible for your husband's death. Can you suspect her of hating you so much that she could want to do all this to you?"

She stared before her like a cold statue, with every emotion locked inside the living stone. "I didn't think anyone could hate so much," she whispered. "The irony of it is that I was trying to take her advice. I was trying to get Richard back, if only as a brother, for the sake of his reputation, and I think I could have done so if given a little more time . . .

"Inspector," she said.

"Yes, Mrs. Huntingdon?"

"I—I—do you mind leaving now? I think I want to weep for the first time in my life, and I'd hate anyone to witness my humiliation."

Knollis left without a moment's hesitation and returned to police headquarters, sinking wearily into the chair facing Bamford.

"Where the heck have you been?" asked Bamford.

"I've been to Red Gables," he said slowly. "I've been acting inquisitor to Dinney's faith. I've transformed a tortured woman into a raving fury, and I've thrown her, complete with teeth and claws, into the Montague dovecote. God forgive me if I've made a mistake, because if I have it is the most wicked action of my life."

Bamford grunted.

"Can you get me a cup of tea?" asked Knollis.

Bamford lifted the house telephone. "A pot of tea and two cups, instanter, please."

To Knollis he said: "You look uneasy, cock!"

"I'm feeling uneasy," confessed Knollis. "I've played a great game, and taking it all the way round I've scored the winning points."

"But what?"

"Those letters were not written by Dickens. That is firmly established. On the other hand, they don't appear to have been written by Maud."

"It could have been a partnership, you know," suggested Bamford. "John Willie and Maud, with John Willie doing the writing."

"And the Grenson 'phone call?"

"It might never have happened," Bamford said blandly.

"You've only John Willie's word for it, and it might have been a put-up job between them."

Knollis looked up with astonishment. "Bam, you've got a brain. The possibility never occurred to me."

"What? The possibility of me having a brain? Oh, yes, I've had one for years now. I don't use it much, of course, but—"

"Don't be an ass," snarled Knollis. "I mean about the 'phone call. I'll have a cup of tea and then go straight up to Montagues' and talk to Maud about psychology."

Bamford sighed wearily. "Why can't you learn to relax? Last Saturday afternoon I said I would like to see you at work. Well, I've seen you at work, and Lord help me but the very sight of your activity tires me out."

"There are two lives, two young lives, in grave danger, Bamford. Andrew Montague and Dorrie Huntingdon."

Bamford bounced forward. "You mean a conspiracy to murder them?"

Knollis snapped his fingers contemptuously. "Physical murder is a mere trifle comparatively, Bam. It is when anyone tries to murder a soul, and especially a young soul, that I really get mad and go to work!"

"Heaven help us!" exclaimed Bamford. "Here's the tea. For God's sake take a cup, and you'll feel better."

Chapter XIII
THE EVIDENCE OF MAUD

KNOLLIS HAD BY NOW, in his own estimation, a substantial body of evidence against Maud Montague, and in accordance with his usual practice he listed each item in his notebook:

Facts:

Maud was responsible for the Grenson call.

The Montagues are joint trustees of the Huntingdon fortune in the event of the deaths of both Richard and Dinney, and that until Dorrie reaches the age of eighteen.

A matter of fifty thousand pounds is involved. Both are of the opinion that Andrew is not getting the education to which his genius entitles him.

Maud was in the vicinity of the crime at the time of its commission.

Maud bought the decoy yacht and sold it.

She hated all the Huntingdons.

Possibilities:

That Maud wrote the decoy letters.

That she bought the yacht, sold it, and again bought it from Loseby.

That Maud shot R.H. from the cover of the trees.

That she did not allow for me seeking corroboration of the "long chat" with Mrs. Brownson.

That Maud sent the birthday-present yacht as part of her plan.

That taking advice from her alleged book on psychology she took action rather than blow up as the result of suppressing her hate.

That Dinney might yet be in danger.

That I placed too much importance on the presence of the Bishop and Jacland in the plantation, and . . .

That the primary importance of the letters was to draw police attention to Grenson's affair with H.*Questions:*

If Maud wangled the two faked telephone calls, how did she do it?

Where did she get the pistol from, and where is it now?

Was she hoping to kill Dinney as well?

Would she have done so if Drayton had not appeared on the scene with the patrol car?

And then Knollis threw his pencil down on the desk and went into a reverie, with his hands clasped over his waistcoat.

This notebook work was all very well, but how the deuce was he going to prove the case against Maud? Burton had seen a cycling woman fooling about on the slip road to Coleby, which was Brookdale Road, but that didn't prove anything—not even that it was Maud. The tyre tracks, even if proved to be of the same type of tyre as she used, could not be used as proof that she had been in the lane. They might easily be the tracks left by some townee as he made a tryst with a girl from one of the farms or cottages in the neighbourhood, and the marks on the hedge might mean no more than that some cyclist had paused to 'wash his hands'.

Again, going back to the Loseby-Montague yacht, it could only be proved that Loseby had re-sold the yacht to Maud by pushing Loseby's imagination, and by suggesting her identity until he came to believe it was she who had bought it back—and such tricks were not done these days, for no investigator who valued his integrity would stoop to such measures.

On paper it was easy to consider Maud as a vile and calculating murderess, but it was just as easy to prove in the opposite that she was as innocent as a new-born lamb, and yet, while feeling that she was the guilty party, he could not bring his intellect to agree. Even the feeling was not one of certainty, but rather a feeling that she *should* be the culprit according to the circumstantial evidence.

"Heck!" he exclaimed, and rose to stamp impatiently round the office.

Bamford joined him. "Well, that's the plasticine trick done. Quick work, eh? The tracks and the cast are identical, Gordon. The lad noticed a cut on the tyre, and took the cast from that section of it. You were correct. Mrs. M. was in the lane, and there's no two ways about it."

Knollis paused in his peripatetic meditation. "Stand on four feet if we have to take it into court?"

"Solid as a rock," Bamford retorted. "Even expert defence witnesses couldn't rake up a denial or an alternative theory. No, it's safe enough, Gordon."

"I've been wondering," Knollis said slowly, "how the deuce we're going to prove the case. I think Maud was responsible for Huntingdon's death."

"I may have some news for you about the pistol before long," said Bamford. "Hall and Grayson are out on the job now. They're working their way round the acquaintances of the suspects. By the way, you know it was fired from an army revolver?"

Knollis shook his head. "No, I don't. I haven't paid the slightest attention to the weapon until a few minutes ago. What calibre?"

"Point four-two."

"Heavy service type, eh? Should be useful! What are you doing? Looking for war service in your suspects?"

"That's the usual way," said Bamford. "Huntingdon was in the final stages of the last do, you know."

"He may have been, and he may have possessed a revolver, but he couldn't shoot himself in the back!" Knollis retorted dryly.

"That's no reason why somebody else couldn't have shot him with his own revolver," Bamford answered hotly.

Knollis looked up and grinned. "Sorry, old man! This case is getting me all hot under the collar. Frankly, I don't think the weapon matters a great deal. What I want to know is how I'm going to corner Maud. And at the moment it looks to me as if she is going to beat me."

He took up his rambling again, wandering aimlessly around the office while Bamford threw himself into a chair and fidgeted.

"You know," said Knollis after a time, "I have the feeling that we've overlooked the major clue. It's in your mind, and in mine as well."

"Well," demanded Bamford, "what is it? For heaven's sake get it off your chest!"

"I don't know," said Knollis. "That is the irritating part about it. It's at the back of my mind and I can't pull it forward. It's like having a name on the tip of the tongue and not being able to get it out. From past experience I know there's only one thing to do—try not to remember it. That's difficult."

"I don't see it," Bamford said impatiently.

Knollis came to a halt in front of his friend. "Think it's easy, eh?"

"Well, why not?"

"How good is your power of visualization—as if I didn't know?"

"Pretty good. I have what they call a photographic memory."

A puckish twist came to Knollis's lips. "Good enough! Can you visualize a piebald horse?"

Bamford half closed his eyes. "Easily!"

"Now think about it without thinking about its tail!"

"What the dickens are you playing at? Nursery games?"

Knollis wagged a finger under Bamford's nose. "There is a fool saying to the effect that anyone seeing a piebald horse will be lucky all the day—providing he doesn't think about its tail. That is the snag. Just so long as you remember that you have to forget, well, you remember! It's the Coue-Baudouin Law of Reversed Effort again. I *want* to forget this fact or item which is hanging around the back of my mental stage, but just because of that fact I can't dismiss it so that it will come in its own way!"

"A piebald horse and don't think about its tail," murmured Bamford. "Oh, hang it! I can't do it! There's more tail than darned horse now! It's all tail!"

"That," said Knollis, "is the point. The only way I can dismiss the half-tail in my mind so that it can grow into a full-sized one is by occupying my mind to the full. Look, Bam, I suggest that we go along to Maud's and try to break her resistance. Hammer questions into her until she grows tired, relaxes the guard on her tongue, and lets slip some damaging statement."

Bamford shook his head. "I don't like it. Savours too much of third degree."

"Hammer was the wrong word," said Knollis. "We'll have a nice quiet talk with her, and include plenty of questions, taking it in turns to shoot them in. Keep up a conversational style, and lull her into a false sense of security."

They were interrupted by the telephone bell. Bamford lifted the receiver. "Inspector Bamford here."

He drew a jotting-pad towards him and made notes as he nodded his head and said yes and no from time to time. He then rang off.

"You're a lovely worker, Gordon!"

"What is it?"

"Grayson and Hall have traced the gun. Well, not actually traced it. Huntingdon had one. He lent it to Maud all those years ago when John Willie went to Streatham for the month. She was nervous of living alone while he was away, and Huntingdon thought that even minus ammo it would give her a sense of security."

"That lets us into the house," said Knollis. "I've been looking round for an excuse. Nothing else on, have you?"

"Not a thing," replied Bamford. "By the way, the information came from Mrs. Huntingdon. She told them that she hadn't seen the gun since Richard got it back from Maud. The no-ammo part is what I don't like. Where could she obtain that?"

"A determined woman could get it somewhere or other," Knollis said grimly, "and I regard Maud as a determined woman."

"Then let's go and bone her about it!"

Maud Montague invited them into the dining-room, where John Willie was pecking at a sandwich on one side of the hearth, while his son loudly sucked up his tea on the other. She pushed the tea-wagon aside and invited them to be seated.

Knollis looked Andrew over. He was dark, and possessed of a high forehead and a long, sloping head. His ears were largish and when he eventually lowered his cup his mouth was seen to be full and wide. Clever he might be, but Knollis silently cast him for Snow White's eighth dwarf.

Bamford looked at Knollis in enquiry.

"Your job," muttered Knollis.

"Information has reached us," said Bamford, "to the effect that you are in possession of a service revolver which belonged to Mr. Huntingdon. We would like to see it, Mrs. Montague. In fact we must ask you to hand it over to us. I don't suppose you have a licence?"

"I have neither licence nor pistol," Maud Montague returned quickly. "I admit that it was lent to me by my brother-in-law, but it was returned to him—"

"About two years ago," interrupted John Willie. "I remember the occasion. Richard said he wanted to hand it in to the—"

"To the police," said Maud. "That is right, John, and it would be about two years ago. He lent it to me years ago when I was staying alone in the house, and I put it away and completely forgot its existence until he came for it."

"It was in the trunk in the box-room," said John Willie.

"One Sunday morning it was when he came for it. There had been several shooting cases in the papers, and the police were asking for arms to be turned in to them. Richard said the newspaper reports had reminded him of his own pistol, and he thought it should be put into safe custody."

"You haven't seen it since?" asked Bamford.

"I haven't," said Maud Montague.

"I certainly have not," added John Willie.

Bamford turned his head. "Knollis?"

"We are needing your help on another matter," said Knollis, taking up the questioning. "There would seem to have been unusual activity in the neighbourhood of Hampton Knoll and

Three Crows Corner on Saturday afternoon, and we are wondering, considering that you were on the Brookdale Road—"

John Willie bent forward, his cup half raised to his mouth. "You on the Brookdale Road, my dear? I thought you went shopping?"

Maud looked horribly confused for a moment, and then she tossed her head defiantly. "I went for a run round, but I don't see what it signifies!"

"We were wondering," went on Knollis as if there had been no interruption; "we were wondering if you saw any stranger, or for that matter any person you know, in the neighbourhood of the Three Crows."

"I saw a large car turning on the corner," she replied quickly.

"Which way did you return home?" asked Knollis.

"The way I came. I felt like a run, so I cycled as far as the Norton Birchfield road junction, and then turned and rode straight back."

"I see," said Knollis. "We are to understand that you saw no one on the road?"

"Not a soul, Inspector."

Knollis signalled to Bamford and they left.

"Now what?" asked Bamford.

Knollis fingered his ear reflectively. "I'm blessed if I know, Bam, and that is the truth. The woman has got me tied up, and I can't move! Between being seen by Mrs. Brownson at twenty past three, and arriving home at half-past four, there isn't a single witness to say where she was. We think that she murdered Huntingdon, but how the deuce are we going to prove it?"

They returned to headquarters and slumped into opposite chairs in Bamford's office.

"I'll try Norton Birchfield and see if they have got anything on the Brookdale Road enquiry," said Bamford, reaching for the 'phone. Five minutes later he turned away and shook his head. "Maud seems to have had the road to herself. Narry a soul about to help us."

"Of course," said Knollis, "we are certain that she was on the road, because she mentioned seeing the car. As Burton saw her, that clinches that—if only in our own minds. The trouble is that she so casually admitted her presence on the Brookdale Road, and offered no explanation other than that she felt like a run. If she had made some excuse or other we could have tried to break her down. The woman is either clever or innocent, and I'm beginning to doubt my own intelligence."

He pushed back the chair and stamped round the room.

"Heavens! What a case!"

"Looks like going into the unsolved file," Bamford grunted despondently.

Knollis seated himself on the corner of the table.

"Look, Bam! What have we got and what haven't we got?"

"I'll tell you, Gordon! We've two letters, two yachts, one body, a first-class suspect with a first-class motive, and no joy."

Knollis nodded. "I guess that just about sums it up."

He dropped from the table and sauntered to the door. "I'll see you later."

"Where are you going?" Bamford called over his shoulder.

"Mad, I think," replied Knollis, and closed the door.

He intended walking round until his brain had cleared, but a few yards from police headquarters ran into John Willie Montague, sidling along close to the wall, his clothes hanging from his rounded shoulders, and his brow deeply furrowed in thought. Knollis deliberately stepped into his path, so that he looked up.

"Going to police headquarters, Mr. Montague?" he asked hopefully.

John Willie nodded. "I was going to look for you, Inspector."

"Want to talk to me?"

"Well, yes," John Willie said hesitantly. "I've no statement or anything like that to make. I just wanted you to clear something up for me. I'm worried."

"It's a warmish day," said Knollis, "so suppose we cross the road and sit in the gardens. It is quite private there."

John Willie gave a shy smile. "That will be nice. I hate walls—and especially those round a police station."

Knollis led him across the road, through the gateway, and down the tarmac path until he found a seat in a secluded corner. He offered John Willie a cigarette, lit it and his own, and then sat down and waited.

"Er—this is entirely unofficial, Inspector?" John Willie ventured nervously.

"Unless it has any direct bearing on the murder of Huntingdon," replied Knollis. "You know very well that I can't accept any reservations."

"Yes, I see that, Inspector. The fact is that I'm worried—about Maud. It was your attitude when you called an hour ago. I mean, you aren't suspecting *Maud* of—well, you know!"

"Did you gain that impression?" Knollis asked blandly.

"Frankly, I did, Inspector. You didn't say anything, but you left it clear that you were unsatisfied with Maud's explanation of her cycle ride on Saturday afternoon."

"Well?"

"Er—well, it was just coincidence that she happened to choose that direction for her ride."

Knollis considered the matter for a few moments, while John Willie peered anxiously into his face.

"You know," Knollis said slowly, "you couldn't have annoyed me more, Mr. Montague. Coincidence happens to be my pet aversion. Some day I'm going to write an essay or a monograph on coincidence. Coincidence is supposed to be a fortuitous happening. Now I contend that there is a cause for everything, and a coincidence only appears to be fortuitous because we cannot immediately see the cause. I'll give you an example. Are you aware that the Bishop of Northcote walked from the plantation some thirty minutes after Huntingdon died?"

"I have heard a rumour about it," Montague said quietly.

"Well, he had been in the plantation for a considerable time; in fact he was there when your brother-in-law was shot to death. He was walking with nature while he meditated on the speech he was to give that evening at a meeting. Pure coincidence on the face of it—and yet when we investigated the matter thoroughly we found that there was a cause for his presence there, a cause directly associated with Huntingdon's death."

Montague made a funny little noise which Knollis failed to interpret.

"I'll give you another example," went on Knollis. "Your sister was first married at Streatham. Now you spent the previous month at Streatham. Pure coincidence, wasn't it?"

"It does look peculiar now I come to think about it," murmured Montague.

"Your sister hasn't told you?" Knollis asked quickly.

"Told me what, Inspector?"

Montague shifted nervously on the seat, and stared down at the grass.

"That we know the whole truth about that apparent coincidence. That your presence in Streatham was not a coincidence. That you were there to satisfy a residential qualification so that your sister could marry at the registry office. That you masqueraded as Froggatt, and went through a form of marriage with your own sister."

"Oh—h! So you know all about that!"

John Willie Montague stared bleakly before him. "I knew it was bound to come out some day," he whispered. "I told Dinney that we'd all get into trouble, but she persuaded me. I was all against it. It was a wrong thing to do. We'll go to prison for it, won't we, Inspector?"

"I can't say," Knollis answered him. "The affair is out of my hands. It rests with the Director of Public Prosecutions."

"You—you know about Froggatt as well then?"

"I know everything except who killed Huntingdon," said Knollis, "and I've more than a suspicion about that."

"Then you do suspect my wife!"

"Her movements, unless more satisfactorily explained, seem to be highly suspicious," Knollis said non-committally.

"But she can explain them!" Montague said fervently. "She isn't keen on doing so, but after you and Inspector Bamford had gone she said she could explain if it came to a pinch."

Knollis turned his head and looked straight into Montague's eyes. "Don't you think it has come to the pinch, Mr. Montague?"

He nodded miserably. "I suppose so, Inspector. If this goes on, it means that my boy will suffer. She must explain! Will you come back with me now?"

"I'll collect my sergeant and we'll come straight back with you, Mr. Montague," said Knollis, rising.

"Must we have anyone else there?"

"We must, for my own protection," explained Knollis. "On odd occasions when a detective has examined a witness alone he has been accused of threatening, bullying, and even worse."

They called for Ellis, picked up the car and drove to Chestnut Road. John Willie ushered them into the house as if introducing two undesirable characters. "My dear," he faltered, "I've had a chat with the inspector, and I really think you should tell him about Saturday afternoon—you haven't told me yet, you know!"

"You!" she ejaculated in a scornful voice. "Inspector Knollis, you suspect me of shooting my brother-in-law!"

"I wouldn't say that, Mrs. Montague," Knollis said in what he hoped was a pacifying voice. "It is just that your movements are unsatisfactorily explained. We work on the principle of elimination, you know, and the sooner we can eliminate you from the scene the sooner we can concentrate on—well, on certain other people who were in and around the immediate neighbourhood."

She threw up her chin. "How much do you know?" she demanded.

Knollis took one second to decide his course of action, and then took the plunge.

"I know that you met Mrs. Brownson at twenty past three, paused for no longer than a few minutes, and then cycled along the Brookdale Road. You cycled to the junction with the Norton Birchfield road, and then returned to the side-lane. You cycled along it for approximately three-quarters of its length, and then parked the machine in the hedge-bottom while you walked towards Hampton Knoll and the stile that leads into the plantation. I *suspect* that you went into the plantation."

Maud Montague cleared her throat. "It was sheer coincidence that I happened to be in the neighbourhood—"

John Willie gave a discreet cough. "The inspector doesn't believe in coincidence, my dear. He thinks there is a cause for everything!"

"Then he must thank heaven for leading me that way," she snapped sharply. "It was sheer coincidence that I happened to be that way."

"Then why did you park your cycle and walk into the plantation?" asked Knollis. "Not another coincidence, surely?"

"No, I saw something," she replied frankly.

"Such as?" prompted Knollis.

"A large black car running up and down the road. The driver got out and walked to the stile—but perhaps I had better explain that it was my intention to cycle up the lane, over Hampton Knoll, and return home via Coleby Rise and the Hedenham Road. I had seen the car reversing on the Three Crows Corner, and when I was half-way along the lane I saw the driver behaving suspiciously."

"The time was then?"

She shrugged her shoulders. "I don't know. Somewhere between half-past three and four o'clock."

"In what way was the driver behaving suspiciously?"

"He was walking backwards and forwards between the stile and the road. He walked to the stile, peered into the trees, and then walked back to the middle of the road and looked up and down. He repeated this several times, and then got in the car and drove up the Knoll. I was intrigued, and so I left the cycle and went forward on foot to—"

"Spy!" John Willie interrupted. "Spying is the name for it, my dear, and I'm ashamed that you should admit it before these two gentlemen!"

"Be quiet!" she snapped savagely, and John Willie shrank back as if she had struck him with a whip.

"I went into the plantation," she said, turning again to Knollis. "There was nothing to be seen, but it was pleasant there, and so I walked on."

Knollis did some rapid mental arithmetic, and then said: "So you heard the shot that killed your brother-in-law, Mrs. Montague?"

"Yes," she replied. "Yes, I heard the shot, Inspector. For a moment I thought it was someone shooting rabbits, and then my mind went back to my childhood. My father used to shoot, and this sound did not seem like the one I used to hear from his shot-gun. I was curious, so I went on. I—I found Richard. That is, I saw him lying on the ground, with blood pouring from his back. I turned and ran back. I got my cycle and cycled back home as hard as I could—that is, until I reached the town, when I made a more sedate pace so that I would not draw attention to myself."

Knollis lowered himself to the arm of the settee, and looked wonderingly at her. "Tell me, Mrs. Montague; did you see or hear anyone else in the plantation?"

"There was movement, but I couldn't place its direction. It seemed to be over on my right, but I couldn't swear to that."

"Tell me another thing," said Knollis. "Did you at any time emerge from the shelter or cover of the trees?"

She shook her head. "I did not! I peered out of them and saw him lying there."

"And the yacht?"

"Yes, that was floating on the dam, Inspector."

"You know," Knollis said reproachfully, "you could have told us all this before to-day!"

"Do I look like a fool?" she demanded angrily.

"That is the last word I should use to describe you, Mrs. Montague," Knollis said ambiguously. "Nevertheless, I still do not understand why you could not have placed this information at our disposal before this."

Her face came forward and pushed itself under Knollis's nose. "Think about it as I saw it, Inspector. By next morning I knew that the yacht was what you would call a vital clue in the case. I had already bought a similar yacht for Dorrie, and sold it again. I was in the neighbourhood of the dam when Richard was killed. Looking at it my way, it seemed that all my actions would appear to be suspicious, and so I kept quiet."

"And you still insist that it was sheer coincidence that you were in the Brookdale Road district on Saturday afternoon?" said Knollis.

"Can you suggest any other reason, Inspector?" she asked sarcastically.

Knollis rose. "At the moment, I cannot, Mrs. Montague, but I still do not believe in coincidence, and I am not satisfied with your statement. I believe that you had a very good reason for taking your cycle ride."

John Willie shuffled forward an inch, pointing a shaky finger at his wife. "You are not helping the inspector, my dear, and he needs all the help he can get. This is a murder case, you know, and it is very important that it should be cleared up."

Maud turned to look at him. Her lips tightened into a thin straight line, and her eyes blazed.

"You should talk!" she barked at him. "Suppose you help the inspector! I've practically run my neck into a hangman's noose, and all because of you! You tell the inspector why I went to the dam! You and your fancy woman! You underhanded and detestable little rat! For two pins I'd—oh, heaven give me strength to keep my hands off you!"

John Willie shrank against Ellis for protection.

"I—I—I—" he whimpered.

CHAPTER XIV
THE EVIDENCE OF DISSENSION

KNOLLIS CAST a thoughtful glance at the Montagues.

Maud was a raging fury; John Willie a scared—and badly scared—little mouse whose eye yet held a spark of angry defiance. It should be possible to do something with the two of them. By throwing them against each other who knew what might eventuate?

He forced a smile to his lips. "Well, I consider that I know men by now, Mr. Montague, but you've fooled me completely! A lady-killer, eh! Well, well, well!"

Montague stayed hard by Ellis's side. "I don't know what my wife is talking about, Inspector! I really don't! I'm not interested in any women."

He screwed up his courage to the full and glared at Maud. "That includes you."

She snatched her handbag from the sideboard, opened it, and thrust a dirty grey envelope under his nose. "Then explain that!"

"Pardon me!" said Knollis, taking it from her. He slid a note from it, which read: *"I'm meeting R.H. at Three-Acre on Saturday at four and giving him the bullet. It should be worth watching."* It was not signed.

"Well?" asked Knollis, fixing John Willie with an accusing frown.

"What is it?" he whispered. "I don't know what it is."

Knollis held it out so that he could read it.

"I've never seen it before," he protested faintly.

"I found it in your coat pocket," said Maud, "so there is no need to lie about it. It came on Saturday morning. I saw you reading it in the entrance hall, and you pushed it into your best jacket, which was hanging behind the door. You never said a word to me about it, so I took it out and read it for myself."

John Willie nodded. "Well, yes, that is right. I did read it, but I couldn't make head or tail of it, so I just pushed it in my pocket and then forgot it."

"What construction did you put on it, Mrs. Montague?" asked Knollis.

"The obvious one," she snapped. "The Grenson woman was packing in Richard and taking my husband as her—oh, I can't say it."

John Willie summoned up enough spirit to retort. "Nonsense! You're the most suspicious woman who ever lived."

"And this note breaks down the coincidence motif you introduced," said Knollis to Maud Montague.

She dumped herself heavily on the settee. "Yes, that is the truth, Inspector. I thought that John would be there, and I wanted to catch them together."

"But this note isn't signed," Knollis pointed out.

"Who else could it be from but the Grenson woman?" she asked.

"Any one of a number of people," Knollis replied. "You jumped to a conclusion, if I may say so."

"Well, right or wrong, I went to catch them, and I've told you what happened, Inspector!"

"You went to the dam?" Knollis asked John Willie.

"I was in the greenhouse all afternoon, Inspector. I forgot the note. I should not have gone if I had remembered it." He added: "Plants are more satisfactory than women. If they are weak, or if they annoy you, you just pull them out and throw them down to die. You can't do that with human beings, can you?"

"You can," said Knollis, "but we hang you for doing so."

John Willie nodded. "That is it, Inspector, so I live my life down there, and everything else is just nothing to do with me."

Maud stared at him. "Against my will, I'm beginning to think you didn't understand this note!"

She turned to Knollis. "Can you explain it?"

"I can, but I'm not going to do so," he replied.

"But who killed Richard?"

"We may learn that if we can get at the truth behind the conflict between yourself and the Huntingdons," Knollis answered her.

"He knows the whole story," John Willie said wearily, "so you may as well rake up the rest of the dirt. There has been no peace in this house since Dinney was first married. That event ruined our married life, and in spite of all her psychology-reading Maud hasn't had the sense to let the past slip by and forget it. She doesn't understand any loyalties between blood and blood, and she's hag-ridden me all these years for helping my own sister. There have been times when I've boiled beneath the surface, but I've gone down to my plants and looked at the never-ceasing miracle of nature and then I've asked myself why I should let myself become angry over one foolish woman."

"Foolish woman!" exclaimed Maud, half rising. "Why, you—"

John Willie raised a hand. "That's enough, Maud! I've had enough of it, and this is the end. I've held myself in far too long. The inspector has asked you a question. Answer it, or you'll find yourself swinging at the end of a long rope—and that wouldn't be nice for Andrew!"

There was an air of quiet determination in John Willie's manner, and Maud quailed before it. "Ye-es, John," she said.

She knuckled her eyes miserably. "I couldn't bear it," she said in a whining voice. "It was the Huntingdons, always the Huntingdons! Whatever we wanted to do, the Huntingdons were always there before us. It started when Dinney wanted John to help her out after her husband's suicide. He wouldn't tell me the truth about why he was going away, but as soon as I heard that Dinney was getting married, I knew! John was taking his place. Things were never the same between us after that, and I said be damned to him and that I wouldn't bother about him any more. And then the next year Richard brought her back as his wife, and she just treated me like so much mud! Every time I was asked to organize something she stepped in and took it from under my nose, making me look a fool. John had done all the work that made Richard's money, and they never as much as said thank you. We wanted our boy to have a good education like Dorrie is getting and will get, but we couldn't afford to do it, and Dinney used to put a sneer on her lips and say how unfortunate it was that Andrew could not have his chance. Some weeks ago I taunted her with Richard's unfaithfulness, and she turned round and asked me if I was blind. She said that Richard was shielding John, and that it was really he who was—you know!"

She sniffed into her handkerchief. "I couldn't afford to fall out with her, because of John's job. He isn't a young man any longer, and if he lost his job at the works we wouldn't have anything, and there's Andrew, you see!"

"You've been a bigger fool than I thought," said John Willie. "From now on I'll take charge in this household."

"All this is getting us nowhere," said Knollis. "I'll ask a few questions. Apart from the driver of the car, did you see anyone else on Hampton Knoll?"

"No one, Inspector."

"And you returned straight home after the shot?"

"As fast as I could. I was frightened."

"What was the first thing you did when you got home? Did you go down to the greenhouse to make sure that your husband was at home? I mean, did it occur to you, even momentarily, that he might have been responsible for Huntingdon's death?"

She shook her head. "Oh, no! I never thought that for a minute. I ran upstairs and took off my outdoor clothes, and then went about preparing tea. I wanted it to look as if my outing had been no more than the usual shopping run. I didn't want anybody to know that I had been near the dam."

"So that you never told your husband when you called him for tea?"

"I didn't call him. He came in from the garden about ten minutes to five, and I did not tell him where I had been."

"Now the Sunday morning telephone call," said Knollis.

She regarded him with silent suspicion.

"Miss Grenson did not call you," Knollis said accusingly.

"No-o!" she replied hesitantly. "How—how did you guess that?"

"I did not have to guess," Knollis informed her. "The telephone exchange had no trace of an incoming call to this house at the time stated. It was obvious that you yourself made the call."

She lowered her head in silent assent.

John Willie sat watching her for a time, and then re-entered the arena. "I think I've got it now," he said at length. "Thinking the note was from Gloria Grenson, and that I was mixed up with her, you made me think that you were her, and made me give her away to the police. I'm learning a lot about you to-day, Maud. You have a very nasty mind; a suspicious, jealous, and intolerant mind! I've been a good boy for a good many years, and you've underrated me. From now on you shall see what I really am like! I'll clamp down on Dinney as well! The pair of you shall throw up all these silly societies—and your bridge parties—and attend to your homes. I'm going to be the man in both houses from now on! Women—my heavens!"

He turned to Knollis. "My apologies, Inspector. This is as distasteful to me as it is to you, but at any rate it should have cleared away your suspicions of my wife's complicity in Richard's death. She has merely been a very foolish and suspicious woman who has eaten out her own heart with hate. It is all my fault. I should have been the master in my own house as I am master in my office. These silly antagonisms!"

Maud Montague sobbed quietly into her handkerchief.

"By rearranging the furniture," said John Willie, "we can get the egg cabinets in this room. They will occupy three of the walls, and—oh, excuse me, Inspector, do have a cigarette!"

He took a packet from his pocket and handed it to Knollis and Ellis. He took one himself, and happily blew the smoke to the ceiling.

"Well, Inspector," he said, "I must not detain you. You are a busy man, and will be wanting to get on your way."

Knollis smothered a smile. "We'll let ourselves out, Mr. Montague. Thanks for the interview."

On the way out, Knollis held the knob tightly so that the catch was held back. He closed the door with a thud, and then gently opened it again. John Willie Montague was laying down the law to his tamed shrew. ". . . and if I get any more nonsense I'll strike you! You and your psychology! You think you understand people, don't you? Well, even a domestic cat has claws—and primitive instincts, and there are times, Maud—you are listening, aren't you, my dear?"

Knollis quietly closed the door.

"How now, brown cow?" said Bamford as Knollis and Ellis entered his office.

Knollis chewed his lower lip and shook his head.

"Not so good?" asked Bamford.

Knollis released his lip. "Not so good. Truth to tell, I don't quite know what to make of the blessed case. Maud can still be responsible for Huntingdon's demise, but how the deuce I'm going to prove it is another matter."

He swung round on Ellis. "What did you think of the interview?"

Ellis brushed his heavy moustache from his mouth. "She was disarmingly frank all the way through. She told us everything—except what we wanted to know. Even that last scene where John Willie regained the steering-wheel may have been an act—in which case she will be now bashing his head with the stout bottle."

"Disarmingly frank," repeated Knollis. "That describes her manner accurately."

He threw the grey envelope to Bamford. "She found that in John Willie's jacket pocket, and went out to the dam in the hope of catching him and Grenson in *flagrante delicto*. She did not. She heard the shot, saw Huntingdon's cadaver, and beat it for home on the bike. Pardon the alliteration."

"She approached the dam from which direction?" Bamford asked with interest.

"Hampton Knoll," replied Knollis. "Must have been on the Bishop's heels—or at any rate on the same track."

"So that gives us the Bishop on the south of the dam, Jacland about south-east, and Maud on the west, with Burton patrolling the road on the north. I remember you saying, earlier in the case, that our man must have had a hectic time cramming everything into the time. Well, he was just as busy with the available space, or so I see it!"

"We only need a helicopter hovering above the dam and we've got all three dimensions covered," said Knollis.

He stamped across the room to stare through the window. Over his shoulder he said: "Bam, where's the catch in this case?"

"If you, as the specialist, can't see it, how can you expect me to do so, Gordon?" Bamford said gently.

Knollis nodded. "That's fair comment."

He was silent for another minute, during which the only sound in the room was the rapid ticking of the clock on the mantelpiece.

"You any ideas, Ellis?" Knollis asked stiffly.

"Search me, guv'nor," Ellis replied.

Knollis gave vent to a bitter laugh. "I'll soon begin to suspect young Dorrie!"

"It has happened before," said Bamford. "Nevertheless, I see the inference."

Knollis turned, half sitting on the window-sill.

"It's been a clever piece of work, Bam, whoever did it. By all the rules of the game we should have had our man in the cells two days ago. It was a complicated job to organize, and it went without a hitch—unless he meant to bump off Dorrie as well."

"You've given up the Montagues, Gordon?"

"Not given them up, but merely stuck with them," Knollis admitted with a grimace. "They have the perfect motive. They were sufficiently in touch with the Huntingdon family to know every move they made or were likely to make. And Maud could have done it. She approached from the right direction to shoot him in the back as he stood facing the dam. She was there at the right time. Oh, it all fits in well and truly, but the evidence is so circumstantial that I just dare not present it to the Prosecutor."

"The physical clues haven't helped us a great deal," Bamford grunted. "The Spencers can't tell us who bought the yacht. Loseby can't tell us who rebought Maud's yacht. We haven't a clue to the letter-writer. We can't find the pistol—Dinney has allowed my two blokes to search the house; I forgot to tell you that, I think. Of course, the two telephone calls are the vital clue. They, to my mind, hold the secret of the whole thing."

"True enough," commented Knollis. "You know, Maud is clever. If, as we suspect, she wrote those letters, or caused them to be written, then she used her brains. She sends John Willie one of them, and then has a perfect reason for going out to the dam—and unless we can prove that she wrote them, or caused them to be written by someone else, then she has us just where she wants us. On the face of it, it is just another attempt to blacken the character of yet one more member of the Huntingdon circle."

"What about Grenson?" asked Bamford. "Can we have over-looked her?"

"Apart from her intimacy with Huntingdon she is as pure as the driven snow," Knollis replied. "No motive, no opportunity."

"Dickens?"

Knollis shook his head. "No motive—and if he had one we'd be stumped with his alibi."

"Then what do we do?"

"I don't know yet, but it will come. I'm annoyed with myself, but I'm not really worried. The thing has an explanation, and we have all the available facts. It's a bit like one of those wire puzzles. You know, two bent nails twisted round each other! You twist and turn 'em, and all at once there is a click, and the thing is done."

"Hope you are right," muttered Bamford. "The Chief Constable rang up to-day. He's beginning to fret."

"He needn't bother," Knollis smiled wryly. "I'll pull it out of the bag."

"By the way," said Bamford, "we'd better not tell her yet, but the Eastbourne police will be requiring Dinney Huntingdon in a day or two. Had a word with the super to-day. They are exhuming Telsen. The job has caused quite a stir at the Home Office. Dinney and Dickens look like getting it in the neck."

"So will John Willie when 'Z' division get weaving on the faked marriage at Streatham," added Knollis. "Well, they have sowed, so they must reap."

He turned to Ellis. "You can knock off. I'm going to take the car and have another look at the scene of the crime. I must have missed something somewhere. There's no other explanation for it."

"Like me to come with you?" said Bamford.

Knollis shook his head. "No offence meant, but I would not. I want to stooge around and soak up the atmosphere. In fact, if I haven't got it soon I'll be looking for a reputable hypnologist to rescue the clue from the lumber-room of my brain. And that wouldn't be a bad idea either! One of these days I'll slip out to Uxbridge and try it."

"Uxbridge?" said Bamford.

"Old friend of mine. Marvellous chap. See you in the morning."

He closed the door and went out to the street. He dismissed the driver, tucked himself under the driving-wheel, and set a course for the dam. Here he pulled in to the verge, locked the doors, and then vaulted the fence.

The whole position, he admitted, was stupid. A man had been shot, and the killer was at large after almost a week. It was a slur on the force as well as on himself as an individual, and something had to be done about it.

See, Huntingdon walked along here, turned here, and was shot in the back. The blood still stained the short turf. The killer must have come from the same direction as both Maud and the Bishop, and Maud must have been on his heels, if, indeed, she was not the killer. If she was the killer, she had half an hour in which to get home to Chestnut Road. In fact she had exactly the same time if she was not the killer, for she admitted being in the plantation when the shot was fired. Now Bamford had made a rough guess at the time it would take her to get home, and rough guesses were no good in a game of this kind. Factual evidence was needed.

Knollis returned to the car, and drove over the Knoll until he reached the stile. Here he left it, and went through the plantation in the gathering darkness until he was once more on the spot where Huntingdon had met his death. He took out his watch and noted the time, then set off back to his car at a fast pace. Once in the driving seat, he swung into the narrow lane, driving at five miles an hour until he reached the point where Maud Montague had parked her cycle.

He now put more pressure on the accelerator. Twelve miles an hour was a normal touring pace for a cyclist, and Maud was in a hurry, so he gave her the benefit of two more miles per hour, and continued at that rate until he was in the business centre of Coleby. He now decelerated and sauntered at ten miles per hour, ignoring the curious glances of pedestrians and the irate hooting of a car behind which wanted either to pass or continue behind him at a higher rate of speed. Arriving in Chestnut Road, he consulted his watch. Forty-one minutes. And that on comparatively clear roads. Maud's ride had taken place on a busy Saturday afternoon, and a market day to boot.

He backed the car to the bottom of the road, and left it; then walked back to the house adjoining the Montagues', and rang the bell.

In an undertone he introduced himself and asked the owner if he could step inside for a moment. Once the door was closed he explained his errand.

"Your neighbour, Mrs. Montague," he explained glibly, "has been able to put into our hands certain vital information concerning the death of Mr. Huntingdon. Unfortunately, she is unable to fix the time, and we think you may be able to help us. Did you, by any chance, happen to see her return from her shopping expedition on Saturday afternoon?"

The gentleman gave a short laugh. "My wife is the person you want to see, Inspector. I was out, golfing. If you'll follow me—"

He led him into his wife's presence and repeated Knollis's request. The lady nodded. "As a matter of fact I did see her return, Inspector. It was the girl's day off, and I was in the kitchen, preparing tea. Mrs. Montague returned at a quarter to five. She came in by the back gate, almost threw her cycle against the wall of the cycle shed and hurried into the house. I wondered if something was wrong, for she was hurrying as if seeking her husband, or as if dashing to the telephone."

"And her husband? Surely he was in the greenhouse?"

"No, he came in about five minutes later, and put his cycle in the shed. He then took his wife's into the shed, after which he went up to the house."

Knollis heaved a sigh of satisfaction. "Thank you very much," he said. "That fixes the time very satisfactorily. I'm greatly obliged to you. Please accept my apologies for disturbing you."

At the door he said: "Do the Montagues sleep at the back or front of the house?"

"Well, Mr. and Mrs. Montague sleep at the front, but the boy sleeps in the back bedroom."

"He would!" said Knollis.

"Pardon, Inspector?"

Knollis coughed. "I was intimating that it was the normal arrangements. Thanks very much. Good night!"

Back in the car, he stared keenly through the windscreen. The fog was beginning to clear now. It cleared considerably during the next five minutes, so that he suddenly started the engine, rammed in the bottom gear, and tore round the corner. He was in top gear twenty yards farther on, racing for police headquarters. He came to a skidding halt and ran up the steps into the building.

"Inspector Bamford still here?"

"Why, yes," replied an astonished sergeant. "In his office, sir."

Knollis took the stairs two at a time, and flung open the door of Bamford's office. Bamford and Ellis were busily re-reading the evidence in the case, and both looked up in astonishment. Then Ellis brushed his moustache and buttoned his jacket, grinning. "Here it comes! The penny has dropped."

"Into the car!" Knollis shouted. "I've got it! Birds' eggs! That's the solution! Birds' eggs!"

CHAPTER XV
THE EVIDENCE OF THE BEES

THEY WERE WELL CLEAR of the town before Bamford asked mildly: "Who are we chasing this time, and how do birds' eggs come into the business?"

"John Willie, of course," Knollis said impatiently.

"For shooting Huntingdon?"

"For what else?"

"I don't get it," said Bamford, "and I can't see where these eggs come into the case. It doesn't make sense."

"It will," said Knollis. "We are now on our way to Grenson's cottage. I'll park some distance from it and we'll finish the journey on foot. Ellis is to go to the back door, knock, and keep her talking for at least five minutes. The main idea is to keep her away from the front of the house—and you might ask her, Ellis, if she happened to be at the front of the house round about four o'clock on Saturday afternoon. That is rather important."

To Bamford he said: "Is there a torch in the car?"

"Should be one in the side pocket. Yes, here it is."

"Then bring it along with you, please."

Two minutes after Ellis had vanished behind the house Knollis moved cautiously along the drive with Bamford on his heels.

"What the deuce are we looking for?" whispered Bamford.

"The telegraph pole, of course."

"Oh!" exclaimed Bamford. "But why of course?"

"Here it is. The whole thing will be self-evident."

He focused the rays of the torch on the brown surface of the pole, slowly shifting them upward until the pole was obscured by the overhanging branches of the trees on the boundary.

"See 'em?"

"The indentations? Yes, I see them."

Knollis flicked out the light. "That's it, then. We can return to the car and wait for Ellis."

Bamford asked no questions. He accompanied Knollis back to the car, and together they waited until Ellis rejoined them.

"Well?" asked Knollis.

"She was not only at the back of the house, but some distance from it," said Ellis. "Her apiary is behind the house, and as far as I can make out from her somewhat long-winded dissertation they—the bees—have been packed down for the winter, and now the temperature has risen above the sixty mark she is slowly going through them, whatever that might mean in basic English. She started this going-through business shortly after lunch on Saturday, and was in the apiary all the afternoon except for the period during which she was interviewing the Bishop."

"I thought she was nattering with the Dabell woman?" Bamford murmured doubtfully.

"They were together, whatever they were doing," said Knollis. "The point is satisfactory from my angle."

"That's something," Bamford remarked in a dry tone. "Suppose you now explain the egg part of this mystery—that is if I'm not presuming too much! This may be a puzzle party, but I'm supposed to be on your side."

"It's this way, Bam," Knollis explained as he drove back to town. "I've been seeking an explanation of the telephone calls. According to the exchange they came from the Grenson number. Now both Grenson and Miss Dabell deny that the instrument was used, so that means that the wires leading to the house *were* used!"

Knollis paused, and paused for so long that Bamford's patience snapped. "Well, let's hear the rest of it!"

"How was the trick done?" Knollis mused aloud. "That was the question I had to ask myself. It was an awkward one. I pondered over it until my head ached, and then the solution presented itself all at once. The answer is that John Willie was an egg collector in his younger days."

"Still doesn't click," said Bamford.

"Ever seen his collection?"

"Ye-es. I once spent an afternoon in the museum when it was raining."

"Do you regard it as a complete one?"

"Very complete," said Bamford. "I used to collect them as a kid. He has eggs in that collection for which I'd have given my right arm in those days."

"Are they all the eggs of birds that nest in hedges or scrapes in the ground?"

"Oh, no, it is a pretty comprehensive collection."

"So we'll say," suggested Knollis, "that he has a rook's egg among them?"

"Yes, of course he has! What are you getting at?"

"How would he get it?" Knollis asked simply.

"Climb for it . . ."

Bamford's voice trailed away. After a moment he turned to Knollis in the darkness of the car. "You're a clever so-and-so, aren't you!"

"Got it now, old friend?" asked Knollis.

"Those indentations. Climbing irons, eh?"

"Climbing irons," said Knollis. "You'll probably find them in a long banana box in his greenhouse—and if you don't I'll willingly eat the box and hinges."

"That means a search warrant."

"I'm afraid so," replied Knollis. "I fully intended organizing an unofficial entry, but learned that the son sleeps in the back bedroom. I'd risk waking Maud and John Willie, but precocious sons are more easily roused, and he might easily let fly with an air-gun or something equally sinister, such as a catapult. So a search warrant it will have to be."

"We'd better do it right away, Gordon!"

Knollis nodded. "One other job first, and that is to contact the post office engineers and make sure that they use ladders on that particular pole. If they don't, then I'm afraid we are up against another stumer."

"We'll call at Hefford's house on the way down. I'll direct you. He's the chief linesman."

"Only a ladder," said Knollis ten minutes later. "That is highly satisfactory. Only a ladder, and any marks of irons are not the work of the authorized staff. Look, Bam, we won't bother about a warrant, but go straight to the house and tackle him."

"We can do that," agreed Bamford. "We may be able to bring him in at the same time. Let's wind up the case as quickly as we can. You've got him on the hip, and as soon as he realizes it he will pack in."

"We hope!" said Knollis.

John Willie answered the door, and they were immediately made aware that it was a new man who faced them, a man resurrected from the grave of his self-induced inferiority. He faced them boldly, and with an annoyance far too evident for Knollis's liking.

"Isn't there any peace in this world?" he complained. "I was just thinking of going to bed, because I'm tired with all this questioning and investigating. Surely you've asked all the questions you can think of by now? Or perhaps this is a social visit—not that I issued any invitations!"

Knollis pushed past him so that John Willie turned with him. Bamford and Ellis dodged through the gap and closed the door.

"We aren't asking questions this time, Mr. Montague," said Knollis.

"Then what in the name of heaven do you want?"

"Your climbing irons—if you have no more telephoning to do, that is!"

John Willie's head came forward. "My climbing irons! Are you mad?"

"You do possess a set of climbing irons?" asked Knollis. "Or am I being too inquisitive?"

"Of course I have a set. They are a relic of my old collecting days. They are in the greenhouse—"

"In the banana box?"

"How the devil did you know?" demanded Montague. "You surely haven't been poking round there without my permission!"

"Talking of permission, Mr. Montague, may I have permission for my sergeant to fetch them to the house?" John Willie Montague nodded. "Yes, I suppose so. I don't profess to understand what is in your mind, but you may borrow them."

Ellis went through the house to the garden. He returned with the long banana box in his arms. He laid it on the carpet and threw back the lid. The irons, with their leather straps, lay in the bottom of the box.

"When were these last used, Mr. Montague?"

John Willie ran his tongue round his mouth in a speculative manner. "Why, about a month ago!"

"By yourself?"

"No!"

"There is no need to confine yourself to simple negatives and affirmatives," said Knollis. "We shall be pleased to hear you expand on the subject."

"How the devil do I know what you are wanting to know?" snapped John Willie. "I'm not a thought-reader."

"Very well. Who did use them?"

"Richard. Richard Huntingdon."

Knollis's jaw fell. Then he clamped his mouth tight. For a second he stared unbelievingly at John Willie, and then rapped out: "Huntingdon used them? What on earth for?"

"As far as I understood it," John Willie said wearily, "some child had been flying a kite near Gloria Grenson's cottage, and it dropped across the wires. Richard couldn't attempt to borrow a ladder from any of her neighbours—for obvious reasons—and so he borrowed my irons and fetched the kite down late one night."

"How long was he in possession of them?"

"One day only. He borrowed them one evening, and brought them back the next."

"And you still persist that you haven't used them yourself for any reason?" asked Knollis.

"For any reason such as?"

"Climbing telephone poles."

John Willie shook his head. "I've never climbed a telephone pole in my life, Inspector, and I'm too old for climbing trees. By the way, you wouldn't still be trying to connect my wife and myself with Richard's death?"

"I can best answer that question by asking you if you can account for your movements on Saturday afternoon," said Knollis. "We know that you were not in the greenhouse, as you first stated."

A puckish grin appeared on John Willie's face. "No, I was not in the greenhouse, nor yet in the garden, Inspector."

"Then where were you?"

It was the new John Willie who answered; no longer the hen-pecked, mousey little husband of a day ago.

"Find out!"

"Eh?" exclaimed Knollis, shocked by the unexpected defiance.

"I told you to find out, and I mean it!"

"Listen," said Bamford, breaking into the conversation; "the inspector has asked you a question."

"As a detective it is his job to find the answers to questions," retorted John Willie. "I refuse to answer his question. If you think I killed Huntingdon, then you should arrest and charge me, and also warn me! Oh, yes, I know the law! If, on the other

hand, you have no reason for charging me, then I remain an individual who knows his rights—and I don't have to answer any
questions if I am not so inclined!"

"Well—!" Bamford ejaculated.

"Now get out of my house," barked John Willie. "Oh, yes, you
can take the irons—once you have given me a receipt for them.
That is all you can take, for I have no intention of telling you
where I went or what I did on Saturday afternoon."

Knollis turned and walked from the house. Bamford and
Ellis followed him, slamming their respective doors as they got
into the car.

"Well, I'll be blowed!" said Bamford. "What's he been taking?
Dope?"

"Got top-side of his missus after a goodly number of years
and he's feeling his feet," said Ellis. "Defiant little what's-it,
isn't he?"

"He happens to be in the right, too," Knollis grunted. "We
tried to pull a fast one over him, and it just didn't work, so we
can't grumble."

"It means that we've got to start work again," grumbled
Bamford. "As you say, he's well within his rights, and we haven't
enough evidence on which to charge him. That is what I've to
report to Hedenham to-night! The Old Cock will be as mad as
a hatter!"

"Can't be helped," said Knollis. "Ellis and your men must
start working on John Willie's movements, checking still further on Maud, and making another attempt to find the gun."

"Getting convinced about the value of the pistol at last, are
you?" said Bamford.

"I'm getting convinced about the value of every penny pin
that comes into the case, Bam. I'm not too proud to admit it,
either!"

"And what do you and I do in this game?"

Knollis turned the key in the switch and pressed the starter.
He gave a tired and sardonic laugh. "Pray, as Solomon did, for
wisdom and understanding."

The next three days remained in Knollis's mind as the most unproductive he had ever spent on a case. Sergeants, detective officers, and uniformed constables trailed round Coleby and the surrounding district for hour after hour, asking questions, taking statements, and asking more questions. Knollis and Bamford, in the office at police headquarters, sorted the rigmaroles as they came in, and discarded a hundred per cent of them.

"It's the old story," moaned Bamford. "We can't mention John Willie by name, and so we ask for a sight of a little man with bent shoulders and so on and so on. Imagination is a valuable faculty in an intelligent man, but a powerful and uncontrolled one in the generality of the population. I honestly believe, so help me heaven, that if we asked for people who had seen a unicorn in the market square at five o'clock of a summer evening we should have thirty thousand witnesses with thirty thousand different descriptions of it. Lord help us and save us!"

"The little man on the cycle has been seen everywhere," agreed Knollis, wearily turning over the sheets of statements. "He was cycling out of Hedenham at half-past three. At the same hour he was biking into Linford, miles away and over the hills. He was in five different parts of Coleby at the same time. He was eating ice-cream on the bridge in the centre of the town. He was taking tea in three cafes. He was buying fish and chips in a back-street saloon a mile away. He was angling in the reservoir, begging in Church Street, and accosting a young woman in a field. The town has gone mad."

"It never was very sane," grunted Bamford. "What hope is there for mankind?"

"One," said Knollis.

"What's that?"

"Let's leave it all and go for a drink. A pint of your Coleby mild-and-bitter is just what we need."

Bamford grabbed his hat. "That's the best idea you've had yet."

They left headquarters and sauntered down the street, Knollis with his eyes focused on the pavement, and Bamford idly regarding the shop windows.

Knollis had walked some yards before he realized that Bamford was not at his side. He turned to see him looking in a shop window. He went back. "What's the interest?"

"Pictures," Bamford said shortly. "The missus asked me to look out for a suitable present for a couple who are getting married. Pictures seem to answer her cry for help. Like those water colours of York Minster?"

"All right if the couple know York Minster," said the sardonic Knollis, "but hardly appropriate if they have never been in York."

"Suppose so," grunted Bamford. "Still, they are easy on the eye!"

"Yes, they are pretty good reproductions," agreed Knollis. "I like that sort of thing on my own walls. Hasn't public taste changed during the two wars? All the old heavy stuff has gone, and now even the general public can appreciate pictures like— well, say those Greuze reproductions . . ."

He did not finish the sentence, and Bamford turned to see what had happened to him. Knollis was staring at the centre of the window, one finger pointing. "That's interesting!"

"What is?"

"That picture!"

"The one of the little boy being questioned by the Roundheads?"

"Mm!"

"It's a famous one," Bamford informed him gratuitously. "In the Walker Gallery at Liverpool. It's by Yeames."

"Darn the gallery and hang the artist—with all due respect to both," said Knollis. "Look at the title, man! Look at the title!"

"And when did you last see your father?" read Bamford. And then he ran a ruminative tongue over his upper lip, and a gleam of interest appeared in his grey eyes. "You've got the most peculiar mind I've ever encountered. It has more twists and turns in it than a maze. You know! I think you've got something!"

He again looked Knollis up and down. "How the deuce do you do it?"

188 | FRANCIS VIVIAN

Knollis turned his gaze on Bamford's face, but his mind was far from the busy Coleby street.

"John Willie was confident. He was super-confident. He didn't care two hoots whether we found out where he was, or whether we didn't. That means that his movements haven't anything to do with the case! He's fooling us. He's deliberately sent us on a wild-goose chase, deliberately made us waste time, and for no other reason than sheer devilment born of his escape from spiritual imprisonment. The question we now have to ask ourselves is where was Andrew on Saturday afternoon?"

"He was—"

"Playing cricket with his school!"

"We've had that drink," mourned Bamford. "We'll have to get the car and run round to the school. Come on, *maestro*! Back you come!"

The sports master provided John Willie with a perfect alibi in less than two minutes. He had sat with him. It was a trial match before the opening of the season proper. Andrew's captain won the toss and elected to bat first. Andrew went in as fifth man, and his father stayed until the end of his innings. He left the field shortly after half-past four.

"Just in nice time to get home by ten to five from here," said Bamford. "Well, we'd better get back and call off the hunt. The little so-and-so has made nice fools of us, and no mistake!"

Then he asked Knollis: "What's up with you?" Knollis was standing with his trilby on the back of his head, stroking his forehead.

"I dunno, and that's the truth. I've still got the stupid notion that the solution is staring us in the face. We've either overlooked a point, or misconstrued one. Hanged if I can pull it to the front of my mind. I'll borrow a car once I've dropped you at headquarters, and take a jaunt in the country. The atmosphere of the office cramps my style. I can't think within four walls. And yourself?" Bamford pushed out a pugnacious jaw. "I'm going, in service parlance, to tear a strip off John Willie. I'll not be made a fool of by man nor beast—"

"Ssh!" said Knollis. "Don't let the man realize that he won the round. He can't get off scot-free, because he still has to pay for the Streatham wedding farce. Keep still and don't let him know that we've sorted him out."

Bamford expelled a great breath of air. "I hate doing it, but I suppose you are right as usual. Here we are then; the car is all yours. Don't go picking up dumb blondes."

Knollis grinned, slid under the wheel, and drove out of town. Inevitably he drove up the Hedenham Road, four times he made the journey between the top of Coleby Rise and the Three Crows, and then idled along the main road, one eye tracing the telephone wires as they ran along on his right. In due course he came to the entrance to the midget Grenson estate, and having driven past it he brought the car to a halt, changed into reverse, and backed down to the gate. It was newly painted in green and white. In the centre of the top panel was the notice-board advertising her honey; a white board with yellow lettering: *Honey For Sale.*

Knollis blinked. He hacked the car across the road to the opposite verge, where he parked it. He got out and strolled back to the gate, where he stood in silent contemplation of the notice.

After some minutes he turned and walked back to the gate leading into the plantation, and passed through. Instead of taking the path which led to the dam, he forced a new one between the young trees, keeping as near parallel as he could judge with the boundary fence on the north-western side of Gloria Grenson's garden. He proceeded in this direction for a hundred yards, and then made for the fence. Making sure that he could not be seen from the cottage, he pushed his head through the hedge and regarded the scene in an earnest manner.

He was overlooking the apiary. Twelve white hives were set out in a large triangle; six on the rear row, three on the next, two on the next, and one single hive leading the phalanx. They faced south-east, and a narrow path ran in the grass behind the rear row. Knollis twisted his head, ignoring the defences of the protesting hawthorn hedge, and saw that the path continued for a considerable distance and passed into a large orchard.

"Might be possible!" he murmured aloud. He withdrew his head and regained the cover of the trees. He continued on a course parallel with the hedge and the three-strand wire fence. When he judged that he had reached the corner of the orchard he again pushed his head through the gap and looked round. The path ended at a newly-made gap in the hedge.

He withdrew from the thorny pillory and dropped on his hands and knees, crawling until he was round the corner and level with the gap. He looked to the right. The bracken, new and mostly unfurled, was flattened as surely as if a herd of buffalo had passed over it, and the new path thus formed continued as far as he could see through the thick cover, and the broken fronds lay in the direction of the dam.

He grunted and backed away, making his way back to the main road and the car. He turned it and hurried to Coleby in search of Bamford.

"Well?" Bamford asked hopefully. "Has the brain functioned as anticipated?"

"I want a bee-keeper," said Knollis.

Bamford stared. "A bee-keeper? Now why in the world would anyone want a bee-keeper?"

"A bee-keeper. A bloke with a world of information to give away to an enquiring policeman," said Knollis, making no attempt to explain his need.

Bamford sighed. "Well, if you want a bee-keeper I suppose I must find one for you. The bloke with the best reputation round here is an old fellow by the name of Hetherington, who lives in a nearby village. Like me to take you out to him?"

"Please," Knollis said simply.

Bamford shrugged his shoulders helplessly and descended to the street level with Knollis. Not a word was spoken all the way, and Knollis only came to life when Bamford had introduced him to the bee-keeper.

"This is my friend, Inspector Knollis. He wants to know if you would mind answering a few questions about your craft, Mr. Hetherington."

"I'll try," said the old man. "I've been keeping them for sixty-odd years now—since I was a lad of ten—so I may be able to do something for him."

"What happens to bees in the winter-time?" Knollis rapped out without preamble.

"It used to be flies when I was a lad," Bamford remarked jocularly, but subsided under Knollis's severe glance.

"We pack them down, to keep them warm and dry, you know. Most of mine are still packed down. It's been a very severe winter, and the stocks are weak, so I haven't disturbed many of them yet."

"You have looked at some of them?" asked Knollis.

"Three hives. I went through them yesterday," the old man nodded.

"Saturday," said Knollis; "was it a suitable day for doing this—er—going through them business? Or would it be too cold?"

"Some bee-keepers might have worked last Saturday, but not me, Inspector. I decided to give them a few more days."

"I see," Knollis mumbled, more to himself than to Bamford and Hetherington. "Now suppose I was to take you to an apiary I have in mind, could you tell whether the hives had been gone through or not?"

The old man hesitated. "Well, yes and no. If the owner had unpacked them for the spring, I could. If he'd only looked at them and packed them down again for a week or two, then the answer would be no. On the other hand, if he was feeding them with syrup, I could tell roughly when he last opened the hive."

Knollis nodded thoughtfully. "So that an inspection of a hive last Saturday would have been in keeping with the normal practices of your craft, Mr. Hetherington? It would have been in order to have looked through a hive last Saturday?"

"Oh, yes. And then again, no. I'm a wee bit cautious. You see, Inspector, bees are sensitive insects. The sun was warm, but there was a coolish breeze blowing, and you have to be careful. A bee's legs are paralysed in a temperature of less than fifty degrees, and they can't use their wings when it's less than fifty-nine. My thermometer was registering a level sixty, and I prefer the benefit of a few more degrees."

"So that we can say that a sensible bee-keeper would not have opened his hives last Saturday?" persisted Knollis.

"You can say that," said the old bee-keeper.

"Thanks very much," said Knollis, and walked away.

"You've got one in your bonnet, haven't you?" asked Bamford as they returned to Coleby.

Knollis did not answer. He was looking straight ahead. His eyes were reduced to mere unseeing slits, and his facial muscles were tense.

CHAPTER XVI
THE EVIDENCE OF TRUTH

KNOLLIS CALLED ELLIS from the sergeants' office, and then stood at the foot of the stairs flicking over the pages of his notebook. "I'll need a driver who knows Hedenham," he said shortly.

"You do, eh?" Bamford muttered through his teeth. "That is extremely interesting."

A faint smile crossed Knollis's lean features. "How long will it take to drive to Hedenham?"

"Three-quarters of an hour. Less if you are in a hurry and driving a police car."

Knollis nodded. "Good enough. Here is the set-up. I'm going over to see Miss Dabell, and taking Ellis with me. While we are away I want you to 'phone Dinney Huntingdon and ask her to bring Dorrie down to the station. In exactly an hour's time I'd like you to invite Gloria Grenson similarly; we want her to read through the statements made by John Willie, Maud, and Dinney Huntingdon. She and Dinney are not to be allowed to meet. Oh, and ask for Dorrie to bring the yacht with her. That is important. Now, can you lend me a screw-driver?"

"The garage can provide one."

Knollis turned to Ellis. "Get a largish one and wait in the car for me."

Ellis hurried away.

"Now suppose you tell me what this is all about?" said Bamford in a pained voice. "I am supposed to be the head of this crime bureau, and the murder did occur in my diocese! I am—herrum—also supposed to be your personal friend. Mind you, I don't want to force any confidences!"

Knollis laughed. "I know I'm a queer bird when on a case, Bam, but I've made fools of the pair of us on several occasions during the course of the investigation, and I'm going to make sure that I don't do it again. All I can—or will—tell you now is that Grenson and Dabell hold the secret between them. You've heard me holding forth about the value of positive evidence all the way through. Well, for once I've made a mistake. I've been looking for people who *saw* something. I should have looked for someone who *didn't* see something. Is that a riddle?"

He paused, and then continued in an earnest manner:

"You examined the baker's man who delivered the bread to the Grenson cottage. What did he tell you?"

Bamford shrugged his shoulders. "Just what you could expect him to say. The lady took in the bread and a few pastries and then paid the bill. He gave her the change, marked the account in his delivery book, and then returned to his van."

"In that statement lies the crux of the whole matter," nodded Knollis. "Three people took a single fact for granted. You, the baker's man, and myself."

"Interesting, old cock," said Bamford, "but hardly enlightening. Are you suggesting that I interview the fellow again?"

"It's an idea," said Knollis. "It will help matters as well as keep you busy until we get back in about two hours. See you later."

Miss Peggy Dabell was thirty-four, tall, lank, and bright-eyed. She was also inclined to be naive, so that Knollis's assumed air of all-is-well-with-the-world induced a reciprocal manner in herself, and she smilingly invited them to forsake the doormat for the sitting-room chairs.

"It must have been simply thrilling for Gloria," she enthused as she placed ash-trays beside them. "Fancy getting oneself mixed up in a murder case! It was a good job I went over to see her, wasn't it? I mean, it was my evidence that saved her from unjust suspicion!"

"It was indeed," Knollis purred. "It was a lucky thing you happened to be there."

"I had promised her, days before, you know!" she confided. "She rang me and simply insisted that I should go over on the Saturday. It was just as if something had told her that the horrible thing was going to happen!"

"She was not in the cottage when you arrived, was she?" asked Knollis.

Ellis gave him a startled glance.

Miss Dabell waved the fact away with an airy hand. "Oh, that didn't matter. She'd left a note for me on the table, and the money for the baker, so I was all right. I never go to the apiary, you know!"

"You don't like bees, Miss Dabell?"

"They don't like me," she corrected. "Gloria says I am too excitable. I just can't avoid swiping out when one settles on my hand, and then, of course, that is that! You can guess what happens!"

"You don't wear gloves?"

"Gloria doesn't, so on the very odd occasions when I've gone down with her I've followed suit. She says I upset them too much, so I don't go these days."

"I see. The apiary cannot be seen from the cottage, can it?"

"Oh, no! There is the big hedge between it and the house. What is it—*cupressus macrocarpa*? The one that separates the rose garden from the apiary and the orchard."

Knollis took out his notebook and considered his notes, or made a pretence of doing so. "See, it would be about a quarter past four when Miss Grenson came in from the apiary? That is correct?"

"About that," replied Miss Dabell. "It might have been twenty past. I can't say exactly."

"You arrived at the cottage about ten minutes to four? Or perhaps it would be earlier?"

Miss Dabell shook her head. "We-ell, a little later actually. The bus halt is down the road, and I have a four-minute walk. Five minutes to four is more like the time."

"I am satisfied, providing you didn't arrive at a quarter to four," Knollis said with a grim smile.

"I couldn't have done that!" Miss Dabell declared emphatically. "The bus is more inclined to be late than early. It's like a milk-round on the Hedenham route, with the bus stopping every few hundred yards. The houses are so scattered, you know!"

"I see," murmured Knollis. "I note that you paid the baker's delivery man?"

Miss Dabell agreed that she did.

"When did you first hear about Mr. Huntingdon's death?" asked Knollis.

"Someone rang Gloria about six o'clock. She was awfully upset—naturally! I didn't quite know what to say to her, because while I obviously knew about *him*, his name was never mentioned. He was—well, understood! You know!"

"I know!" said Knollis. He pushed the notebook in his pocket and prepared to leave.

"On her return from the apiary you spent the remainder of the evening together?"

"Oh, yes, of course," she replied as she followed them to the door. Then, with a queer frown creasing her forehead, she said: 'Er—Inspector!"

Knollis turned in the doorway. "Yes, Miss Dabell?"

"Haven't you forgotten something? Surely!"

"I don't think so, Miss Dabell."

She fanned the air with an uncertain hand. "Well, I mean, you must have come to see me about something!"

"I called on business, and my business is completed," said Knollis. "I thank you for your assistance."

He bade her a good day and left her hanging to the edge of the door with a large question mark written on her face. She suddenly wheeled round and hurried indoors, a movement on which Ellis commented.

Knollis nodded. "She's trying to 'phone Grenson, which is why I asked Inspector Bamford to get her down to headquarters."

"Hear the pennies dropping, count them as they fall. Only two more to make the shilling," said Ellis as they raced back to Coleby. "This is getting exciting. Any halts on the way?"

"Grenson's cottage," Knollis said briefly.

He eventually ordered the driver to pull in at Miss Grenson's gate. Then he gave Ellis a push. "Got the screwdriver? I want the honey notice from the gate. Get going. We are in a hurry."

Ellis climbed to the road. "You going nuts?"

"Get to work," said Knollis.

The foot-square notice was parked in the car, and they returned to headquarters, where Knollis straightway asked for Dorrie Huntingdon.

"In the room on the right, sir," said the station sergeant.

Knollis strode in. He removed his hat and smiled at Dinney Huntingdon. "I'm sorry to put you to this trouble," he apologized, "but I assure you that it is very necessary. Ah! Dorrie has brought the yacht. May I borrow it, Dorrie?"

The child nodded mutely.

"I'll look after it," Knollis promised. He turned to her mother. "Can you supply me with a programme of Dorrie's movements on her birthday?"

Dinney Huntingdon smiled wanly. "I continue to be reminded of my neglect of the child. I am afraid that I was out nearly all that day. She had a party after five o'clock, but beyond that— well, I just can't say. I'm sorry, Inspector!"

"You won't object if I question her?"

"If you wish to do so, Inspector."

Knollis seated himself so that he had little advantage of height over the golden-curled Dorrie. "I want you to tell me something, Dorrie, my dear. A few days ago you said that you had seen yachts like your own in three shops—"

"Miss Franklin's, Spencers', and the one in Hedenham Road," she recited gravely.

Dinney Huntingdon lifted her finely pencilled eyebrows. "I'm afraid I don't quite see the point, Inspector!"

"In which case I must explain," said Knollis. "Mrs. Montague bought a yacht which she intended to give Dorrie as a birthday present. Dorrie telephoned her shortly after breakfast to tell her about her presents, and she mentioned the yacht which had been sent anonymously. Mrs. Montague, not wishing to duplicate the present, sold the one she had bought to Loseby on the Hedenham Road. That was mid-morning on the twenty-first of March—Dorrie's birthday. He sold it shortly before half-past six that evening. Now as he does not normally sell yachts of this type, Dorrie must, obviously and inevitably, have seen it during that day. See the point?"

Dinney nodded. "You want to know who was with her when she saw it? Well, it couldn't have been myself, and it couldn't have been Richard because he went to a conference."

She turned to Dorrie. "Darling, we want you to tell us who you were with? Or perhaps you were alone in town—and you know that is forbidden on busy days! Still, you must tell us."

Dorrie drew her bottom lip into her mouth and chewed upon it. She looked from one to the other in childish perplexity.

"Well, Dorrie?" said Knollis gently.

"*Well*, darling?" said Dinney Huntingdon.

Dorrie continued to look from one to the other uncomfortably, and then, in obvious imitation of some adult she had heard in conversation, she said: "There's going to be a dam' awful row!"

Knollis laughed involuntarily, and quickly straightened his features.

"Why should there be a—a dam' awful row?" asked her mother.

"It was Daddy's secret, and I promised never to tell, cross my heart and hope to die! He said you would be mad if you got to know."

Dinney Huntingdon took a deep breath. "I won't be mad, darling, and that is my promise. Your promise does not count now that Daddy has gone. He would want you to tell Mr. Knollis now."

Dorrie took an even deeper breath than her mother had achieved. "I was with Auntie Gloria!"

"Auntie Gloria!" screamed Dinney Huntingdon. She flopped back in horrified surprise, to come quickly forward with an urgent question on her lips. "How did you come to be out with—with Auntie Gloria!"

"I used to go round town with her every Saturday afternoon," Dorrie informed her. "I met her once with Daddy, and she is ever so nice, only Daddy said you didn't like her and I mustn't ever tell you about her. He let me go out with her, but only when you were playing golf."

Dinney Huntingdon laid a hand against her cheek. "The whole town must be laughing at me!"

"So you noticed the ship while shopping with Auntie Gloria, Dorrie?" said Knollis.

"Mm! We stood and looked at it in the window and I told her all about the one I had, and she said what a pity it was that no one had time to take me to sail it. Daddy hadn't time, she said, and Dinney couldn't be bothered. She was going to take me to the water where Daddy was taken ill, and we were going that day only there was the party at Sally Castle's."

"Please excuse me," said Knollis. "Don't go away yet. I may need you again."

He hurried from the office, the yacht under his arm, and chased up the stairs to Bamford. He found the Chief Constable of Hedenham and the County C.I.D. Superintendent waiting for him.

"I got the notion that something was about to break," explained Bamford, "so I passed on the news."

"Where's Miss Grenson?" Knollis demanded.

"Down below. Wanting her?"

"We'll all go down if that is convenient," said Knollis. He offered no explanation as he led the way downstairs to the room in which Gloria Grenson was waiting. She rose to meet him. "You have kept me waiting a long time, Inspector Knollis!"

"I am going to keep you waiting longer than you can anticipate," Knollis replied grimly. "I am charging you with the

murder of Richard Huntingdon. I have to warn you that anything you may say will be taken down in writing and may be
used in evidence."

"You—you seem pretty sure of yourself," she retorted.

"No mistake, Inspector?" the Chief Constable muttered
behind his hand.

"None," Knollis said crisply. "Miss Dabell has given a statement to the effect that Miss Grenson was not in the house
when she arrived from Hedenham. She was supposed to be
in the apiary, but she was busy shooting Huntingdon with his
own pistol."

He swung round on Bamford. "The baker's man was new to
the round?"

"How the deuce did you reach that one?" asked the astonished Bamford. "Yes, you are correct. The driver of the van was
showing him the round. He stayed with the van while the new
man made the deliveries and collected the weekly accounts. The
driver was the original roundsman, and he says that he told all
his customers that the new man would be taking over on that
day. He told them a week in advance. So the new chap didn't
know whether he was serving Miss Dabell or Miss Grenson."

"Exactly!" said Knollis.

"But how did you reach the conclusion?" repeated Bamford
anxiously.

"It was the only possible solution," explained Knollis. "Once
we discovered that Maud had a genuine reason for being in the
plantation I knew we could dismiss her from the list. That left
Miss Grenson, and only Miss Grenson. Her alibi was so simple,
and yet so tight that there was bound to be something wrong
with it. It rested on the evidence of Miss Dabell and the baker's
man. My examination of the plantation where it abuts the Grenson orchard proved that someone had made a track from the
cottage to the dam, and who else could it be but Grenson? The
undergrowth, which is mainly very young bracken, was pressed
down in the direction of the dam, indicating beyond doubt that
the traveller had gone *from* the cottage and not towards it. The
return journey had done little to disturb the broken bracken,

which mainly evidenced the direction of the original journey. The rest came fairly easily when once I had started thinking round Grenson. For instance, she sent the birthday-present yacht to Dorrie! That is correct, Miss Grenson?" he asked, turning to her.

"Steady!" the Chief Constable reminded him. "Judges' Rules, you know. She has been warned, and you can only question her to clear any points in a statement voluntarily made. As she hasn't made a statement—"

Knollis flapped a weary hand in recognition of his mistake. "I must tell you the story myself at that rate, and I repeat that she sent the yacht to Dorrie Huntingdon."

"How do you arrive at that conclusion?"

"Who else among the Huntingdon family and social circles would want to give the child a present, and be unable to sign it?" demanded Knollis. "Who, indeed, but her father's mistress. The child has just informed me that she and Grenson, to whom she refers as Auntie Gloria, were good friends—unknown to Mrs. Huntingdon. Even supposing that Grenson had no sincere wish to send a present to the child, it would at least be a politic action if she wished to retain Huntingdon's interest. Huntingdon would know, even if Grenson had not told him, that she was the giver of the present, and he could hardly reveal the fact in his own home, so that however curious Dinney and Dorrie might be, he just remained silent."

"That's logical," granted the Chief Constable.

"You still haven't *proved* that she sent it," interrupted the superintendent. "The theory is sound, but we must have proof."

"The notice-board, Ellis!"

Ellis came from the rear of the room and laid the board on the table beside the yacht.

"Miss Grenson, did you write this notice yourself, or was it written by a professional sign-writer?"

"I wrote it myself," she answered reluctantly.

Knollis pointed to the yacht and the neat *Doreen* written on each side of the hull. "You can take two guesses as to who wrote that, sir!"

"Looks like he's got something," said the Chief Constable. "Neat point that. Shouldn't have noticed it myself."

"And the pistol?" demanded the superintendent, who evidently came from Missouri and had to be shown before he would believe.

"It will be found in Miss Grenson's possession, and probably in her cottage," said Knollis. "You see, he lent the same pistol—I'm referring to Huntingdon—to Mrs. Montague several years ago when she was left alone in the house during her husband's absence in Streatham. Now Huntingdon was a remarkably consistent character. Having acted in one particular manner in one particular set of circumstances, he was likely to act in a similar way should the circumstances be repeated. He was a man with chivalrous instincts, as we have seen all the way through the case. He regarded woman as the weaker vessel, someone to be guarded and cared for by mankind. Grenson was living alone, and in a deserted spot. Huntingdon was concerned for her safety. Ergo, I submit that he lent the pistol to Grenson for her own protection."

"That can be proved if we find the pistol on the premises," nodded the superintendent. "Have you an explanation for the two telephone calls?"

"That is the simplest question of all to answer," said Knollis. "My first idea was moderately sound. I assumed that another person in possession of climbing irons climbed the pole in Grenson's garden and tapped the wires, so that the calls appeared to come from her cottage. Miss Grenson had deliberately fostered his idea by providing climbing marks in the pole, this being done by persuading Huntingdon to borrow Montague's irons and rescue a kite from the wires. I fell for the trap and assumed that Montague had done the job. It was really then that I began to wonder how he had done it without being seen. I enquired whether Grenson had been at the back or front of the house that afternoon, and the first inkling of the real solution occurred to me.

"Montague could have tapped the wires in this way. It was possible, but not probable, for surely—I reasoned—someone would have seen him, either from the road or the cottage. And

202 | FRANCIS VIVIAN

so I had to find another explanation. The simplest explanation was the most obvious one—*that the calls did actually come from the cottage.* This theory came into direct conflict with Miss Dabell's original statement. I have requestioned Miss Dabell to-day. The calls were made about ten minutes to four, and Miss Dabell could not possibly arrive at the cottage earlier than five minutes to four! Miss Dabell found a note awaiting her, stating that Grenson was busy in the apiary. Miss Dabell is afraid of bees; she excites them, and they sting her, and so she did not go down to her friend, but waited in the cottage. The calls were already made, and so she could truthfully back Grenson's statement that the instrument had not been used. Instead of attending to her bees, Grenson was on her way through the plantation. She went through the apiary, through the orchard, and made a path through the new bracken to the edge of the dam. The Bishop of Northcote was on the southern side. Jacland was on the south-eastern side. Burton was back and forth on the roadway. Maud Montague was making her way from the western edge of the plantation—coming due east. Grenson was cutting across her path, and running! She had to run, in order to be in her place before Huntingdon arrived."

"Then it was Miss Grenson who telephoned him!" said the Chief Constable.

"Of course! And we can now see why Huntingdon accepted the message without question. Dorrie has proved that she spent Saturday afternoons with her Auntie Gloria. Knowing Huntingdon's lack of interest in home affairs, we know or can guess that he wasn't at all sure where the child was likely to be, but would have a good idea that she was out with Grenson. When, therefore, she rang to say that the child had met with an accident by the dam, he would accept the statement without question—and he obviously would not tell the maid who had informed him. As for the message to Dinney Huntingdon, we can only assume that the golf club secretary had no idea whether it was a man or a woman who had 'phoned. We unconsciously put the idea into his head that it might have been Huntingdon, and just as unconsciously he accepted that!"

"There's a point," said Bamford uncomfortably. "I hate to cast doubts on your case, but the decoy yacht; she would have to pass the Bishop, and possibly Jacland, if she put the yacht into the water. Or if not pass them, at least run the risk of being seen by them."

"Didn't Jacland say that the yacht was on the water when he arrived?" asked Knollis. "I can't prove this, but I'm prepared to say that she went down by the normal track earlier in the afternoon to plant the yacht, and long before the Bishop unexpectedly turned up. She expected him at the dam, but not at the cottage, and that must have made her anxious about the success of her plan. It was only by insulting him that she got rid of him. I suggest that the whole thing leapt into her mind on the afternoon of Dorrie's birthday. Dorrie tells me that she and her Auntie Gloria stood looking at the yacht in Loseby's window, and she also states without realizing it that Grenson made her more anxious to sail the yacht than she already was.

"We'll come to motive in a minute. The next points I want to deal with are the red herrings she strewed across the trail. She had to cast suspicion on someone, and she chose the Montagues. She knew the contents of Huntingdon's will, and she knew that the Montagues benefited only if both Richard and Dinney died and Dorrie was left in their charge, so she wrote the note to John Willie Montague hoping that he would turn up at the dam. She wrote letters to the Bishop and to Jacland in the hope that they also would be present and see John Willie Montague there. Two excellent witnesses, prominent public men! Those two letters, signed apparently by Dickens, also drew our attention to Dickens, and thence to the early life of Dinney Huntingdon, which in turn led back to Dickens and John Willie and the Eastbourne affair. Maud Montague's action in ringing John Willie in Grenson's name was just the action of a spiteful opportunist. Now, is there anything else?"

"The distance from the cottage to the dam," said Bamford. "That is still worrying me."

"Look at the sketch map," advised Knollis. "She didn't have to do the hundred yards down the road and then follow the winding track taken by the Bishop. She cut straight through the plantation, and ran it. I can walk a mile in ten minutes if I'm in a hurry, so I'll leave the rest to you."

"Looks as if you've nicely stitched up the case," said the Chief Constable.

"Except for the motive," said the superintendent.

"Yes," interrupted Grenson. "You've made out a pretty case against me, so you may as well tell me why I killed him!"

"Up to now," said Knollis, wagging a didactic finger, "the facts have proved to be exactly opposite to the statements you have made, so I'll suggest that the same principle applies in the matter of motive. You told me in an earlier statement that Richard Huntingdon had almost pleaded with you to allow him to make financial provision for you in his will. You told me that at no time had he given you money. I am prepared to believe the latter statement, but not the first. We again take into consideration Huntingdon's character and his chivalrous trait. Richard Huntingdon would convince himself that the affair between himself and you was a pure love-affair, and would consequently believe that no money should pass between you lest such should automatically change your status from that of an unmarried wife or mistress to that of a—pardon me!—prostitute. Huntingdon could rationalize the relationship existing between you for just so long as there was no monetary settlement. For that reason alone he refused to contribute to your upkeep, or to make provision for you after his death."

Gloria Grenson sneered. "You make it sound high and mighty and all Sir Galahad! That was Richard all over! He thought he was Sir Galahad, whereas he should have thought more about Lancelot. Unethical, he said; unethical it would be to let money come between us. It would spoil the true and unsullied love that had miraculously come to us. I was at the end of my tether for money, and sick of his self-righteous and sanctimonious blather. There were times when he made me sick!"

"You're admitting that you shot him?" asked Knollis. Then he caught the Chief Constable's eye and hastily added: "Perhaps I was mistaken."

"Don't be a ninny," she replied. "Of course I shot him. Haven't you proved it! I did it all exactly as you've described. The pistol is in a hat-box in my wardrobe. I was saving that for Dinney. Then the Montagues would have taken Dorrie, and with anything like luck I could have fixed it so that they both took the blame for that even if they had got away on the score of Dick. I love Dorrie! She's a sweet kid!"

"I don't think a great deal of your idea of love," Knollis snarled angrily. "Shoot her parents, hang her aunt and uncle, and leave her stranded!"

"She wouldn't have been stranded," Grenson said slowly. "I thought it all out very carefully. I knew all about that phoney marriage of hers. Richard knew, only he never let her know that he knew. He was too big-hearted and chivalrous—the half-wit!— to do anything about it. I was relying on Dickens, or Froggatt, finding a way of explaining the second marriage as bigamous and taking charge of his own child. Then I should have let him know that I knew the truth, and got the money I never got out of Richard—for I think the courts would have given him Richard's money in trust for Dorrie. A long way round? Well, I've plenty of patience! You must have patience if you handle bees. You have to learn to handle them slowly and confidently. And it looks as if I've been stung!"

She was led away, her head in the air defiantly.

Knollis licked his lip for a moment, and then begged to be excused. "See you shortly," he muttered as he hurried away.

He pushed open a door and smiled grimly at Dinney Huntingdon. "It's all over," he announced.

Dinney Huntingdon silently mouthed the words *Gloria Grenson*.

"How did you guess?" said Knollis.

"A woman's intuition, Inspector," she replied. "I think I knew all along."

"In which case you beat me at my own game," Knollis said with something approaching a smile. "Now, have you an hour to spare in a good cause, Mrs. Huntingdon?"

"I've all eternity before me, Inspector. Why?"

206 | FRANCIS VIVIAN

Knollis gave an embarrassed laugh. "I was wondering if we might go down to the pond in the gardens, there to eat ice-cream and sail a yacht. Dorrie can't have her own yacht back for a time, but I know where I can buy one just like it."

Dorrie jumped up and down with excitement. Her mother stayed her with one hand as she anxiously asked: "There is one matter I must first ask about, Inspector. My first marriage? What is going to happen to me?"

Knollis bit his lip. "You'll probably get your knuckles rapped—very lightly. Circumstances were all against you, and discretion may be given in your favour. More than that I cannot say. I can't help you there, and I would not do it if I could. My job is to uphold the law in both letter and spirit, and my own feelings are not allowed to enter into it. You do see that?"

"Yes. Yes, I do see that, Inspector!" She lifted her chin. "Well, Mr. Knollis, shall we go?"

Dorrie regarded him earnestly. "What's your first name, Mr. Knollis?"

"Gordon," he said.

She grabbed his hand. "Come on, Uncle Gordon. There is the loveliest yacht in Miss Franklin's."

He re-entered police headquarters exactly six hours later. His trousers were soaked to the knees. His hair stuck out from under his hat at comical angles. There were crumbs round his mouth. There was also a happy light in his eyes.

"Where the devil do you think you've been?" demanded Bamford. "Here I am with a deskful of reports, statements, and—"

"Nuts!" Knollis replied happily. "We can't spend the whole of our lives playing at bloodhounds and hangmen. To-day, my lad, I've been a sailor. I've sailed a pirate ship round the Barbary Coast. I've helped to dig for buried treasure on Cocos Island. I've won the America Cup in the finest yacht that was ever built!"

Bamford relaxed. "Been with Dorrie Huntingdon?"

Knollis nodded.

"'Struth!" exclaimed Bamford. "I do believe you're human after all!"

THE END

Printed in Great Britain
by Amazon

25298316R00126